THE FUDGED UP

MURDER

Trust the truth!

Priscilla J. Krahn

Dedicated to my cousin Abby. Thank you for all the late-night talks, mystery brainstorming sessions, and for being my partner in crime. I'll always love the memories of us watching mystery movies together.

Table of Contents

Chapter One

DECEMBER 20th

Instinct said to call the police, but Jessaca Anderson hesitated. If she went down on record as the person that found the body, things could get messy. If she just walked out of the cafeteria, no one would know. Someone else would find the body, and she could stay in the clear.

It was too late to do anything for the man. He was obviously dead. Jessaca took one last look to survey the scene. The man was older, probably in his fifties. It could just be a heart attack or something, but . . . well, even if it wasn't murder, she couldn't get involved.

With every fiber of common sense screaming against her, Jessaca headed for the front exit. Glancing out the glass of the front door, she spied two figures approaching. The elderly

Martin sisters held hands as they moved along the icy sidewalk of Middle Ridge, Minnesota.

Jessaca backed up and glanced both ways. The back entrance would have to do. Besides, then she could stop by the superintendent's office and leave the papers with him. That's why she'd come wasn't it?

Jessaca shook her head and tried to think straight. Why was this bothering her so much? Swallowing hard, she knew that it wasn't the body; it was the fact that she couldn't get involved. She'd always fought for the truth. The truth had to be known, but . . . could she risk it?

The clacking of her heeled winter boots echoed down the empty corridors as she half-ran down the hall. Reaching the superintendent's office, she paused. It was empty. He'd said he would be there. Could he have something to do with the death? The room was void of any Christmas décor that usually creeps into offices the week before Christmas, and his chair was pushed back like he'd left in a hurry. She took a step into his office. Should she investigate why he wasn't here?

"Stop it, Jessa," she whispered to herself. "You've got to forget about this! Forget you ever saw the body!"

She dropped the files on the desk and left.

Officer Clayton Martin raced for his car. It had to be a natural death. Austin Royce had a record of severe health problems. Besides, the last homicide in Middle Ridge had been over twenty years ago. Yet, as Clay drove towards the school, he couldn't still the uneasiness in his stomach. Everyone hated Austin Royce. If it was murder, how would the town handle it? Especially a week before Christmas.

It took all of fifty-eight seconds to drive across town and be parked at the Middle Ridge School. Not highschool, or elementary school, just school. Although twice the size of any other building in town, it ranked on the side of 'puny' in comparison with other schools from larger towns.

Clay parked in front of the school and briefly glanced around the area.

Christmas wreaths hung from the double doors, fresh snow covered the shrubs along the school, and the icicles hanging from the entryway seemed to glow orange in the early morning sunlight.

Everything seemed peaceful. Clay slammed his car door and raced for the double doors. Besides the crunching of the snow under his boots, everything seemed slightly muted. Even the morning birds seemed quieter than normal. A distant train horn blared, raising goosebumps under his coat. With an ominous feeling lurking at the back of his mind, Clay pulled the door open, and headed inside.

Despite its small size, it fit the need of any youngster in town who needed an education. Clay rounded the hall and entered the cafeteria from a side door.

The usual clamor of children was missing, and Clay silently thanked God that this had happened during Christmas break.

The tables had all been rearranged to accommodate the school fundraiser that was supposed to take place that afternoon. Hopefully, it would bring in enough money to allow the school to replace the security system. Homemade Christmas decorations plastered the walls. Apparently, the teachers had been having fun with their kids.

Clay glanced around the top of the room. With no cameras in the room, it would be hard to determine exactly what happened prior to the death. The school certainly needed a new security system. The current one had been in place for over thirty years and didn't have cameras to cover even half the rooms.

"Clay!" a distinctly elderly woman's voice called.

Clay cringed. "I should have known," he muttered.

Swallowing hard, Clay entered into his 'cop' mode. "Auntie Bertha, Auntie Donna, please step away from the body."

"It's murder!" Donna squealed. Something that looked frightfully like ecstatic excitement pulled at the corners of the elderly woman's eyes. Donna, the younger of the two elderly sisters stood over the body. Her dark hair was wind-blown, and her cheeks were tinged pink. Whether from too much make up or the cold, he couldn't tell.

"It's not murder," Bertha insisted, tapping her pearl handled cane on the linoleum for emphasis. "The greedy man ate too much fudge and died!" Slightly stooped over, Bertha didn't try to conceal her age.

Clay knelt by the body and felt for a pulse even though everything about the body screamed that he was dead and had been for a few hours.

"He's already dead," Donna said, pushing her glasses up. "I poked him with my foot to make sure."

"I told her it wasn't proper to touch a dead body," Bertha said.

Clay stepped back from the body and surveyed the scene. As he took in the details, he said a silent prayer for the family of the deceased.

5

Austin Royce was lying face down. A half full plate of fudge rested a few inches from one hand, and in his other hand, he clutched a half-eaten piece of fudge.

"I declare! Any man who steals other people's fudge deserves to die!" Bertha said. "Especially on a day like this! Imagine having the nerve to die in our school on the one day that the entire town is going to be coming here!"

Clay grabbed his radio and relayed the situation to Sheriff Vicklund. When he set his radio down, he turned to his elderly aunts. "Ladies, please, step back. The coroner will be here soon and they don't want the scene being disturbed."

"Then it was murder?" Bertha asked. Her voice trembled slightly.

"We don't know that," Clay said. "There's no sign of a struggle, but it's standard procedure."

"It was murder," Donna said. "See that note?"

Bertha started to reach for it, but Donna grabbed her hand. "Don't touch that, you'll disturb the evidence!"

Bertha huffed. "Evidence. I declare, this man ate too much fudge and died. It's not a murder. You need to stop living in a dream world and get practical!"

Clay forced himself between his aunts and the body. "You need to stay back."

6

Donna frowned. "How many people do you know of that died from eating too much fudge? And he's too young to die of a heart attack. He's just a young whippersnapper. Why I bet he's not even fifty yet. And that note, we didn't write that. It's obviously murder."

Bertha raised her chin slightly. "Oh, for nonsense. You read too many mysteries. If I didn't know better, I'd say that you killed him just so that you had a crime to solve."

Donna gasped. "You don't think that everyone will blame me, do you? I mean, it's my fudge!"

"It's our fudge," Bertha corrected. "And, of course they'll blame you! How many of your old wrinkled friends find bodies lying around? None of them. So naturally, everyone will assume that you killed him. You're always talking about murder and reading those dreadful novels."

"Old wrinkled friends?" Donna huffed. "I would have you know that most of my friends aren't half as old as you are!"

"I declare, I . . ."

"Aunties, please!" Clay glanced from Donna's younger face and dyed hair to Bertha's unashamedly white head. "You need to stay calm."

"Calm?" Bertha asked. "I'm always calm!"

"I might have known it would be the Martin sisters," Sheriff Vicklund boomed.

Donna and Bertha turned to watch the middle-aged sheriff approach, and Clay let out a sigh of relief. Natural or not, this was the first body he'd had to deal with in small town Middle Ridge.

Sheriff Vicklund's face was serious, but his eyes twinkled. "I don't believe I've ever come upon a crime scene like this and found two old ladies arguing about their age while standing over a dead body."

"So, it is a crime scene?" Donna asked stepping forward.

Sheriff Vicklund's face went blank. "No. Austin Royce has a known history of medical complications. That's why he was going to retire from being school janitor and security guard after Christmas. I'm sure it's just natural causes. However, I will need you ladies to step back so we can do a complete inspection and make sure nothing is missed."

Donna took another step towards Sheriff Vicklund and lowered her voice. "I think it was murder, just look at that plate!"

Sheriff Vicklund nodded. "It's got fudge on it. You two made the fudge, didn't you?" He turned to include Bertha.

Bertha smiled slightly. "If you're trying to get us to give you a piece, it won't work. It's going to the benefit and you have to make a donation if you want some."

"Of course, we made the fudge," Donna said, interrupting her older sister. "There's not another person alive who can make cookie dough fudge like we do. But we didn't put it on that plate. If you look closely, you'll see that the fudge on that plate was taken from our bigger platter. Someone wrote the note too." She pointed towards the note that was still taped to the edge of the plate.

"*Samples for the school board*," Sheriff Vicklund read. "What's strange about that? It's a benefit for the school, you ladies donate fudge, doesn't it make sense that someone would want to give the school board some fudge to sample?"

Donna clucked her tongue. "You can believe whatever you want, but I still think it's murder!"

Sirens sounded in the distance and Clay couldn't stop the smirk. Excitement was so rare that whenever something happened, no matter how small, everyone showed up. Like the time newlywed Mrs. Olson burned a frozen pizza and set off the fire alarms. The neighbors called the police and the poor Olson's ended up with three squad cars, an ambulance, and two firetrucks in their driveway.

"Clay!" Sheriff Vicklund snapped his fingers. "Where are you? We have an investigation to do."

Clay nodded. "Yes, sir." Trying to stop his shaking hands, he glanced towards his aunts. How could they be so calm after finding the body?

"Will the benefit still be able to be held this afternoon?" Bertha asked as Clay escorted the women to chairs along the wall.

"There's no reason why it shouldn't be able to continue as normal," he said. He glanced at the portable walls. Yes, they would be able to block this area off nicely, and then . . .

"Is our fudge table part of a crime scene?" Bertha asked, her knuckles turning white around her cane handle.

"I wouldn't call it a crime scene," Clay said. "But it's standard procedure when someone dies without a witness present to verify the cause of death, to make sure nothing is missed."

"So, there will be an autopsy?" Donna asked. "I hope they do a toxicology report and check for cyanide. That would be my guess as to the cause of death. Although you'd better guard this table! People might try to steal our fudge. Dennis Nordlum and his wife have been after us for years to give them the recipe! They might slip in here and try to analyze our fudge."

Clay nodded. "Yes, ma'am. Now, if you're sure you're both okay, I have some questions I need to ask."

"Oh, we're okay, honey, but you don't have to treat us like the suspects!" Bertha said.

Clay cringed. Being called 'honey' in front of his co-workers was something he knew he'd never live down at the office.

"We'd love to answer your questions and help solve this murder!" Donna said.

Clay took a deep breath. He glanced over his shoulder. Shelby was taking pictures, the diamond on her engagement ring caught the light, and Clay frowned. For a guy as thrifty as Isaiah, he sure hadn't gone cheap on a ring.

Shelby's fiancé, Isaiah, was on his hands and knees. With gloved hands, he slipped the plate of fudge into an evidence bag. Sheriff Vicklund barked orders, and the paramedics zipped up the body bag. The coroner would have his work cut out for him. Everyone seemed totally comfortable with their job. Everyone except him.

"Why were you here this morning?" Clay winced at the harshness of his own words. Then, realizing he didn't have his notebook in hand, he reached for it and clicked his pen open.

"We set up our table yesterday with the fudge and came by this morning to put some holly on the table," Donna said. "Then, we were going to go to the community center to help with the finishing touches on the Christmas costumes we're sewing. For the church pageant, of course."

"Donna thought we should hang mistletoe over the booth." Bertha huffed. "Imagine hanging mistletoe in a school! We can't have kissing in front of the children! Besides, the mistletoe they sell these days isn't like the stuff we had when I was a kid. Why, when . . ."

"Auntie Bertha!" Clay swallowed hard. "What time did you find Austin?" Clay jotted furiously to keep up with his aunts as they rattled off answers.

When the last question was answered, he clicked his pen off. "Thank you, I think that's all." He scanned his pages of notes. From all the pages he'd had to fill out, he was beginning to think that it would have been easier to ask the ladies what they hadn't seen, than what they had.

"Who do you think wanted him dead?" Donna asked.

Clay ran a hand through his hair. "*If* it was murder, then . . ." he sighed. "It'd be easier to ask who didn't want him dead. He didn't have many friends." Clay winced. "I can't be talking about this with you two."

"Martin?" Sheriff Vicklund asked. "You done?"

Clay nodded. "Yes, sir."

"Good, stay with your aunts till I'm done here, then I've got a few questions of my own." The sheriff turned to another officer. "Get the superintendent in here. He should be in his office."

Clay pulled a chair around and straddled it. Facing his aunts, he leaned his arms on the back of the chair. "Are you sure you two are alright? It must have been very difficult to find the body."

"Nonsense," Bertha said. "I've seen dead bodies before. At least this one was natural, and not chocked full of liquor."

Clay inhaled sharply. How strong these women were!

Donna shrugged slightly. "I don't care what you think. I still say that something about this death is as natural as windshield wipers on a woolen sweater."

"Forget about poor Austin, what are we going to do about the school benefit? All our fudge is behind those walls." Bertha nodded towards where their fudge display had sat. Now it was blocked off by moveable walls.

"Forget about the fudge, will you?" Donna rummaged in her purse for a notebook. "Do you have a pen?"

Bertha huffed. "You carry everything in that suitcase size purse, guns, sleeping bags, and who knows what else, but you don't have a pen? What would you do without a big sister?" She reached into her small handbag and pulled out a pen. "Don't lose it."

"Thanks, Bert." Donna flipped the notebook open and started scribbling.

"I declare, if you call me 'Bert', one more time, I'm going to hogtie you to the kitchen table and feed you fruitcake the rest

13

of your life!" When her rant about Donna's least favorite food didn't create a storm, she leaned forward. "What are you writing?"

Clay found himself leaning forward too.

"Everything I can remember about the victim and today's crime. You never know when it will come in handy."

"This isn't one of your murder novels! This is real life." Bertha huffed. "Your fascination with mystery will come to no good. Mark my words it won't."

Clay swallowed hard. The old sisters seemed fine, but . . . "Are you sure you're okay, Auntie Bertha, you look a little pale."

"Pale!" Bertha flushed. "I declare, who raised you, child, to be so rude?" She paused, and Clay smirked.

"Now don't get impertinent with me!" Bertha pounded her cane on the floor. "I was tough enough to raise you. I'm tough enough to find a body."

"Now, Auntie, don't get upset," Clay said. "It's not like I think you can't handle it, it's just that . . . well, finding bodies isn't the easiest thing on a person's nerves and . . ."

"And you think we're two old geezers who might keel over and die at the slightest fright," she finished for him. "Sonny boy, I'd have you know that half the people I've known are dead!"

Clay bit his lip to keep from laughing. "You two are the most amazing women I know!"

"And that's funny how?" Bertha asked.

Donna snorted. "What's funny is the idea of proper and polite Clay calling anyone an old geezer."

"Officer Martin? May I have a word with you?"

Clay glanced over his shoulder. "Be right there." He turned back to his aunts. "You'll have to excuse me."

Donna grabbed Clay's hand. "You are still coming over for supper tonight, aren't you?"

Clay frowned. "Is anyone else going to be there?"

Bertha and Donna exchanged a look.

"I thought so." He turned to walk away.

"Clay!" Bertha spoke up. "It's just our new neighbors, and they don't know anyone yet. We wanted to invite them by to get them acquainted with the townsfolk."

Clay sighed. "Alright, but this had better not be another set up. After the last four dates you've tried hooking me up with, I'm done with girls forever."

He turned and hurried away.

"What's gotten into you?" Shelby stopped him. "Your aunts are sweet. Why wouldn't you want to go to supper with them?"

15

Clay snorted. "You'd be surprised how many girls they've tried matching me up with!"

"What's wrong with that?" Shelby asked. "It's about time you get a woman in your life." She winked. "Besides, you owe it to them. It makes them so happy to see you, and they did raise you, and your father for that matter."

"The last girl had pink hair, was a vegetarian, and blamed us cops for all the bad politicians." Clay shook his head. "I'm not on the market."

Shelby nodded slowly. "It's been eight years since . . ."

"That's not long enough," Clay cut her off. Guilt washed over him for being rude to her. She'd always been there. Her and Isaiah had been there when . . . but no, he couldn't think about it. *God,* he prayed silently. *Please help me to stop snapping at people.*

"Officer Martin?" Sheriff Vicklund was practically growling. "A word with you?"

Clay stepped towards the sheriff and lowered his voice. "Sir?"

"From the brief analysis that the coroner did, he says it was death by asphyxiation. We won't know what caused that until he's done with his examination. I'm putting you as the lead on this case."

"Sir?" Clay opened his mouth, and then paused.

"Is that a problem?" Sheriff Vicklund raised an eyebrow.

Clay slowly shook his head. "Sir, I have the least experience at this sort of thing. Wouldn't it be better to put an older, more seasoned officer on the case?"

"Look, chances are, it was natural causes. Then your job will be easy. If foul play is involved, then I'll call about getting a homicide investigator in here. Whether it's natural causes, or murder, whether there's a homicide investigator or not, I want you on the case."

"Why me?" Clay bit his lip. What right did he have to question his superior?

"Clay." Sheriff Vicklund stared into his eyes. "None of us have dealt with this kind of thing. You're the freshest out of college, and I'm betting that you still remember more of what they taught you about an investigation than most of the guys do."

"What about Isaiah and Shelby?"

"Really, Martin?" The sheriff shook his head. "They're planning a wedding! The last thing they need to think about is murder. And Isaiah, well, he's a great forensic guy, but you and I both know that he's more effective when he's not in charge." The sheriff rubbed one of his silver temples. "I would take the lead, but I'm kind of busy with the whole lawsuit. If you'd rather deal with the state lawsuit . . ."

Clay shook his head. "No, thank you." It all seemed ridiculous to Clay. Suing a police station for switching the brand of tires on their cars just proved that some people had too much time on their hands.

"Clay!" Auntie Bertha called.

Chapter Two

"Excuse me, for a moment, will you?" Clay asked the sheriff. The sheriff nodded, so Clay hurried back to his aunts.

"I just want to make sure you come at the right time. Supper will be ready at six o'clock." Auntie Bertha pounded her cane for emphasis. "Don't be late." She turned to go and then paused. "Oh, and wear something nice."

"Auntie!" Clay started after his aunts.

"Clay, get back here," Sheriff Vicklund called. "You've got an investigation to lead. I want the fundraiser postponed. The superintendent says he's been in his office all morning. He's the only one that's been in the building to our knowledge. Confirm that. You'll also want to question him about any detail he may have seen or heard and . . . sorry. It's your case. You lead."

Clay stole one last glance at his retreating aunts, and then turned back to the Sheriff. "Yes, sir. I'm working on a plan of action."

"Good, because I have paperwork to do at the office. This is your crime scene." The sheriff pointed at Shelby. "Once you've got everything, put that camera away and help Clay."

"Can we call it a crime scene when we're not even sure that it was murder?" Isaiah asked.

"It wasn't murder," Clay said.

Sheriff Vicklund shrugged in Isaiah's direction. "Follow Clay's lead."

"So, you're sure it wasn't murder?" Isaiah asked once the sheriff was gone.

Clay resisted the urge to straighten Isaiah's tie and stared at where the body had been. "No, but Royce had a history of medical problems. Diabetes, heart surgeries, you name it and he's probably had it. Any number of his health issues could have caused death by asphyxiation." He silently hoped he was right, but something felt wrong.

Isaiah grinned. "Do you have his medical records memorized?"

Clay shook his head. "Not all of them, just the highlights. He had a police record too, you know."

20

Shelby's eyes widened. "You remember his medical records from when he was in jail three years ago?"

Clay shrugged. "I didn't want to be the cause of him dying in our jail, so I memorized his health statements."

Shelby whistled, and Isaiah grinned at his fiancé.

"He's as smart as they come," Isaiah said.

A grin spread across Shelby's face. "I do know one man that is smarter." She winked at him.

Isaiah blushed. "Well, I would say you're the smartest woman, but you fell for a guy like me so . . . you may not be playing with a full magazine."

Shelby raised an eyebrow. "You better be careful! The woman you just called crazy, happens to have a loaded gun, and is friends with the sheriff so . . . beware! And, I will agree that Clay must be pretty smart, because he was your best friend before you met me."

"Hey now!" Clay said. "I'm still his best friend."

Shelby batted her eyes at her husband-to-be. "I think I'm his best friend."

Isaiah groaned and held up his hands. "Come on, you two! I'm both of your friends."

Clay allowed a smile to ease his tension. With Isaiah and Shelby working with him, how could they not get this case wrapped up?

His attention drifted to the man entering the room. Nels Christianson, the school superintendent. It was time to get serious.

Donna waited at the car for her sister to catch up. Age hadn't treated Bertha well.

"What are you staring at?" Bertha asked.

Donna opened the car door for her sister. "Nothing, Bert."

"You call me nothing?" She stamped her cane. "Just because I don't spend half my time and money on looking young, dying my hair, and other such nonsense, doesn't mean you can stare at me like I'm some old goat!"

"I just think you'd feel younger if you made up your mind to look younger." Donna said.

Bertha eased her way into the car. "Hogwash. I've lived a long full life, and if it's left me looking old before my time, I'll not hide it."

Bertha was right, life had given her more stress than any woman should have, and it had left her looking every bit as old as her eighty-seven years. The ten-year age difference wasn't the only reason that Bertha looked older than Donna.

"What are you thinking?" Bertha asked. "And where are we going?"

Donna swung the car onto the main road and took off into the country. Talking about the years of trials that Bertha had been through didn't seem like a good idea. At Eighteen, when their parents died, Bertha had been left to raise her young siblings. Spending the majority of her younger years raising siblings, and then, after their brother died, raising their nephew, she'd never taken the time to get to know anyone special. Now, with no hope of marriage, she continued to serve others. Bertha's serving spirit often made Donna feel guilty. Sure, she'd helped with raising Clay, but only after her own husband had died. She'd never been the sweet servant that Bertha was.

"Did you hear me?" Bertha asked. "Where are we going?"

"We're going to visit Sally Landean."

"Why?" Bertha asked.

Donna rolled her eyes. "Why do you think?"

"If you're going to accuse her of murder . . ."

"Don't be silly. I'm not going to *accuse* her of murder. If she confesses, so be it." Donna glanced down. A plate of cookies still sat between their seats. "Besides, we should give her some cookies as a consolation for losing a loved one."

23

"Loved one!" Bertha harrumphed. "Sally didn't love her brother any more than I did! She had more cause to wish him ill than anyone. Besides, those cookies are for the sewing group."

Donna smiled. "Forget the sewing group. They've got plenty of help, and this is more exciting. You're right about Sally having motive. That's why we're going to find out if she's the killer."

"Clay wouldn't like it," Bertha said.

"I know, but that dear boy can't be worried about something he doesn't know about, and if we don't find anything out, he won't have to know." Donna swung the car down a narrow dirt driveway. A police car was leaving as they pulled up to the house.

"We shouldn't be bothering her so soon after she heard the news. She needs time," Bertha warned.

"Time for what? She isn't going to be grieving, and I don't think she needs time to feel relieved. Just the same, we should be thoughtful sympathizers." Donna parked and walked around the car to help her sister.

At the door, Donna knocked, and they waited. Jazzy Christmas music from the '60s blared through the house, and Donna knocked again.

"Come in!" a male voice yelled.

"Ken is home," Bertha said with disgust.

Donna opened the door and followed the music. The kitchen smelled of fresh paint.

Ken glanced up with paint brush in hand. "Well, if it isn't the Martin sisters. A pleasure." There was nothing in his voice that indicated any pleasure.

"Is Sally home?" Donna asked. She glanced around. What kind of man finds out his brother-in-law was murdered, and then goes back to his painting and music as if nothing was wrong?

"Sally? Oh, she's in the basement. Organizing some magazines or something. You're welcome to go down and see her." He gestured towards a door exiting the kitchen. "It's right through there."

Donna smiled. "Thank you." She set the plate of cookies on the table and grabbed Bertha's arm.

"I knew they wouldn't be grieving," Bertha whispered as Donna helped her down the stairs. "But I never thought they could be so indifferent! Imagine painting in this closed up house! They'll probably get sick from the fumes!"

"You hoo! Sally!" Donna called.

Strange noises came from behind a row of dusty shelves. Donna and Bertha worked their way around the shelves, and found Sally sitting on a dusty pew with a box of magazine, sobbing her heart out."

Donna and Bertha exchanged a look. Bertha raised an eyebrow, and Donna shrugged. Was this remorse because she had been the one to kill Austin?

"Oh, Sally, we're so sorry for your loss," Donna said, patting Sally on the back. "We came as soon as we could."

Sally blew her nose into an already soiled handkerchief. "My little brother is gone!" she wailed.

Donna stared into Sally's eyes. The tears were definitely real. "I know what it's like to lose a loved one," Donna said. Sitting down on the pew beside Sally, she slipped her arm around her. "There, there, go ahead and let the tears come."

Donna glanced at Bertha's skeptical face and shook her head. Sally's pain was real. Donna knew it. Hadn't she been through her own pain? Losing her parents, a brother, and a husband?

Donna sat in silence for a bit and let Sally cry.

"I'm so sorry," she repeated when Sally's tears were beginning to subside.

Sally wiped her eyes with violently trembling fingers. "I hated him so much." Her words were hard and Donna sat back a bit. That was what she'd been expecting, but the tears . . . well, she hadn't expected both.

Sally sniffed loudly and straightened. "I'm sorry too. Sorry it didn't happen sooner. I'd have killed him myself, but . . . well, I don't want to spend the rest of my life in jail. Whoever killed him deserves a round of applause."

Bertha jerked back a little. "The police told you it was murder?"

Sally shook her head. "Not in so many words. They actually said it was probably natural causes, but they wouldn't know for sure until they got the autopsy results. But I know it was murder. I can feel it. Austin was too tough to let simple health issues kill him."

Donna sank back and held a hand to her head. "I'm a little dizzy. First, you're crying like you lost your best friend, and then you're glad someone killed him?"

Sally laughed.

Donna reached for her arm. "Are you okay? Should you be seeing a doctor?"

"I'm not crazy, if that's what you think." Sally said. "I'm realistic. I was crying because I was remembering our childhood. He had potential. He did. We got along great as kids." She started tearing up again. "Then, he fell in with the wrong crowd, and has been trying to make an easy buck ever since." Her face hardened. "I'm sorry our childhood is gone. I'm not sorry that the adult Austin Royce is dead." Sally's forehead wrinkled, and her eyes flickered with something like confusion.

Donna sighed. "How's Ken taking it?"

Sally shrugged. "He's glad, but he's pretending we never knew Austin. He doesn't want people to blame us for it."

Now's my chance! Donna thought. "Well, you have to admit, having your brother con you out of most of your life savings and get away with it is pretty bad. Then you add the fact that he was responsible for Ken losing his dream job, and the fact that he's sued you twice, and people will think you definitely had a motive. I don't mean to speak ill of the dead, but Austin wasn't exactly a saint. If anyone had motive to do him in, it was you or Ken. Especially since rumor has it that Austin was planning on suing you again over that incident with his flower garden."

Donna raised an eyebrow. Austin had probably planted those flowers in front of his door just so that someone would step on them and he could accuse them of vandalizing his property. "I can see how people would suspect you." She paused for a moment. "Unless you have an alibi . . . people could point fingers."

Sally folded her unsteady hands in her lap. "Ken is my alibi, and I'm his. Obviously, that wouldn't hold up in

28

a court of law. But unfortunately, I didn't do it. Oh, I wanted to do it, but I didn't. I never could have. He was my brother."

Donna stared into Sally's eyes. She'd always thought herself to be a good judge of character, and at the moment, she believed Sally.

"What about Ken?" Bertha asked. "He hated Austin too."

Sally twisted her handkerchief between her trembling fingers. "Well . . ." Doubt flashed through her eyes. "I don't know. But if he did it, he'll never be caught. Ken is too smart. Besides, he has too much to lose. I don't think he did it."

"What do you mean you don't *think* he did it?" Bertha asked. "Didn't you say you were his alibi?"

Sally nodded. "I am, but he was up before me this morning, and since breakfast, I've been down here most all morning. He could have slipped out sometime." Sally's eyes narrowed. "Why are you asking all these questions? You're not the police. You're not going to try to get us arrested for murder, are you? We didn't do it!"

"Oh, no," Bertha said. "We just wanted to stop by and offer our condolences. We also brought a plate of cookies."

Sally's frown deepened. "If you'll excuse me. I have work to do." She turned back to her box of magazines as if no one else were in the room.

Donna and Bertha said good-bye, and then headed for their car.

"I think it was one of them," Bertha said with confidence. "That is, *if* it was murder."

Donna shook her head. "I don't think so."

Bertha harrumphed. "You always disagree with me."

"I don't *always* disagree with you," Donna said. "Only when you're wrong."

"And you think I'm wrong." Bertha frowned. "If I'm wrong, those two need to be examined by a psychiatrist. They're both a few bells shy of a full sleigh."

Donna nodded. "There's definitely something strange. Sally's tears were unnatural for someone who hated their brother so much. It almost seemed like she had done it and was feeling guilty."

"See?" Bertha said. "I told you."

"And Ken, well, he was awful calm about it. They could have done it together."

Bertha smiled smugly. "I knew you'd see it my way if you thought about it."

Donna shook her head. "But I think Sally was telling the truth. She looked . . . well, she looked like she was telling the truth. And Ken, if he had done it, I think he would be trying to act a little bit sad to cast suspicion off of himself. I mean someone who shows no remorse over the death of their brother-in-law ought to be considered suspicious. I think he's smart enough that if he was the killer, he would at least act sober about it to cast suspicion off himself."

Bertha turned away from Donna and stared out the window. "How would you know if Sally was telling the truth? We need to go to the police station and tell Clay."

Donna nodded. "I want to stop by the grocery store first."

"What on earth for?" Bertha asked. "Are you . . ." her voice trailed off. "Seriously?"

Donna slowed the car as they entered city limits. "It is possible."

"Larry Erickson isn't anymore a killer than I am!" Bertha said.

Donna glanced at her sister. "Are you a killer? I hadn't thought about that. You didn't exactly like Austin either. Did you do it?" Donna bit back the laugh that rose in her throat.

"How dare you accuse me!" Bertha said a little louder than necessary. "Austin Royce was a scoundrel, and I haven't liked him since he accused your Harold of stealing. But as much as I didn't like him, I couldn't have hated him enough to kill him. In fact, I was trying to learn to love him. After all, that's the right thing to do. Love your enemies."

"I'll make sure the police know he was your enemy." Donna smirked.

Bertha grabbed the hand grip on the door. "Slow down! It's icy!"

Donna tapped the breaks and slowed for the next turn. "It's not that icy."

Donna parked at the grocery store and paused. "In all honesty, you make me feel guilty sometimes."

Bertha stared at her but didn't say anything.

"I was just starting to feel good about my attitude towards Austin. I mean everyone hated him, and it was my husband that he accused of stealing. But you're right. I shouldn't be mad at him. Loving people like Austin isn't easy."

Bertha nodded. "No, it's not, but God doesn't call us to do the easy things. Anyone can do easy things, but only with God's help, can we do extraordinary things. Do you think it was *easy* for Jesus to die on the cross? We celebrate Christmas with joy, but we shouldn't forget that the reason Jesus came, was to die for our sins. That includes Royce's sins, and our sins of not loving him like we should."

Donna sat in silence for a moment as she contemplated it. Jesus had shown his love for her by dying on the cross, and yet she couldn't even love her neighbors. She shook her head slightly. It would sure take some work, but she would do it. *I'm sorry, Lord,* she prayed silently. *Here I hated Austin Royce when you call me to love my enemies. Please help me to do just that in the future.*

"Are we going?" Bertha asked. "If Austin had a say in the matter, I reckon he'd want us to figure out who killed him."

Donna nodded, grabbed her purse, and then got out. Waiting for Bertha, she once more resolved that she would try to love her enemies. No matter how hard it was.

Inside, Donna picked up a box of candy canes so she had an excuse to go up to the counter. "Hey, Larry!" She set down the candy canes. "How have you been?"

Larry rubbed his chin and stroked his mustache with his forefinger. "Oh, busy as ever. Between here and the café, I feel like I'm always working. I'm surprised to see you two out. I hear you've had quite the morning."

"Word travels fast," Donna said.

"At least bad news does," Bertha mumbled.

"It must have been awful strange to find a body. Let alone Austin Royce's." Larry rang up the candy canes. "Of course, it's no surprise. Everyone hated him." Larry's face hardened.

Donna glanced at the price on the register and began digging in her purse. "I suppose you're glad you don't have to sell that land now," Donna said as she deliberately took her time trying to find a pen in her purse.

Larry shrugged, causing his mustache to wiggle. "I suppose everyone knew about our little bet."

"Little bet?" Bertha asked. "When you lost, you owed him everything you had!"

Veins bulged in his neck, and his eyebrows lowered. "It wasn't a fair bet. He shouldn't have lied to me."

"So, you gain a lot by his death?" Donna asked, finally putting her checkbook back and pulling out a ten-dollar bill.

Larry typed on his screen and the till popped open. "Everyone benefited by his death."

"You more than others," Bertha said.

Larry counted the change back to Donna.

Donna slowly began trying to put the money in the right spot in her purse. "Some would say you had motive to kill Austin."

Larry crossed his arms. "If you two ladies think you're going to pin the murder on me, you've got another thing coming."

"Did you do it?" Bertha asked bluntly.

Larry's scowl deepened. "I've got to get ready to go work my shift at the café." He walked away, mumbling under his breath.

"He looked awful mad," Donna whispered as she grabbed the candy canes.

Bertha raised her brows. "Now to the police station?" she asked.

Donna nodded. "Now to the police station."

Chapter Three

Clay leaned his hip on the counter and circled his hands around his navy-blue cop mug. The aunts had gotten it for him for Christmas the year before, and he'd appreciated having an actual mug at the station instead of the typical Styrofoam cups.

"And that's the last one," Shelby said, tacking up a picture on the cork board that ran all around the office.

Isaiah walked around and let out a low whistle. "I got to hand it to you, honey. You sure know how to document a crime scene."

Shelby tucked a strand of her light brown hair behind her ear and flashed a smile. "It's my job."

"What's the plan?" Isaiah asked, looking at Clay.

Clay swirled the coffee in his cup around and glanced at the wall they'd dedicated to the mysterious death. "If we find out it was murder, then we find out who did it."

Isaiah's eyes widened. "Really? I thought we were going to play elves and drop the case."

"The sarcasm dripping from your words is thick enough to drown a cat!" Shelby grinned as she gave Isaiah a playful punch in the shoulder and Clay frowned.

"This isn't something to joke about," Clay said.

The grin disappeared from Isaiah's face. "Then let's get serious. I already know that we're going to try to find out if it's murder, but how are we . . . Would you stop that?"

"Stop what?" Clay stared at his friend's frown.

"Swirling your coffee. You're going to spill it."

Clay glanced down. Isaiah was right. The brown liquid was almost up to the brim of the mug. Clay set the mug down and sighed. "Okay. So, you want a plan of action. Here it is. The medical examiner is with the body now. He'll get back to me sometime today with his initial report, and depending what he finds, he's going to take samples and send them in for a toxicology test. The closest place that does that is . . . oh, maybe four hours from here? Anyway, the results from that may take up to several weeks. In the meantime, we keep our eyes and ears open, and stay calm. We don't want people getting worked up over a murder if he died of natural causes. If we find out it's murder, there's a certain amount of information we'll need. Information that we can start gathering now."

"That sounds simple," Shelby said.

Clay ran a hand through his hair. "It's not. The sheriff said you two could help me, but if you'd rather stick to your regular work, I understand. I mean with all the wedding planning and stuff . . ."

"Are you kidding?" Isaiah said. "We're in all the way. Murder or not, we like working with you. Besides, this should all be cleared up by the wedding."

Clay nodded. "Okay, our first step will be to interview the suspects and get alibis for the ones we can."

"Who are the suspects?" Shelby asked.

Clay sighed. "Pretty much the whole town, but we'll start with Ken and Sally Landean, and Larry Erickson."

"Martin?" Officer Harrison stuck his head in the room. "Brad's here to see you."

Clay groaned.

"Do you want me to take it?" Isaiah asked.

Clay sighed. "No. But thanks for offering. Examine those pictures and see if you can find something that doesn't belong. I'll deal with Brad."

In the reception area, Brad Gustafson stood with an ancient fedora cocked at what he probably thought was an artistic angle. With notebook and pen in hand, he looked like a reporter from an old movie.

Clay sighed. *God, I'm going to need patience here,* he prayed silently as he approached the man. He wanted to knock the guy's hat into place, but that didn't seem like a very good display of Christian character. It certainly wasn't something Jesus would have done.

"Brad," Clay nodded. "What can I do for you?"

"It's what I can do for you, Mr. Clay Martin!" Brad said with a sly grin. "As this town's only radio station, people hear what I say. If you have something to say, I can relay it to the public, and I hear you're in charge of the murder investigation, so I'm sure you have something to say."

Clay stared at the older man, he was about Austin's age . . . he could have . . . but no, Brad hadn't moved to Middle Ridge till a year ago. He didn't have any quarrels with the deceased.

"What do you have to say? How are you going to ensure that this never happens again? People are panicking that a killer is on the loose, and you could put them at ease if you could tell them what you're doing."

Clay frowned. He knew exactly what Brad was doing. "I'm sorry, Brad, but I'm not going to be able to tell you about the investigation. If you want to give the people a message from me, tell them that we don't even know if it was murder."

"You might not know it, but the town thinks it."

"Then tell the public that I'm going to do my best, and I don't take my job lightly."

"You hoo!" a high-pitched voice screeched. "Clay, darling!"

Clay welcomed the interruption. "Hello, Aunties."

"We have some information for you," Donna said. "You see, we were . . ."

"Aunties!" Clay glanced at Brad. "Let's go to my office to chat, shall we? Brad, I'll see you later."

"Oh yes," Bertha said. "The chairs in there are more comfortable anyway."

Clay glanced back and caught Brad's frown. Brad touched his fedora and turned to go.

Of course, Brad wouldn't be happy. Since he'd come to Middle Ridge, he'd done a phenomenal job getting news for the radio and he wasn't used to being left in the dark. On the contrary. People loved to tell him everything they knew and more.

Once he'd shut the door behind him, Clay gestured towards the chairs along the wall. "Have a seat."

Clay noticed the devious grin on Donna's face and frowned. "Please don't tell me you've been interfering with my investigation."

Donna's grin widened. "We can help you! Remember the time we helped you find the man stealing the political signs?"

"This isn't a theft!" Clay took a deep breath. He had to stay calm. "I want you two staying out of the way. If for some reason it does turn out to be murder, it could get dangerous."

"Wait till you've heard what we've been up to this morning," Donna said. "I'm sure you'll be surprised."

Clay reached for his coffee. Surprises. That was the last thing he needed.

Jessaca Anderson refilled her coffee mug and turned up the volume on the radio.

"... *statement from Sheriff Vicklund,*" the radio announcer said. *"Brad, play the recording."*

There was the sound of wind over a microphone, and some indistinct sounds. Then a voice came on.

"Sheriff, is it murder? Do you have a statement for us?"

"I'm not saying it's murder," the sheriff's voice sounded strained. *"My statement is that Officer Martin is in charge of the case and he will give a statement when he is ready."*

"You're leaving a murder case to Officer Clay Martin? Isn't he a bad choice for this investigation. Everyone knows that

41

he is insecure and slow to react." The nasally voiced reporter sounded mocking, and Jessaca could imagine that he probably had his nose upturned.

"*Martin is a good man and perfectly capable of handling this. And like I said, we don't know that it was murder.*"

"*But Sheriff, don't you . . .*" the crackling sounds took over and then it switched back to the radio announcer. She sounded young.

"*With the mysterious death of sixty-three-year-old Austin Royce, a resident of our usually peaceful town of Middle Ridge, Minnesota, Sheriff Vicklund has taken a move that, in my opinion, wasn't very smart. He's appointed an inexperienced officer who is rumored to be very insecure. Thirty-two-year-old Officer Clay Martin is a resident of Middle Ridge and has been most of his life. Although the sheriff hasn't mentioned any suspects, our sources suggest that Liam Bennett should be on the top of the list. Not only is his father still in jail, but he's been out of the juvenile detention center less than four months. Brad, do you have any comments?*" The woman paused.

"*Well, Zoe, I think we need to give this Martin guy a chance, but honestly, I wouldn't expect him to solve it.*" The nasally voiced reporter said. "*I mean honestly, Austin Royce had more enemies than friends, and half the town would have done him in if the chance had arisen. Finding a suspect is going to be nearly impossible. Especially when the police don't even believe that he was murdered. We all know Martin isn't exactly good at what he does. Of course, if Liam is the killer, it shouldn't be too hard to figure out. I'm sure the whole department is going to get some flack over letting that violent kid out of jail."*

Zoe's voice came back on. *"I've been looking into Martin's background, and it seems that he has had a rough life. He was raised by his aunts after his parents divorced. It seems he's also been engaged twice, but both girls jilted him."*

Jessaca clicked the radio off and frowned. How vulgar could people be? The idea of discussing a man's life on the radio as if his past somehow would keep him from doing his job!

Glancing at the clock, Jessaca sighed. "Twenty minutes," she said out loud. "That's just enough time. Not that I want to go, but . . ." she paused. How would she face the sisters? All they'd want to talk about was the body they'd found. The body that she'd found first.

"Callie! I'm going to the store!"

The Pomeranian dog ran into the room at the mention of her name, her nails clacking on the tile flooring.

Jessaca crouched down in front of the dog. "You be a good girl while I'm gone, okay?"

43

The dog rubbed its head against Jessaca's hand and she giggled. What would her sister say if she could see her talking to her dog? "We don't care what Laci would say, do we, Callie?"

Jessaca got up and grabbed her purse. If Laci were here, then she might not have the need to talk to her dog, but being all alone . . . Jessaca glanced around the small kitchen. The marble topped counters, and the tile flooring was what she'd always wanted, and the window above the sink framed the frozen Minnesotan view. It was a beautiful home, but so empty. She hadn't even had time to decorate yet. Nothing about her house felt like Christmas, and she sighed. Her mom would have decorated long before now.

With one last glance at the clock, she grabbed her phone off the charger and hurried for her beloved car. As rusty, and beat up as her red PT Cruiser was, she wouldn't consider trading it for any car in the world.

"God, please let it start," she whispered a quick prayer as she turned the key. It clunked a bit, and then revved to life. "Thank you."

Halfway to the store, she began wondering why she drove. The gas station that did double duty as the grocery store was only a hop, skip and a jump from her town house, and there was a stop sign in there. Walking would have been almost as fast.

Jessaca glanced at the curb where she had parked on her first day into town. It left an easy quick path to the door and back. However, at the moment, the parking spot in question was occupied by a four door, jacked up truck.

"Seriously?" Jessaca said out loud, tapping her brakes. It wasn't that often that she was in a hurry. Why did this guy have to pick this time to park there?

With a sigh, Jessaca pulled up in front of the truck and parked. She glanced at her fingers and listed off the three things she needed to remember. "Dog food, coffee, and eggs." Grabbing for her purse, she unbuckled.

"This shouldn't take long," she mumbled, and then winced. She was going to have to learn not to talk to herself one of these days.

Officer Clay Martin swung his police cruiser into the parking lot and let out a sigh. Supper at the aunts' house wasn't the worst thing in the world, but it had to be close. Especially when they couldn't keep out of an investigation.

Clay forced himself to stop thinking about all of the girls they'd invited over to introduce him too, and instead scanned the parking lot. If he hurried, he could get in the store, buy some cold cereal and be back in time to hit the station, drop off some paperwork, and make it to his aunts on time.

He took a deep breath. It would take some careful talking to avoid more talk about the death of Austin Royce.

He glanced over the cars parked along the curb. Mr. Hanson's truck was easy enough to recognize, but that red cruiser wasn't familiar.

He did a double take and groaned. If he didn't do anything, no one would ever know that it was parked halfway in front of the yellow curb line, but if he did nothing, and the driver got comfortable parking in front of yellow lines . . .

There's a lot of snow, they probably don't even know where the yellow line is. It's no big deal, he tried to tell himself, but he knew that it was. If the driver parked along yellow curves, it could block someone's view, like Liz's. He winced. That was the last thing he needed to think about, but he couldn't get the images of the wreck from his mind. His throat tightened and a tingling sensation filled his nose. Blinking the extra moisture from his eyes, he cleared his throat. He had to stay focused.

Clay grabbed his notebook and headed for the cruiser. He jotted down the license number and headed back to his car.

Typing in his laptop password, he scanned the area again. When he was sure that no one was around, he began his research. He'd meant to find the name of the owner and the hometown of the owner, but as he began research, he found himself digging.

"Jessaca Maria Anderson," he mumbled. "Age, thirty-one." He paused, a year younger than him. A woman that age ought to know the rules better. She was totally getting a ticket.

"Height, 5'2. Hundred and twenty-three pounds. . ." He scanned her information, and then clicked around on the screen until he was in a deeper website. He glanced over his shoulder. What right did he have to do all this research? The woman had just parked wrong! Clay ignored the feelings and kept researching. Strange. According to the local school website, she was here to be a music teacher, but she hadn't been hired yet. Before that . . . she didn't exist.

Shutting his laptop, he leaned his head back. A teacher. Right before Christmas was an odd time for a teacher to show up. Unless she had something to do with Royce's death . . . Clay bit his lip. *Stop it,* he chided himself. *You can't assume that everyone is hiding stuff.* But the fact remained. A woman

47

with no background had moved to town for a job that she hadn't even been hired for yet! If that wasn't strange, then he didn't know what was!

A woman exited the store, tossed some change into the Salvation Army bucket, and then headed for the cruiser. Clay grabbed his ticket book. The woman's long dark hair was loose and looked slightly wild and unkept. She seemed rushed.

Clay stalked towards her. Her hand was on the door, and she was juggling a grocery bag and a backpack size purse. At least she fit the description of the owner so he wouldn't have to check her license for the information he already had.

"Miss Anderson, I have a ticket for you."

The woman stopped without turning around. "A ticket for what? A symphony orchestra? Or maybe a movie? I think it's quite forward of you to assume I want a date, because I don't. I don't date and I never have. I'm happily single. Besides, I have a dinner date tonight in just a few minutes and I need to go." She shoved her grocery bag into the car and turned to face him.

Her eyes bugged. "Oh! I . . . I didn't realize . . . I mean . . . that is . . . I didn't see your uniform and . . . I thought . . ."

Clay fought the smirk. "This ticket, is for the parking job." He nodded towards the PT cruiser. "You're by the yellow curb."

Jessaca Anderson glanced from her parking job to his face. "I . . ." she huffed, and her breath hung in the cold air.

He raised an eyebrow, waiting for a response. *"Come on it's lovely weather for a sleigh ride together with you!"* The loud speaker blared Christmas music, and Clay frowned. Who had picked this song to play at this moment?

"I also have a supper date tonight, so if you'll take your ticket, I have to go."

Jessaca stared at the ticket. "Seriously?" She walked around the front of her car and scraped her shoe in the snow. "I couldn't see the line at all. But I'm only half in front of the yellow, I'm also half in front of the grey. Does that count for anything?"

"The front end of your car could block someone's view and cause an accident. Now take your ticket. I have to go."

Jessaca stared at the ticket for another moment, and then took it. "Well, thank you, sir, for being concerned for us drivers, and for doing your job." She paused, and Clay tensed. It wasn't often that he was thanked for giving out a ticket, but the tone in Jessaca's voice said that more was coming.

She raised an eyebrow. "But despite you doing your job, if I'm late tonight to dinner, I'm going to blame you. Is that

49

alright?" She didn't look mad, but Clay shifted anyway. You never can tell about women.

"You can blame me all you want, but only if I can blame you for my late entrance at supper tonight."

"Deal!" She flashed a bright smile, and then hopped into her cruiser. "Merry Christmas!" she said before pulling her door shut.

"Merry Christmas," Clay muttered as he turned towards the store. A figure dashed around the corner of the building and Clay sighed. It was probably nothing but . . . Clay glanced at his watch and frowned. He was already late, what was five more minutes?

He approached the building and slipped around the side. Keeping to the shadows, he scanned the mostly empty parking lot. No one seemed to be anywhere nearby. Clay stilled and waited.

A faint whimpering carried through the crisp air. The sound came from behind a crooked pile of pallets.

With painstaking steps, he approached the pallets. The snow crunched under his feet and he paused before taking a few more slow steps.

". . . won't know where we went." The fringed breeze carried a young voice. "Just eat. You'll feel better."

"What's going on here?" Clay asked stepping around the pallets.

The high-school guy's gentle posture went rigid and he shoved a little girl behind him. "We didn't do anything wrong."

Clay stared at the young man, and his mind played through his file. *Liam Bennett. Age, sixteen. Served nine months in a juvenile detention center for possession of illegal drugs.*

"It's not a crime to sit behind pallets." Liam's face was hard and masked any emotions, but his eyes flickered with hidden feelings. Clay frowned. If only he could read those feelings.

"No, it's not a crime." Clay paused. "Is this your sister?" He stepped to the side, but Liam rotated with him, hiding the child.

Liam's eyes glanced from the back of the store to the clump of trees beyond with a look like a hunted animal. Like he might bolt at any moment. The little girl's hand was visible behind him, and it clutched a napkin with a hotdog sticking out of it.

"Liam," Clay fought to keep the interrogating tone from his voice, and sound less threatening and more friendly. "For all the time we've spent together, I don't feel like I know you really well, would you care to step inside and I could buy you a coffee or something?"

Liam gave a jerky head shake, without taking his eyes off of Clay.

Clay sighed. How do you help someone that doesn't want to be helped? He could walk away, but if he found out later that Liam had stolen the food, he knew he would regret it. "May I see your receipt for the hotdog?"

Liam's face tensed again. "You got a search warrant?"

Clay shook his head. "No, but all I have to do is go inside and ask the clerk if you bought them."

Liam shook his head. "I'm not a thief."

The little girl peeked at Clay from behind her brother. Clay fought to remember her name. Was it . . . "Hi, Clara." Clay waved at her.

The little girl stepped out. "How did you know my name?"

Clay breathed a slight sigh of relief. "I remember your mother mentioning it during one of our meetings."

"You mean one of the times you arrested Liam?" The girl's bottom lip stuck out.

Clay shrugged. "Yeah, something like that." The girl's thin jacket hardly seemed enough in the December air. Snow began falling, and Clay sighed. "Does your mother know where you are?"

Liam's silence was answer enough. "Look, I took the hotdog from the garbage can after some rich kid bought more than he could eat. There's no crime in that. So, buzz off, and leave my sister and me alone. We're not hurting anyone. Besides, lots of teens are out at night. Why pick on me?"

Clay sighed. "If it was just you, I wouldn't be worried, but having an eight-year-old girl out here in this weather without her mother's knowledge isn't a good idea."

Liam grabbed Clara's hand. "We'll go somewhere else if we're not allowed here."

Holding up a hand to stop them, Clay sighed. "If you're in need of . . ."

"We're not looking for handouts," Liam cut him off.

"How's your mom's job been going?"

Liam shrugged. "Fine."

Clay nodded. The fact that he'd been getting food from a garbage can spoke volumes of conditions at home. How could he help them without letting them feel like they were a charity case?

"Can we go?" Liam asked.

Clay nodded. "If you ever need anything, don't be afraid to ask me."

Liam nodded, but his hard stare told Clay that he wouldn't even consider asking for help.

Watching them go, Clay tried to keep his feelings in check, but his chest ached. Liam's hard act didn't fool him. Not for a minute. His throat tightened and his eyes blurred. It seemed like yesterday that he had been like that, alone, and afraid to trust anyone. Afraid that people would leave him. *God, please, give me opportunity to help them!*

Chapter Four

Jessaca let out her breath as she drove home. As hard as she had forced herself to be polite, this was the last thing she needed. *Laci will kill me,* she thought. *Getting a ticket my first week in town is not what she meant by keeping a low profile! And finding a body without going to the police was . . . unthinkable!*

At home, she ran a comb through her hair and tried to pull it back. It only half worked, and she shrugged at her image in the mirror. What did it matter? Sweet Bertha and Donna wouldn't mind if she looked like she came from the gym.

"Are you ready, Callie?" she asked the small dog as it ran around her ankles.

She grabbed her coat again, buttoned it, and scooped up the Pomeranian. "Come on, Callie. Bertha said she'd have a treat for you."

Knowing Donna's love for mystery, she felt sure they'd discuss the murder that had been announced on the radio. Part of her was excited, but she knew she couldn't get involved. Not again. And at all cost, she couldn't let them know that she'd been there. Laci would never let her live it down. It was bad enough when she'd solved the kidnapping of the funeral home director, and the time she'd solved the female mechanic's murder. She couldn't get involved this time. Not without serious trouble from her sister. But at the same time, if the lead investigator was as incompetent as the radio had made him out to be . . . well, he might just need the help.

Jessaca trudged through the snow towards her neighbors' house, thankful for her snow boots.

"Jessaca and Callie!" White haired Bertha held the door open as Jessaca stomped the snow off her boots and stepped in.

"I've got a dish of meat scraps from the roast for Callie," Bertha said. "Our nephew isn't here but go ahead and make yourself at home."

Jessaca smiled and headed into the kitchen where Donna bustled about. The younger sister certainly had more flare. Her dyed, brown hair gave her the illusion of being much younger, and her gaudy earrings made her look like she belonged on a bling advertisement of some kind.

"Jessaca, honey!" Donna exclaimed. "I'm so glad you could make it. Merry Christmas!"

Jessaca smiled. "Merry Christmas to you too! It was so sweet of you ladies to invite me."

"Oh, it was nothing," Donna said.

Jessaca set Callie on the floor and unbuttoned her coat. "It was still sweet of you. I mean you hardly know me!"

"Well, moving isn't easy, and with you moving in so soon before Christmas, it's just the neighborly thing to do." Donna finished straining the potatoes, and then added some milk and butter and began mashing them.

"Oh, I can do that!" Jessaca said, crossing the kitchen and taking the potato masher from Donna.

"Thank you, Jessaca!" Donna busied herself with the vegetables. "We have a box of Christmas decorations for you to borrow. No house should be without lights at Christmas time."

"Donna! Don't make our guest work!" Bertha hobbled in on her cane.

"It's alright, Bertha," Jessaca insisted. "I wanted to help."

"As soon as those potatoes are done, I think we're ready," Donna said.

Jessaca glanced up. Both Donna and Bertha stared at her. Donna was wringing her hands, and Bertha looked on the verge of speaking.

"Is something wrong?" Jessaca asked.

The two women exchanged a look.

"There's nothing wrong, so to speak," Bertha said. "But we could use your help."

"I'd be happy to help, what can I do?" Jessaca paused from her mashing and looked from one anxious face to the other.

"It's our nephew, Clayton," Donna said. "He's had an awful hard life, and we had to raise him. The poor boy isn't married and is very lonely. Would you befriend him?"

Jessaca froze for a moment, and then mashed the potatoes with vigor as she tried to think up an answer. "Um . . . ladies, as much as I would love to help, I don't think that's a good idea. I don't know him."

"That's why you're here tonight!" Bertha said. "You can get to know him."

Jessaca tried not to groan out loud. She glanced down. The potatoes were mashed beyond perfection. "I think the potatoes are ready now."

Donna took over, and Bertha led Jessaca to the table. Jessaca smiled at the homey dining room. The candles were lit, and the garland around the room gave it the feel she remembered from her childhood home.

In one corner, a small Christmas tree perched on a bent stand. The haphazardly placed ornaments only partially concealed the ugly tree. Jessa smiled. It was just the kind of tree Laci would like. And the homemade decorations . . . they looked like the ones her little brother Josh had made when he was six. *It's precious!* she thought.

A small manger scene sat below the tree, and Jessa paused. How incredible! That God, had become a man to pay for her sins! He was so much more than just a baby in a manger. He was God Almighty!

"We'd like you to sit here, by our nephew," Bertha said.

Jessaca opened her mouth to argue but forced a smile instead. How bad could one meal be? Besides, the sisters had been so welcoming it would be wrong to not sit where they wished.

Donna set the last dish on the table and stepped back. "Now, where is that nephew of ours? He's always late, just like my Harold."

"How old were you when you got married?" Jessaca asked.

"I was eighteen." Donna pointed to a picture hanging on the wall. That's Harold and me at our wedding."

Jessa stepped closer and examined the old wedding photo. "You two were such a cute couple. Do you mind if I ask what happened?"

Donna shook her head. "Not at all. Harold was an electrician. I don't think I'll ever know exactly what happened, but something went wrong, and the shock killed him."

"I'm sorry to hear that," Jessa said.

"By that time, Bertha was here alone, raising our nephew, so I moved in and started helping out." Donna went to the window and parted the blinds. "Where is that nephew of ours?"

Bertha glanced at the clock. "I say we start without him."

Jessaca glanced around the room. A ball of mistletoe hung in the middle of the doorway between the kitchen and dining room.

"I noticed your mistletoe," Jessaca said. "You have the traditional berries on it!"

Bertha glanced up. "You know them?"

Jessaca nodded. "It's the state flower of Oklahoma. The white berries are . . ." A gust of cold air swept through the room as the front door opened.

"Sorry, I'm late," a familiar voice came. "I had to deal with a belligerent driver." The man had his back to the table as he took off his coat.

He turned to face the table, and their eyes met.

"Belligerent?" Jessaca raised an eyebrow.

It all made sense now. Their nephew, Clayton, was a policeman. The insecure policeman who was supposed to solve a murder. The policeman who'd given her a ticket. Clay Martin.

"Clay," Bertha said. "I'd like you to meet our new neighbors. This is Jessaca, and her dog Callie."

Clay's eyebrows lowered. "I've had the pleasure of meeting her before." His voice didn't sound like he'd had any pleasure in it.

"Why are you still in uniform?" Bertha asked.

Clay shrugged. "I didn't have time to change."

"Please, Clay, sit down there, beside Jessaca." Donna motioned towards the empty place.

Clay gave something between a strangled smile and a snort. "I think we'll be more comfortable if I sit over here." Clay grabbed the extra place setting and moved it across the table.

"You can't face her like that!" Bertha explained. "It'll be like an interrogation!"

Clay waited till the ladies were seated, and then he sat down opposite to Jessaca and folded his arms on the table. "Maybe I like interrogations."

Jessaca fought to keep her face blank. "It's too bad for you that I already know everything about you and I don't need to interrogate you." She cringed at the sass in her voice. That

61

was no way to start a conversation with someone you were supposed to be nice to.

"Oh really? You don't know anything about me that my aunts haven't told you." He glanced at his aunts with lowered eyebrows. His dark eyebrows made his blue eyes stick out, and somehow, even with his eyebrows lowered, he didn't look mad. He looked more like a little kid who just got grounded.

"I know that you're insecure, that you're thirty-two years old, and that you're in charge of the murder investigation. I know that you've had some girlfriend trouble, and that you're a very detail-oriented person." Jessaca smiled at her spiel of information, but he didn't seem impressed.

Clay leaned back and stared at Jessaca, ignoring his aunts. "That's all very nice, but that only proves you can listen to the radio, and my aunts."

"They never told me you were detail oriented. I figured that out myself." Jessaca sipped her water and noted that Clay squirmed slightly before straightening.

His uncomfortable look disappeared and was taken over by a professional cop look. "I believe I'll start this interrogation by telling you what I already know. Your name is Jessaca Maria Anderson. You're thirty-one years old, you're five feet, two inches, and you weigh a hundred and twenty-three pounds. You're a new teacher in town. You're not in any relationships, and you're from Missouri." Clay grinned.

Jessaca began to squirm. "Do you research everyone that you give tickets to, or just me? Because it's creeping me out."

"I only research people who strike me as trouble," he said.

Bertha pounded her cane on the floor. "Let's say grace, shall we? Clay, would you do the honors?"

There was a moment of silence and Jessaca wondered if Clay would stare forever. Then he ducked his head.

Clay took a deep breath. He wanted to thank God for the interruption from the awkward conversation, but wasn't sure how that would sound. "Dear God," he paused. How would this Jessaca feel about him praying? Would it make her uncomfortable? Why would he even care what she thought? "Thank you for my wonderful aunts, and for allowing us all to be here today. Thank you for this food, and . . ." He swallowed hard. "Please help us to have a pleasant time this evening. Amen."

"Amen," the three women echoed.

"Just grab whatever is in front of you and pass it to the left," Bertha instructed.

Conversation restricted to comments about the food for the next several minutes while everyone dished up, but when Clay was contentedly enjoying his aunts' cooking, Donna addressed Jessaca.

"You said something about the traditional mistletoe? Most mistletoe around here has red berries. How did you know they're supposed to be white?"

Jessaca smiled. "Because the plant, mistletoe has white berries. The artificial mistletoe people buy with red berries is a mix between the real mistletoe, and holly. According to tradition, whenever a man and woman meet under the mistletoe, they have to kiss, and then the man picks one of the berries off the plant and gives it to the girl. Once the white berries are all gone. People don't have to kiss under it anymore."

Clay snorted. "Yes, well, as romantic as you may think it is. Mistletoe is a parasite. It grows on trees and lives off of them. Parasites are hardly romantic." He glanced at the mistletoe. There was no way he would ever be caught under it.

"For someone who doesn't seem to be in the Christmas spirit, you sure know a lot about mistletoe."

While her comment stung, Jessaca raised an eyebrow in an innocent way.

"Contrary to popular belief, I'm not Scrooge." Clay frowned. Why was he snapping at Jessaca? He forced himself to breathe deeply. Just because a girl was beautiful and blunt didn't mean he had to be rude to her. *I'm protecting myself,* he thought, but deep down, he knew it was more. He didn't want these feelings. Not again.

Jessaca opened her mouth, but Donna cut in.

"Clay, we want to know all the details."

Clay glanced up with the best blank look he could muster. "Details?" This wouldn't be any better than discussing Christmas traditions.

"About the investigation!" Donna exclaimed. "We still haven't heard how it's going."

"I'm sorry, but I can't discuss an open investigation," Clay said.

"Oh, rubbish!" Bertha said. "You can talk about whatever you want! Donna and I can help."

Clay set his fork down slowly. "We don't know if it was murder." There was no way he would let his sweet old aunts get involved in one of his cases, especially a possible murder case! But, at the same time . . . maybe they could help. "You've already done more than enough." He paused. "But, if you really want to talk about it, we'll talk about Royce. What do you know of him?"

Donna and Bertha looked at each other.

"He was a scoundrel!" Bertha exclaimed. "If ever a man deserved to die, it was him."

Donna huffed. "Well, I wouldn't say it quite like that, since we are all sinners and deserve to die, but . . . well, it's true that he was an awful man. Give me a second." Donna got up and left the table. She was back in a moment with a notebook. "Clay, I'll share my homework with you. I made a list of all the suspects. Of course, Sally and Ken are at the top, followed by Larry. I'm leaning towards Larry right now. He's working at both the café, and the grocery store, and he stood to gain a lot by Royce's death. If that's not enough, his mustache looks sinister."

Clay sighed. "Really, Auntie Donna, you ladies need to stay out of it! I can't let you get involved."

"Making a list is hardly getting involved," Bertha defended her younger sister.

"But going around and interrogating these people is." Clay remained firm.

"But we may have found out something important," Donna said. "Sally's hands were shaking pretty badly. If she has some kind of medical condition that causes that,

66

then maybe that could clear her. Whoever killed Royce, probably had a steady hand."

Clay glanced from Jessaca's amused face, to his aunts excited faces. Praying for patience, he forced himself to relax and smile. "Alright, for tonight, I'm your guest. Tell me everything you think I should know. Who else is on your list of suspects?"

"His cousin, Janet Royce," Donna said.

"Janet Royce?" Jessaca leaned forward. "As in the school secretary? I've met her a few times and while she's perhaps a bit . . . odd? I don't think she's a killer. What motive would she have for killing her cousin?"

Bertha harrumphed. "Who *didn't* have a motive to kill him?"

"The usual motive," Donna said. "Love. Austin swindled her fiancée out of a lot of money. Her fiancée left after that. She may have murdered, hoping that if Austin were gone, her fiancée would come back."

Clay shook his head. "I don't think love is a good reason for murder. Besides, that was decades ago!" Of course, he would check it out, it was possible, but he couldn't let the aunts think that she was a suspect. They'd be sure to go interrogate her on their own.

Jessaca tore a section of her dinner roll and chewed slowly. When she swallowed, she looked up. "Murder is usually committed because of love, greed, revenge, or because the victim knew something they shouldn't."

"Maybe Austin knew something that he shouldn't have known," Donna said. "Like. . . well, like something!"

Clay shrugged. "He knew how to dig, and when you dig, you find dirt. He probably knew stuff about everyone in town that he shouldn't have."

"Then there's . . ." Donna paused. "Why don't you just look at the list. If you have questions, you can ask."

Clay glanced across the notebook page. Doing his best to look disinterested, he tried to memorize each name and the listed motives. If anyone in town knew people and their motives, it would be the aunts.

Clay leaned back and tapped his finger on the page. The list was long, but despite the long list of names, he couldn't be sure the killer was mentioned. It could be anyone.

"I think you can cross Brad off the list." Clay slid the notebook back to Donna, and then helped himself to more potatoes.

"Why?" Bertha asked. "I thought he should be higher on the list than number seventeen."

Clay raised an eyebrow. "You can't accuse a man of murder just because you don't like him. Or because he wears a funny hat."

"It's not that we don't like him!" Donna insisted. "It's that he doesn't like you! Have you heard anything he's said about you on the radio in the last six months? And his fedora is so outdated that *my* grandpa could have worn it!"

Clay shrugged. "Everyone is entitled to their own opinions. Just because he doesn't like me, and lets everyone know it, doesn't mean he's a killer. We have freedom of speech you know."

"But to discuss you on the radio like a criminal!" Bertha huffed. "It's not dignified. Any man who can do that, is capable of murder."

"Oh, and Liam!" Donna said. "We forgot to put him on the list."

"What would Liam possibly have against Royce?" Clay asked. He glanced at his full plate and his stomach lurched at the idea of Liam being involved. "He's been in a lot of trouble but he's not a killer."

"He doesn't have to have a motive," Bertha said. "You know what they say. He's a troublemaker. His teachers can't stand him. He has personally caused at least three nervous break-downs among the teachers in the last two years alone. He's been in Juvie, and his father is in jail. Like father, like son.

Besides, he was arrested for having crack cocaine in his possession. At fifteen years old! With that kind of record, he doesn't need a motive."

Donna nodded. "I've read about killers who kill just for the thrill."

Clay couldn't believe that. Not of Liam. Sure, he'd had his problems but . . . he looked up, and his eyes met Jessaca's. She seemed a bit confused, and Clay felt strangely pleased at her confusion. "So, Jessaca, what do you think of all this?"

"Jessa. You can call me Jessa, that's what most people call me." Jessa leaned back. "As for this whole murder thing, I think you better figure it out before Christmas."

"Christmas?" Clay sighed. "That doesn't give me much time."

"How much time do you want when there's a killer on the loose?" Jessa asked. "The whole town is going to be worried about this until you find out who did it. The truth of who did it, will set the town free from their worry. It would be a fitting Christmas gift from you to the town, don't you think? The gift of the truth. If the truth is that he died of natural causes, so be it." She cocked an eyebrow, and he frowned. He'd never applied that Bible verse to his town before, but suddenly, it made sense. *The truth will set you free,* he quoted in his mind. Resolve washed over him. He had to solve it before Christmas. He had to find the truth.

The women began discussing the crime scene, and what they'd seen as Clay finished his potatoes.

His phone vibrated in his pocket and he pulled it from his pocket. "Excuse me, I have to check this."

He held his finger on the fingerprint reader to unlock his phone, and then clicked on the new text.

Initial examination done. Sending samples to toxicology. Death by asphyxia. Estimated time of death, 5:30 a.m. Cause of asphyxia, won't know till toxicology report. I suspect cyanide. Everything points to that. If it wasn't cyanide, then it's another poison.

"Who is it?" Donna asked. "You look pale."

Clay swallowed hard. "It's from the medical examiner."

Chapter Five

"What did he say?" Bertha asked, leaning forward.

Clay shook his head and pushed his home screen button. "I can't say, but it's a little bit more truth."

"What's wrong?" Donna asked.

Clay shook his head again. How could he tell them what was wrong? "Excuse me," Clay said, pushing to his feet. "I have work to do."

"But you haven't had dessert yet!" Bertha exclaimed. "And we were hoping you would stay and play some games with us."

"Sorry, Aunties, but I really have to go." Clay glanced at Jessa. If it weren't for her, and the text, he'd love to stay and spend time with the aunts, but no . . .

"At least, let me send a piece of pie with you," Donna said, hurrying towards the kitchen.

"I'll help you," Bertha said, following her sister.

Clay grabbed his coat, and stood by the door, waiting. How long could it take to get a piece of pie? And how long would it take to get the toxicology reports back? If they confirmed that it was cyanide . . .

"I'm sorry," Jessa's soft voice jolted him out of his thought.

"For what?" Clay asked.

"For ruining your evening with your aunts. If I'd have known they were going to make it awkward for you, I wouldn't have come."

Clay frowned. Something about her was . . . honest. He let his frown deepen. She couldn't be honest. She was just trying to pull his leg. That was it. She wanted to soften him. Well, it wasn't going to work. "Do you say that to all the guys that you're trying to charm? It won't work. I'm not interested, and you can apologize, and be sweet till the cows come home, but I'm not going to be interested."

A look flashed across her face. Was it . . . pain? Hurt? Embarrassment? No, it was probably guilt at being caught in a scheme.

Jessa pulled herself up to her full, but short height. "I already told you that I don't date, and I'm not trying to get to know you, or make it awkward for you! I'm just friends with your aunts!"

"Is that so? And how many boyfriends have you had in the last fifteen years? I mean come on, you're thirty-one years old, I bet you've played dozens of guys by now."

Jessa's eyes flashed. "I've never been on a date!"

Clay snorted. If it was true, then she was an amazing woman but . . . it couldn't be true. "Now I've heard it all. You've never been on a date? Get real! A girl like you who's . . ." he stopped. He couldn't say she was pretty to her face, that would never do. "A girl like you who's as sly as a fox has probably played dozens of guys."

Jessa's lips trembled. Clay figured it must be rage at being caught. "Am I right?" he asked. "Am I a little right?"

"No!" she said. "You're not!"

Clay smirked. He'd dealt with a lot of female criminals in his time, but none as ornery as her. "Okay," he said in mock surrender. "So why exactly haven't you ever been on a date?"

"You may not believe me, but I'm saving my heart for the man I marry, and until I meet him, I'm not going to go around flirting with other men. I'm not going to date until I find the one that God wants me to marry."

Running a hand through his hair, Clay smirked. "People date. That's what they do. How do you expect to get to know someone if you never date them?" He could keep up the rough talk, but inside, he cringed. Was it possible that she actually was waiting for God's timing? Why hadn't he done that?

Jessa breathed slowly. "It's not my job to find someone. It's the guy's job to ask. If someone wanted to get to know me, they could do it without dating! I've gotten to know a lot of people by working with them, or attending church events. And any guy with any interest in me could always ask my parents or my siblings questions."

Clay shook his head. Either this girl actually believed she was going to get married by avoiding guys, or she was lying. The latter seemed the most logical. "You're going to have to find someone else to pawn your lies on, because I'm not buying. Good evening, Miss Anderson. Auntie Donna! I'm leaving."

Donna rushed out with a small plate of pie. "Don't forget this."

"I won't." Clay gave his aunt a smile, and turned to go, but as he left, he caught one last look of Jessa's face. She looked like he had slapped her.

"Merry Christmas, Clay!" Bertha yelled after him.

He tried ignoring it, but he couldn't erase Jessa's look of hurt from his mind. Her eyes actually seemed to have tears in them. It left a bitter taste in his mouth. He'd seen girls fake-cry before, but Jessa took the cake for being the best actress. Either that or . . . Clay shook his head. No. She couldn't be telling the truth.

The door slammed behind Officer Clay Martin, and Jessa sank back into her chair staring after him. She blinked back the tears that threatened and sighed. She was used to people not believing her, but the open ridicule from an officer was . . . well, uncalled for. People just didn't understand how hard it was to be thirty-one and not be married.

"Well, that was fun," Donna said, sliding a piece of peppermint cookie dough pie in front of Jessa. "We'll have to do it again some night when Clay can stay and play games."

Jessa forced a smile. "I've enjoyed spending time with you two, and it's very sweet of you to invite me, but I think it would be best if I didn't come over when he's here."

"Did he frighten you?" Bertha asked.

Jessa fought to keep from rolling her eyes. Frightened her? "No. I've dealt with a lot of frightening people in my life, and Clay isn't one of them. It's just that he doesn't like being in the same room as me, and I don't want to make it awkward for him."

"Oh, honey, don't judge Clay that fast. You don't know him yet!" Donna said. "He's been uncomfortable around girls for the last few years. It's not your fault. You just don't know him."

"And I'm not going to get to know him. Not while he laughs at everything I say. Not while he thinks I'm lying to him because I think it will somehow help my agenda that I don't have. He's the one that's got an agenda! He's the one who's had all kinds of girlfriends! I don't know what game he's playing, but I'm not playing it." Jessa bit her lip. "I'm sorry. I shouldn't have said those things."

Bertha calmly refilled her teacup. "Don't believe what they say about him."

Jessa raised an eyebrow, but kept her mouth shut. The last thing she needed was to make enemies of her new neighbors, and only friends in the town.

"You see," Donna said. "Clay's only ever had two girlfriends in his life. His first one was what you'd call his childhood and high-school sweetheart. Clay and Liz were engaged, but two weeks before the wedding, there was an accident, and Liz died."

Jessa sagged back in her chair. "That's awful." What pain Clay must have gone through!

"Clay didn't look at another girl until he was out of college. Having lost his parents in a plane crash, and his fiancé in a car wreck, well, he avoided girls to protect himself from losing again."

"Wait a second, I thought his parents divorced? And I thought he'd been jilted twice."

Donna frowned. "Brad is always saying things like that on the radio. He's pretty well got the whole town believing it."

"You mean he blatantly lies on the radio? Why doesn't anyone stop him?" Jessa asked. If the aunts were right about Clay, then the radio had totally warped her perception of him.

"He has the right to say what he thinks," Bertha said. "It's really Clay's fault that people don't know the truth. He could have spoken out, and defended himself, and straightened out the facts, but he'd rather just keep to himself. He was just a little boy when his parents died. I raised him, and while we had tough times, he was always a good kid."

"You said he had two girlfriends. What about the other?" Jessa asked.

Bertha and Donna sighed simultaneously.

"She was a trickster," Donna said. "She came in and drew Clay out of his shell of pain and made him enjoy life again. When she ran off with a mutual friend of theirs, Clay went back into his shell, and focused completely on his job. He doesn't trust many people, and especially not young women."

Jessa frowned. No wonder he'd been so short. No wonder he'd been so . . . so cold, so hostile. As sad as the truth was, it explained his actions. But what did it matter? She was going to avoid him. At all cost, she had to stay out of his way. And out of the way of the investigation.

Clay set aside his last report for the day and glanced at the clock. His shift had ended six hours before, but there was more that needed to be done. Running a hand through his hair, he headed for the coffee pot.

"You do know it's the middle of the night, don't you?" the dispatcher asked.

Clay nodded. "I know."

"Shouldn't you be getting home? You need sleep, you know."

Clay gave a slight smile. Alfred had worked as dispatcher for the night shift for over thirty years, and in Clay's time at the station, the older man had always looked out for him like a son.

"I don't think I'll be getting much sleep till this thing is over," Clay said.

Alfred chuckled. "You know, things might go better for you if you did get a good night sleep."

"Alfred." Clay swirled his coffee almost to the brim. "We've been friends a long time."

Alfred chuckled. "Yep. And I was friends with your dad before that."

"May I ask you something?"

Alfred leaned back and intertwined his fingers behind his head. "Anything."

"Supposing you're at a crime scene, and you have no idea how a victim was killed. Then, a bystander tells you exactly how the person was killed when really, no one should know except the killer. Then you find out that the bystander was right about the cause of death. Do you assume they're guilty? I mean . . . what if the person in question couldn't be the killer?"

Alfred stared at Clay from his slightly reclined position.

Clay sighed and half-sat on the desk. "I guess you might as well know. At the crime scene, Auntie Donna told me to check for cyanide. She told me she figured that was the cause of murder. The medical examiner told me it was cyanide that killed Austin. At least, he thinks it was cyanide. We've got to wait for the toxicology report. The horrible thing is that, well, Auntie Bertha and Auntie Donna made the fudge that Austin was eating when he died. There's no doubt about that. The aunties are so proud of their cookie dough fudge that even if it was responsible for the death of a hundred people, they'd still claim it was theirs. If she put cyanide in it . . ." Clay shook his head at the ridiculousness of what he was saying. Yet as the lead on the case, he couldn't ignore the facts just because he didn't believe his aunt was guilty.

"What do you think?" Clay asked. He looked down at his swirling coffee, and then glanced back at Alfred's frowning face.

Alfred shrugged. "You can't mix your feelings with the facts. Even the best of people disappoint us."

"But Auntie Bertha and Auntie Donna!"

"Clay, every one of us is born a sinner. Your aunts, you, me, everyone! I mean, you don't have to teach a kid how to lie, or steal, we're born knowing how to sin. We're all capable of horrendous crimes. Even your aunts."

Clay set down his coffee and rubbed his temples.

"Austin Royce is beyond earthly punishment, but all his wrong doings, are going to be paid for. When he stands before God, and has to give account for all his sin, he's not going to come out on top. And Hell isn't going to be any party. He's going to be punished for all eternity for what he's done."

"I know, but . . . what's that got to do with whether or not my aunties are the killers?"

"Clay, your aunts know the Bible. They know that God holds vengeance in His hands. They knew that Austin was going to face God. Now why would they kill him when they knew that his days were numbered? When you know that God's keeping an account, and that He will see justice done, it makes you a lot more patient with people. I reckon that even if your aunts hated someone, they'd leave it to God. I mean seriously, why would you hurt someone when you know that God's got it handled?"

Clay raked his fingers through his hair. "Yeah, I guess you're right. I just . . . I don't understand how she could have been so sure that it was cyanide when no one else knew." It didn't make sense. Cyanide? Donna had talked about arsenic, strychnine, hemlock, monkshood, and other poisons, but never cyanide. At least, not that Clay remembered.

"You should get some sleep," Alfred said. "You'll function better in the morning on your quest for truth."

"I guess you're right." Clay headed for the basement. *Truth.* The word echoed in his head. *The truth shall set you free.*

The apartment in the basement of the police station wasn't what you'd call 'homey'. In fact, the cement walls, and low ceiling with florescent lights gave it a prison feel. Clay opened the fridge and saw the piece of mint cookie dough pie the aunts had sent.

Sitting down at the old desk he used for a table, he sighed. At times like this, moving back in with the aunts seemed like a good idea. This hole in the ground was . . . lonely. But despite his own loneliness, he could never put the aunts in danger. Not again. Besides, by paying the county rent, it helped the town as well as his aunts. At least it was warm and dry. His mind wandered to Liam and Clara. Were they home? How often did they wander the streets at night?

His stomach knotted as he thought of Clara's pinched face, and Liam's mask of control that hid his struggles. If he could only help them . . .

He chided himself. Who was he to think he could help the kids? He didn't have experience in that kind of thing. He'd never been a father, he didn't remember much of having a father, and he certainly hadn't been around kids much, but . . . if he got help, maybe he could figure it out.

DECEMBER 21ˢᵗ

Donna pulled the muffins from the microwave and let them cool. Who would know they'd been in the freezer for two weeks? As soon as they were cool, she covered them with plastic wrap and headed for the car. If she wasn't back by breakfast, Bertha would find her note.

Donna turned the radio on and listened to the morning announcements. In five minutes they'd switch to a half-hour gardening show and then Brad would come on. Donna had never been able to figure out why they played a gardening show in December, but the routine never changed. That was one thing about Brad and his radio station. They were consistent. Perhaps consistently mean, but consistent nonetheless. He'd be there fifteen minutes early, and she intended to be there to talk to him before he went on the radio.

"Good-morning, Mrs. Martin!" Zoe said.

Donna smiled at the young woman in front of the welcoming desk and tried not to shake her head at the reindeer head band. "It's a good-morning, indeed. Is Brad in yet?"

"No, Mrs. Martin, but he should be in soon. You're welcome to wait for him."

Donna smiled to herself. *Mrs. Martin.* Even in marriage she hadn't been able to get rid of the name Martin. Harold had joked about it when they had married. How everyone would think he was taking on her last name, but she knew he hadn't minded that they shared the last name before marriage. At least her name wasn't Mary Johnson or something *really* common.

"So," Zoe began in an, I-want-to-know-everything, tone. "I hear you're the one that found the body, and that he was eating *your* famous fudge when he died."

"Hmmm." Donna nodded. "That's true."

"What was it like?" Zoe asked with a sparkle in her eye.

Donna yawned. "Well, it was not what I was expecting." She headed for the door. "I think I'll be going now. Merry Christmas!"

Closing the radio station door behind her, she sighed. Oh, she didn't mind talking about it, but Zoe wasn't exactly going to help solve anything, and with her loud, open-mouth-gum-chewing habits, she didn't encourage conversation. Gossip. That was all people like her wanted. She'd make a good news reporter whenever Brad made up his mind to retire.

Donna leaned against her car. She had more important things to do than gossip. She was going to find the killer, and Brad was the next logical person to talk to.

Across the parking lot, Timmy Berg leaned against a light pole. A huge lit up snowflake hung just below the light, just like the other ones in town. Donna waved at him, but he either didn't see her, or pretended not to see her. She headed towards him.

"Merry Christmas, Timmy!" she called.

Timmy's head jerked up, and he looked around in panic, when he saw her, he relaxed. "Merry Christmas, Mrs. Martin"

Donna never passed up an opportunity to speak to the young man. Having been left in Middle Ridge almost thirty years before by his parents, he'd become part of the town and had never left. The Berg's had taken him in, but in a sense, the whole town had adopted him.

"How are you today?" Donna asked.

Timmy shrugged. "I'm going to shovel snow again for Mr. Brad! And the sun is shining." He grinned his winsome smile, and Donna found herself smiling with him. For having been born with severe mental disabilities, and having flunked through school, he still knew what was important, sunshine, and smiles.

"Are you waiting for Mr. Brad?" Donna asked.

"I'm waiting for Mr. Brad," Timmy said. "He's a nice man. I like his hat." Timmy's eyebrows lowered.

"Is something wrong?" Donna asked.

"He's a nice man, but he doesn't like me talking about the accident."

"What accident?" Donna asked.

Timmy glanced over his shoulders. "The one where Mr. Royce died. Mr. Brad said I shouldn't tell people I saw him at the school that morning. Other people were there too. Mr. Brad is going to be late. He's a slow man."

As if on cue, Brad pulled into the parking lot and got out. His fedora was at its usual crooked angle, and his face was contorted in a scowl. "Timmy! Get over here!" He yelled from his car. Timmy obediently jogged to his car.

Donna sighed. Brad was the only person in town who dared take advantage of Timmy. The rest of the town, well, they just wanted to help Timmy have a happy life.

Donna could see Timmy cringe from where she was, but she wasn't sure if she should approach or not. Brad handed Timmy something that Timmy shoved into his pocket, and then Timmy ran off.

"Were you looking for me?" Brad yelled.

Chapter Six

Pounding footsteps on the metal staircase jolted Clay awake. He reached for his gun. The light flickered on, and Isaiah stood there in full uniform.

Clay bolted upright, letting his hand fall away from his gun. "Did I oversleep?" He glanced at the clock, he still had an hour before he had to be at the office. "What are you doing here?"

"Never mind that now, you need to hear this." Isaiah reached for the radio and clicked it on.

"*. . . question before we go. You've convinced us all that the murderer is a resident of Middle Ridge. I won't ask you who you think it is, but I would like to ask if you think we're safe?*" Brad's voice came through the radio.

Clay frowned. Who would go on the radio, interfering with his case, and advertising that it was a local person? He hadn't even announced that it was murder!

"Well, I can't be sure," Donna said. *"The police are doing their best, but . . . well, I think everyone listening needs to make sure they take extra precautions. Since it was cyanide poisoning, we should be careful what we eat, and watch your back. With a killer on the loose, you never can tell. I believe I'm very close to finding the killer, and until I do, stay safe."*

Brad signed off and the station switched to Christmas jazz music. Clay clicked it off and turned to Isaiah. "What was that all about?"

Isaiah shrugged. "You missed most of it, but Brad interviewed your aunt. Your aunt gave some very convincing arguments that it was a local killer. She also gave details about the crime scene, and you heard her ending. She announced to the town that she was going to solve it."

Clay paced the room. His nostrils flared.

"You worried she'll solve it before you?" Isaiah asked.

Clay stopped and put his hands on his hips. "I wish she would! The sooner the better." He sighed. "I can't believe she did that! I mean she put herself in danger, she probably scared the town, and she's interfering with a case. I *have* to solve this."

Isaiah put a hand on his friend's shoulder. "You know, you don't have to prove anything."

"To you, maybe not, but to the town . . . to Brad and his radio station . . . I'm not sure I can handle what he'd say if I failed this case and let an elderly woman solve it for me."

Isaiah grinned. "So, you're human after all. I mean, Brad's been saying rotten stuff about you for months, I wondered when it would start to bother you."

"It's bothered me all along! I just . . . I can't let his actions bother me. If I do, I'll become bitter and angry. Neither of those are right responses, and I've seen enough people to know that bitterness and anger would hurt me more than him. Jail is full of people who got bitter and angry and didn't love their enemies. No, I have to love him. But it is hard!" Clay slammed his left fist into the palm of his right hand. "It's awfully hard."

Isaiah nodded. "I know. So, forget about Brad for now. You need to get ready for the day. And don't forget to shave."

Clay ran a hand over his rough face as he watched Isaiah climb the metal stairs.

He reached for his Bible and flipped to the book of Ephesians where he'd left off the day before.

He tried to calm his mind as he read. In chapter four, he paused as he read verses thirty-one and thirty-two.

Let all bitterness, and wrath, and anger, and clamor, and evil speaking, be put away from you, with all malice: And be ye kind one to another, tenderhearted, forgiving one another, even as God for Christ's sake hath forgiven you.

Clay sighed. *God,* he prayed silently. *I've been getting angry lately. So many things seem wrong in my life and . . . well, I guess I've forgotten how much you've forgiven me of. Help me today, to do the right thing, and to keep myself from getting angry. I want to live in such a way that people see you in my actions but . . . I need help!*

Clay hadn't been in his office for more than thirty seconds when Mitch rounded the corner. "Sir, I can't deal with this anymore!"

"Deal with what?" Clay asked.

"All the phone calls! Everyone and their brother heard the radio this morning and they're all terrified that they're going to be killed. The phone has been ringing off the hook with concerned citizens!"

As if to prove his point, the phone started ringing.

"It's your turn to get it," Mitch mumbled as he left the room.

Clay picked up the phone. "Officer Martin."

"Martin, I'm not done with the tests, but I figured you want what I've found."

Clay paused as his mind registered the voice. "Yes! Of course, Tina. What have you found."

Grabbing a pen and his notepad, Clay waited for Tina.

"The fudge on the plate had cyanide in every piece."

Clay sank into his chair. "The fudge?" His mind raced. Why couldn't Austin have gotten cyanide some other way?

"Yes, it was in the fudge. The funny thing is, there wasn't enough poison in any one piece to kill a person. There was only enough to make you sick and land you in the hospital. Austin must have eaten at least three pieces in order to get a lethal dose."

Clay sighed. "Anything else?"

"There may be other substances in the fudge as well. We're still running tests, I won't know more for a while, but I'll keep you posted. I worked all night on it, and tonight, I'll probably have someone on it too, so is there another number I can contact you at if I get more information at an odd time?"

Clay gave her his cellphone number and hung up. The fudge. How could it be the fudge unless . . . he shook his head. "No."

"You hoo! Clay darling!" Donna's voice rang through the station.

Clay cringed. Were his sweet aunts, killers?

"Did you hear me on the radio?" Donna stood in the doorway of his office with glee on her face.

Clay took a deep breath. *Remain calm,* he reminded himself. *Forgive, relax, and stay calm.* "What were you thinking?" he asked. Forcing his voice to sound curious instead of accusing.

"Don't you see?" she asked.

"I see that you've terrified the town."

"That was exactly what I was trying to do!" Donna said. "The whole town is afraid. Even the killer is worried that he'll be caught, so what's the killer going to want to do, since he thinks I'm on his trail?"

Clay frowned. If she was the killer . . . then he had no idea what she'd do.

"I'll tell you, he's going to want to kill me! And when he tries to, you'll be there to catch him! And I think it's Brad. Timmy saw him at the school the morning of the killing. Maybe he did it to get more business for the radio station. Anyway,

93

we've got to find out soon. Christmas is on Monday! How can the town celebrate when a murderer is on the loose?"

Clay shook his head. "That doesn't prove anything, and it would never stand up in court. Timmy saw a band of elephants running around the park last week too. A court would never accept his word because . . ."

"Because he's handicapped?" Donna asked. "He may be handicapped mentally, but his heart is in the right place."

Clay nodded. "I know. He was only a few years behind me in school. He's a good kid, but the courts can't make decisions based off of people's good hearts. They need facts that they can guarantee aren't imagined. Now if you'll excuse me for a bit, I have something I need to take care of for the town's peace of mind. I'll be back in a few minutes."

Clay hurried to Mitch's desk. The young man had just hung up from another phone call.

"This has to stop!" Mitch groaned. "I'm going to have a nervous breakdown!"

Clay almost laughed at Mitch's distraught look. "Welcome to the real police force. Anyway, I want to talk on the radio for a few minutes."

Mitch grinned. "I'm on it." He called the station, talked with Brad, and got the okay.

"You're going live in five seconds," Mitch said as he handed the phone to Clay.

Clay listened as Brad introduced him. It seemed kind of silly, the whole town already knew who he was.

"So, Martin, what do you have to say to us?" Brad cued him.

Clay took a deep breath. "I just want to tell each and every one of you here in Middle Ridge, that you have no cause to worry. We are doing our best to wrap this case up, and we don't feel that you are in any danger. While I recommend that you do take precautions, don't panic. We are handling this and will see to it that this doesn't happen again. We will find the truth. This is Officer Martin speaking on behalf of the Middle Ridge police department." He paused. Could he get in trouble for sharing his beliefs?

Making up his mind, he took a deep breath. "What happened to Austin Royce was terrible, and we are doing everything we can to see that it doesn't happen again, but I can't help but ask myself where I would be right now, if I had been the victim, and I think you should ask yourself the same question. I know we shouldn't speak ill of the dead, but Austin Royce was not a good man, and it's easy to point fingers at him. But if you had been the victim, would you be in a different place than Royce? There are only two options. Heaven, or Hell. Where would you be?" Clay hung up and sighed.

"Wow." Mitch shook his head. "I knew you were religious, but I didn't know you were a preacher!"

Clay shook his head. "I'm not. But this is my town, and I care what happens to the people here. I want to know that they know the truth. It's the truth that sets us free."

Mitch shrugged. "Well, at least, that should stop some of the phone calls. But if the boss heard you, he's going to give you a talking to about that religious spiel."

Mitch leaned his elbow on his desk. "You really don't think we're dealing with a serial killer or something?"

"Well, I believe we're dealing with something, but a serial killer? No. Austin Royce had a lot of enemies. Whoever killed him wasn't looking to kill the town, in fact, they probably think they did the town a favor."

Donna hurried out of the station before Clay could return. No sense in giving him a chance to get upset about it.

She hurried home and, after a quick breakfast, she talked Bertha into going for a drive with her. Technically,

96

Donna knew they were supposed to meet with the sewing group, but missing every once in a while, wouldn't make that big of a difference.

"Where are we going?" Bertha asked.

"Larry's house," Donna said.

"Isn't he at work?" Bertha asked.

Donna shrugged.

"What exactly are you planning?" Bertha asked.

Donna shrugged again.

"Now, Donna, I love mysteries as much as you do, but you've got to be practical! We can't just break into someone's house and search for evidence that they're a murderer!"

Donna nodded. "I know, but the back door on his house doesn't have a lock, so we're not technically breaking in. And I don't actually think Larry did it. I think Brad did it, but we can't ignore Larry. Good detectives check out all possibilities."

Bertha opened her mouth, but no words came out, finally she sighed. "If this works, I'll have to write a book about you."

Donna grinned and pulled around the backside of Larry's house. Parking out of sight from the main street, she surveyed the house. "He's gone. We're all clear."

Stepping inside the house, Donna wrinkled her nose. "You can tell a bachelor lives here."

Unwashed dishes littered the counters and kitchen table, and the trash can was overflowing. A dried-out poinsettia plant was the only sign that it was almost Christmas.

"Let's start in his room," Donna said.

Bertha nodded. "Okay but be careful not to leave finger prints everywhere."

The bedroom didn't smell any better than the kitchen. Dirty clothes sat in heaps around the floor, and a half-filled cup of coffee on the bedside table looked like it had been there for over a week judging by the dust around it.

"He needs a wife!" Donna said.

Bertha harrumphed and reached for a stack of papers weighed down by a can of mustache wax.

Jessa walked back and forth in front of the station a few times before working up the nerve to go inside. She didn't want to run into Officer Martin again, but at the same time, she needed to talk to Sheriff Vicklund.

"How may I help you?" a guy behind the receptionist desk asked.

"Thank you, Mitch, I'm looking for Don Vicklund."

The young man's eyebrows dipped. "Miss Anderson, how did you know my name? Have we met?"

Jessa smiled. "No, we haven't met, but that name tag behind you says Mitch."

The young man turned around. When he turned back to her, he sputtered for a bit, and then grinned. "It's nice to meet you, ma'am. Sheriff Vicklund doesn't spend much time in the office. He's probably on his beat right now, but if he is here, he'd be in his office. Just down the hall. You go past Clay and Isaiah's office, they share an office you know, and then you'll see the office where Shelby works, and then you'll see the sheriff's."

Jessa thanked him and headed down the hall.

The first office contained two desks. One was impeccably neat down to the smallest pencil. Sticky notes were perfectly spaced and in a straight line, and the swivel chair was facing the desk and perfectly parallel. This was definitely Clay's desk. Jessa paused, and stepped inside.

The other desk was the exact opposite. A drawer was left open, papers and sticky notes covered the desk at all kinds of odd angles, and the computer screen had a thin layer of dust on it. Christmas garland, lights, and angels hung behind this desk, and starkly contrasted Clay's plain and neat space. But what really caught Jessa's attention, was the huge cork board on the wall.

Jessa glanced over her shoulder, and then stepped closer. It was definitely pictures of the crime scene. Before she had a chance to talk herself out of it, she pulled her phone from her backpack-like purse and clicked a few pictures. She looked over her shoulder one last time, then slipped her phone back into her purse.

Why did I do that? She chided herself. *I can't get involved in another mystery. Not now.* She sighed. *I'll delete the pictures when I get home.*

She reached for her bag again. Why not delete them now and forget about the case? She wasn't even supposed to be in this office? Why couldn't she stay out of a case when she was supposed to?

"What are you doing here?" A frustrated voice asked.

Jessa let her hand fall from her purse and turned to face Clay. "I'm looking for Don . . . I mean, Sheriff Vicklund."

"Why?" Clay's forehead was wrinkled, and his eyes seemed bloodshot. Dark rings under his eyes hinted at a sleepless night.

He had no right to know why she needed to talk to the sheriff, but then she had no right to be standing in his office.

"It's personal," Jessa said.

"If it's a legal matter, I can help."

Jessa shook her head. "It's personal."

Clay frowned, he glanced over her shoulder at the cork board. "You shouldn't be in here. Sheriff Vicklund is in the end office."

Jessa started from the room.

"Jessa," his sudden voice startled her, and she turned to see him leaning against the desk, cracking his knuckles.

"Yes?"

"I'm sorry," he paused. "I feel like I should apologize for my behavior last night. I know I was rude, and I made it awkward for you. I'm sorry."

Jessa smiled. "You're forgiven. I wasn't exactly the politest either."

Clay shrugged. "You were rude because I was rude. I shouldn't have been rude to you. It wasn't a good display of Christ-like love . . ." He blushed deeply. "I mean of Christian kindness."

Jessa paused. "I appreciate you saying that. You're a Christian?"

Clay nodded, and an open look crossed his face. "I wouldn't be here if it weren't for the grace of God."

"That makes two of us." Jessa gave him a final nod and headed down the hall.

"Don?" Jessa knocked on the doorjamb of the open office.

The middle aged man looked up. "Hi! You must be Jessaca Anderson."

Jessa shook the extended hand. "Yep. I guess word travels fast in small towns. And Jessa is fine."

Sheriff Vicklund nodded, then his smile disappeared. "Of course, I knew you were coming before, but I wasn't sure I would recognize you without your brother and sister at your side. Have you heard any word?"

Jessa nodded. "That's one of the reasons I came by. I thought you should know."

Sheriff Vicklund got up and closed the door behind Jessa. "Have a seat."

Clay stared at the closed door. No one ever called Sheriff Vicklund Don. Not even his wife. And he never shut the door on the office. It could only mean one thing.

Trouble. What if Jessa had bad news? What if she was from the state lawsuit?

He sighed. At least, he'd done the right thing in apologizing. He felt better about himself now. Even if she was as much a villain as he imagined, at least he had a clear conscience.

He began making more phone calls, but after the third one, he stopped. What was left to do? He'd already interviewed all the likely suspects, and although most of them were mad that the aunts had beat him to the interrogation, they'd all been helpful, and none of them seemed to be the one. Many of them had wished him dead, but they didn't actually seem like they'd done it. Clay sighed. He'd gotten pretty good at reading people, and he felt sure he hadn't found the killer yet.

He went back to the pictures and stared at the board. Somewhere, the killer must have gone wrong. There had to be a clue. Something that didn't point to the aunts.

Despite his critical gaze, the body of Austin Royce, and the plate of cookie dough fudge stared back at him as if mocking his attempts.

He grabbed his coat. He had to do something.

"Martin," Officer Holm stepped in the room with his arms crossed. "I've gotten some complaints about your radio spiel this morning. While I admire your guts, you can't mix your faith with the job. You've offended some people. Specifically, by implying that they're no better than Royce was."

"None of us are better than Royce. One lie is enough to keep a person out of Heaven."

Officer Holm sighed. "See what I mean? You're mixing your beliefs with the job. That's not acceptable. You can't go around telling our sweet town people that they're no better than Royce. Some of these old folks were baptized before you were born!"

Clay frowned. "I didn't make those statements as Officer Martin. I made those statements as Clay, and they're true. Baptism isn't what saves a person. Only Jesus can wash our hearts clean of our sins."

"People look at Clay and Officer Martin as the same person."

"I am the same person. Whether in uniform or not, I'm the same person, and just like you don't think I can separate my first name from my job title, I don't think I can separate my faith from my work life. I'm not offended when people I disagree with get on the radio and ask me questions, so why should they be offended if I ask them questions?"

Officer Holm opened his mouth, and then paused. "Just . . . be careful. I've been around for a while and I've seen these things get out of hand." He turned on his heel and left.

Clay ran his hands over his face. What was the big deal? And what was Jessa taking so long to talk to the sheriff about? His gaze wandered back to the suspect board and he took a deep breath. Zipping his coat, he headed out.

Chapter Seven

"You hoo!" Donna met Clay in the reception area. "You'll never believe what Bertha and I found!"

"I have no idea." Clay followed the women back to his office.

"Before you scold us," Bertha said, "we want you to know that we're aware of the danger. We understand that you worry about us, but we also know that as a police officer, you can't do certain things without a search warrant."

Clay groaned. "Please tell me that you weren't invading someone's privacy?"

Donna glanced over her shoulder and shoved a crumpled and soiled piece of paper across the desk. "We found that in Larry's kitchen garbage under about two days' worth of trash."

Clay glanced at the paper. "So?"

"Don't you see?" Donna said. "This paper is a letter from Royce to Larry. It's a blackmail letter! And, Larry had a message on his answering machine from the morning of the murder. That means that he wasn't home that morning like he said he was."

Clay tried to breathe deeply. "You ladies searched Larry's house? I could arrest you for that!"

"No, you couldn't," Donna said. "The house wasn't locked, so we didn't break in, and there weren't any signs forbidding entrance. We didn't take anything but that paper from the garbage, and we left the place undisturbed, although, it was tempting to clean it up for him. Is it legal to sneak into people's houses and decorate them for Christmas? Or clean? Even if the man is a killer, he shouldn't live in a pigsty. And can you imagine living in a house the week before Christmas, and not having any Christmas decorations! It's the saddest thing I've ever seen!"

Clay swallowed hard. If the aunts saw his apartment . . . He turned his attention back to the blackmail letter. Larry had told him that he hated him like everyone else, but that he didn't have any specific grudges against Austin. This paper said otherwise.

Clay stood up and motioned for the ladies to follow him from the office. "I'm taking you two home."

"But, Clay!" Bertha asked. "Aren't you pleased with the information?"

Clay fought to keep his voice steady. "Pleased? That you two put yourselves in danger? Pleased? That you could have been killed? No. I'm not pleased. You didn't find out anything worth risking your life for." Clay took another deep breath and let it out slowly. *Please, keep me calm, Lord.*

"But we proved he wasn't home!" Donna insisted.

"You proved no such thing." Clay stopped at the aunts' car. "Sometimes people let the phone ring without answering it. He could have been home and just not answered it." Clay forced a smile. "You have no idea how close I come to not answering my phone when it rings sometimes."

The aunts looked slightly subdued as they got in the car and started for home. Clay followed them closely.

When they got to their home, Clay got out and helped Bertha to the door. "Please, aunties, promise me that you'll stay out of this. It's dangerous! You could get hurt."

"Clay, why is your room here empty?" Bertha asked.

Clay cringed. "It's not empty. I come home every time I get vacation time."

108

"It's been over a year since you've been out of your dungeon of an apartment. Maybe, if you stayed here with us again, we wouldn't worry about you, and we wouldn't try to solve your case?"

Clay shook his head. "You know as well as I do that when I live here, you two are in danger."

"That's silly!" Donna said. "We've only ever had a gunman in here looking for you once. It's not like an everyday occurrence."

"Once is too often. You could have been killed." Clay ran a hand over his face. How could he make them understand? "Please, just stay out of this. If you want to help, the only thing you can do is pray."

"We do pray for you, Clay. Every day." Bertha nodded. "You need it."

Clay smiled slightly. "Yes. Yes, I do."

"We can't promise not to leave the house," Donna said. "But we promise not to bother you about our escapades unless we actually have information that's helpful. Never mind that I thought our information from this morning was worth your attention."

Clay nodded. Of course, their information from the morning was useful, but that didn't mean they had to know about it. The last thing he wanted was for them to think they were helping. "Just . . . be safe."

Jessa hugged Sheriff Vicklund before heading for the door. "I'm sorry I don't know more."

The sheriff nodded. "I'm just glad you're here. Anything you know is more than I know."

Jessa paused in the doorway. "Laci and Josh know more, if you ever want to call them."

"Where is Laci? And Josh? I haven't seen them since the wedding."

"Laci is in Missouri where she works with Dad. And Josh is a doctor, but I can't really talk about his location."

Sheriff Vicklund nodded with understanding. His phone rang and he picked it up. He listened for a moment, and then stood to his feet. "He's here? Where?" The sheriff's face flushed red. He slammed the phone down.

Stepping around Jessa into the hall, he glanced both ways. "Shelby," Sheriff Vicklund growled.

"Yes, sir?" she said, pausing.

"Where's Clay?"

Shelby raised her hands in a shrug. "I have no idea."

The side door opened, and Clay stepped into the hall.

He glanced from Jessa to Shelby, and then to Sheriff Vicklund's frown. "What's wrong. Is this about this morning's radio call?"

Jessa shifted. There was no easy way to slip out of the hall without pushing someone out of the way. But was it right for her to be in on this conversation?

"A homicide investigator is waiting in your office." The sheriff's scowl didn't disappear.

Clay crossed his arms. "Why? I thought we decided I could handle it?"

"We did, but I didn't think he was coming so I didn't tell him we didn't need him." The sheriff glanced down the hall. "He just showed up, and he's waiting in your office."

Clay scuffed his shoe on the floor.

"Don't worry," Sheriff Vicklund said. "You're still on the case."

Clay grunted. "I could just as well not be on the case."

Sheriff Vicklund shrugged. "Sorry, Martin. He's got authority here. But look at the bright side. You could use the experience working with a partner."

"Authority? He might be my superior, but he isn't yours. You're the sheriff!" Clay pleaded with his eyes. "You could send him away. Couldn't you?"

The sheriff sighed. "I could, but I'm nearing the end of my term, and I don't think it would look good to anyone if I sent away someone that could help. Besides, the more people working on the case, the faster it will be solved."

Clay looked skeptical.

"Clay Martin!" a voice boomed. "They're trusting you with a gun now?"

Clay stiffened as the man approached, adding to the already crowded hall. "Lance? Lance Kramer?"

The man straightened. "Sergeant Kramer is my title now. I'd advise you to use it."

Jessa stared at the man. He didn't look like a bad sort, but he definitely had a chip on his shoulder.

"You two know each other?" the sheriff asked.

"We were in academy together," Clay said.

Sergeant Kramer gestured towards Clay's office. "I see you're making it big in the world."

Clay's jaw tightened. "I'm satisfied."

"I told you that as long as you proclaimed that religious nonsense, you'd never succeed. Now, I want the files on this case, and every detail you can tell me."

Clay cringed but gestured towards his office. The two disappeared down the hall, and Shelby sighed. "Poor Clay."

The sheriff nodded. "It'll be good for him. He needs to work with a partner once in a while. I just didn't wish Sergeant Kramer on him."

Jessa left the station and headed home. She didn't envy Clay's position, but at least now she knew she didn't need to get involved. With a homicide investigator in the picture why should she be?

She parked in her driveway and headed inside. An inch of fluffy snow covered the porch, so after leaving her purse and saying hi to Callie, she headed outside to shovel. After shoveling her sidewalk, steps, and some of her driveway, she headed for the Martin's house. If their nephew wasn't going to shovel for them, then she would.

She shoveled the sidewalk leading up to the front door, and then leaned her shovel against the side of the house and reached inside the wreath to knock on the door. There was no answer.

Frowning to herself, she knocked louder. Their car was there, they had to be home.

She tested the doorknob, it was unlocked. "Hello?" she called inside, but there was no answer.

All the possibilities ran through her head. They were probably just taking a nap. But what if they were hurt? Or worse? Jessa shut the door behind her and walked through the dining room. "Hello?"

She stepped into the kitchen and took a deep breath. The fresh smell of molasses cookies drew her gaze towards the island counter where a rack of cookies was cooling. The counter across the kitchen still had a dusting of flour.

Jessa paused. The sisters wouldn't have gone far and left the kitchen like this. Of that she was sure. Small puddles indicated chunks of melting snow. Someone had obviously been outside, and then come in. She squatted down and dipped a finger in one of the wet puddle like areas. It was still cold. That meant it had been recent. She looked towards the front door where the mop was leaned in the corner. Whoever had tracked the snow in had at least tried to clean it up.

The radio softly played Christmas music, and the house felt empty. "Donna?" she called again. "Is anyone . . ." she gasped. Sticking out from behind the kitchen island, were a pair of men's snow boots.

Jessa eased her way around the counter, and her hands flew to her mouth. "Oh, no!" She stared in shock. Who was this man? She reached for her phone and began snapping pictures.

Like a slap on the face, she realized what she was doing. "No!" she said out loud. "This is not our case! I'm not getting involved." She clicked out of her camera and dialed 911. She couldn't ignore this body. Laci would just have to understand.

After explaining the situation, she followed the dispatcher's instructions to get out of the house until police arrived. Standing in the cold, she hugged herself. Where were the Martin sisters? Who was the dead man? How would she explain this to Laci? How would Officer Martin feel finding another victim after broadcasting to the town that they were safe? Was that rolling pin beside the body the murder weapon? Why hadn't there been more blood? Why hadn't . . . Jessa forced herself to stop asking questions. "I'm not getting involved," she said out loud. Hoping it would somehow help her stay out of it.

Clay showed up with Sergeant Kramer following him.

"Stay here," Clay said to Jessa as he passed. He walked into his childhood home with gun drawn.

Jessa stamped her feet to warm them. She'd thought a small town like Middle Ridge would be free from major crimes, but this was the second murder in two days! Jessa groaned as she realized that whoever had done it, had probably left footprints that she'd shoveled away.

Shelby and Isaiah, a few other officers, and the coroner arrived around the same time. Two of the guys went in to ensure the safety of the crime scene. Jessa debated whether she could go back to her house and put on her warmer boots or if she needed to stay.

One of the officers approached her and took her statement. Once she'd signed the statement, she stepped back and waited. Waited for it to make sense. Waited for some answers. Why had she found both the bodies?

"Jessaca! What is going on?" Donna called.

Jessa turned to see the Martin sisters making their way down the sidewalk towards her. Jessa opened her mouth. How could she tell them? She waited until they reached her before speaking. "I'm afraid you'll have to stay out here for now. If you're cold you can go to my place. Where have you been?"

"We were bringing cookies to Mr. Swenson. What is happening?" Bertha asked. Slight panic flashed in her eyes. "Are we being arrested for Royce's murder? We didn't do it!"

"Nothing like that," Jessa assured them. "But . . . well, there's been another body. I found it . . . in your kitchen."

"My kitchen!" Donna started forward. "Who would dare to die in my kitchen?"

Jessa stepped in front of her. "I'm sorry, but it would be best if you waited here."

Bertha stared with her mouth open. Sounds came out, but no distinct words.

Jessa put an arm around each of the sisters. "There, there. Let's not get worked up. I'm sure the police will figure it out and get this awful killer behind bars."

The officers returned declaring the scene safe, and the team entered. It wasn't like some of the city forensic teams she'd seen, but she trusted the small-town officers to do a thorough job. It was personal for them.

Brad and another girl showed up with press badges. His face was tense with the I'm-getting-a-good-story look, and his fedora was at its usual angle. The girl on the other hand, who looked to be around Jessaca's age seemed totally nonchalant.

"Zoe!" Donna said. "This is so awful! You guys aren't going to broadcast that we had anything to do with this are you?"

The young woman shrugged. "Whatever Brad says. He's the reporter, I'm just his tag along wannabe reporter." Zoe turned and sauntered towards the house.

People began coming and going, including Sergeant Kramer, but it felt like forever before the coroner and his team exited the house with the body bag. Jessa bit her lip to keep from crying. Someone was dead. Someone's family would be grieving. Someone didn't have a chance at the American pursuit of happiness.

117

Sergeant Kramer followed the coroner, spoke a few words with him at the ambulance that was taking the body, and then turned to the sisters. "You two are under arrest for the murders of Austin Royce, and Timmy Berg."

"Timmy Berg?" Donna asked in shock. "I just saw him this morning! Who would want to kill him? He was such a gentle young man, and he wouldn't have hurt anyone. Unless. . ." Donna paused, and Jessa held her breath. Had Donna not heard what the sergeant had said.

"It was Brad!" Donna declared. "He was talking with Timmy this morning, and he made Timmy mad. Timmy saw him at the school the morning of Royce's murder and Royce didn't want him to say anything. But why did he kill him in our kitchen?"

"Did you say we were under arrest?" Bertha asked.

Sergeant Kramer nodded.

"But we didn't do anything!" Donna said.

"We'll leave that to the jury." The sergeant looked pleased at his work.

"But we're innocent! If you lock us up, then the real killer will get away!" Bertha exclaimed.

Sergeant Kramer shook his head. "You're the real killer. You two found Austin Royce. He was murdered with fudge that you made. How would your fudge get poisoned if you didn't poison it? You had a lot to gain by Royce's death. He was going to take your house."

Jessa watched the ladies' reaction.

"He was?" Donna asked. "I didn't know that."

"Of course, you knew that. Then we have Timmy. He probably knew too much about you, or maybe you're just a serial killer and wanted to kill again. Regardless, his skull received a compound fractured with your rolling pin. That's how he died. With your rolling pin."

Chapter Eight

Sergeant Kramer began quoting them their rights, and Jessa stared in shock.

Clay came out, saw what was happening, and stormed over. "What is the meaning of this?"

"It's simple. Your aunts are killers." The sergeant was practically beaming at his quick solution, but Clay wasn't about to let them lock up his aunts.

Isaiah grabbed his radio and called for the sheriff. Brad came out with his phone extended towards the two men. Zoe followed behind with total indifference on her face. For being a wannabe reporter, she sure didn't seem to think it was too exciting, and from the way she kept switching her massive purse from shoulder to shoulder, she obviously hadn't learned the pack-light philosophy of a reporter. If she had to push her way through a crowd to get a story, she probably wouldn't be getting it.

Jessa considered stepping between the men, but from the way they were looking. She might just end up with two black eyes.

"I always knew you were a hypocrite," Sergeant Kramer said. "You can talk all you want about living by the Good Book, but as long as you abuse your powers to let the guilty go free, I'm never going to consider stepping foot into a church."

Clay took another step forward and clenched his fists. Then, a look passed across his face. He closed his eyes for a second, and then relaxed. "Lance, you're right. I haven't been the best example to you. I'm not perfect. I never have been, and I never will be. But I've never claimed to be any better than you. The only difference between us, is that I've asked Jesus to forgive my sins, and I stand before God with a clear conscience and my sins are paid for." He paused. "I know you want to make an arrest, but at this time, we only have circumstantial evidence." His voice was quiet, and his face was calm. "I'll admit things point to them, but I don't think the evidence is hard enough to convict them."

"That's Sergeant Kramer to you. And I'd say finding a body in their kitchen that's been killed with their rolling pin or having someone murdered with fudge that they made is pretty stiff evidence."

A car marked *Middle Ridge Sheriff* pulled up, and Sheriff Vicklund got out. "What's going on?" His tone was all business as he stepped between Clay and Sergeant Kramer.

"Martin is interfering with my investigation." Sergeant Kramer accused. "I've caught the killers, and he doesn't want me to make the arrest. If I were you, I would suspend him from duty until he learns what it means to respect his superiors."

"Sir," Clay said, "if you'll let me explain. See I was . . ."

"Martin, that will be all," Sheriff Vicklund snapped. "Sergeant Kramer, go inside, I'll be in there in a moment. I want you to show me your evidence. Brad, you and your sidekick, get out of here. We don't need any of this reported on the radio until we get some facts."

Sergeant Kramer cast a scathing glance at the two elderly women and headed for the house. Brad and Zoe headed for his car. Brad kept glancing back, but Zoe seemed in a hurry to go. *It's probably her first murder case,* Jessa thought. *That could make anyone nervous.* She remembered the first murder case she'd been involved with. Even after all these years, murder wasn't easy to deal with. It never would be. Taking the life of another human was so . . . evil. Something she never wanted to get used to.

"Martin, you're suspended until this whole situation is over," Sheriff Vicklund bellowed.

Kramer paused, glanced back with a grin, and then shut the door behind him.

"Sir! I . . ." Clay's face had paled. "I didn't do anything wrong."

Sheriff Vicklund glanced around at the other officers there. "You all heard me suspend him, didn't you? So, if Sergeant Kramer asks about what I said out here, that's what you heard. Am I understood?"

Each of the officers nodded.

"Good." The sheriff turned back to the wide-eyed Clay. "Martin," he lowered his voice. "Take your aunts and get back to your apartment. Stay put there until I contact you. The ladies are on house arrest, but all things considered, I don't want the public knowing where they're at. They could be targeted by the killer. So, keep them at your place. They're officially in your custody and you're responsible for them. I'll tell Kramer that I have them under house arrest in the custody of one of my men. Which is true."

Clay's eyes widened even wider. "You mean . . ."

"I mean I'll explain later. Do what you're told. You're not in trouble. I just can't let word get back to the big city that

123

we're so backwoods we don't listen to professional detectives. Kramer will continue on the case, but I'm not ready to arrest the sisters. Now git outta here."

Clay escorted his aunts to his squad car and left.

Jessa watched as Sheriff Vicklund sent away the rest of the officers and went inside to talk to Kramer, leaving her standing alone on the sidewalk.

"Hey!" a neighbor across the street yelled.

Jessa glanced up, the guy stood leaning on his garbage can. He jerked his head.

With nothing better to do, she glanced both ways and then ran across the street.

"What's going on over there?"

"Timmy Berg was killed."

The man's eyebrows raced for his hairline. "If that don't beat all. Who'd want to hurt a nice kid like Timmy?"

Jessa shrugged. "Beats me."

"Clay will find him."

She glanced the man up and down. Nothing unusual about his coat and scarf, or his untied winter boots. "You believe in him?"

"Everyone in town does," the man said with confidence. "Oh, sure, Brad's hard on him, and broadcasts stuff about him, but most of us weren't born yesterday.

Brad's had it in for Clay ever since his son was kicked out of academy, and Clay was top of his squad. We know Clay, and we knew his folks, and we know his aunts. Sure, he's kind of slow to make calls, but that doesn't mean his mind isn't working faster than most. Besides, he's helped almost everyone in town at some point in his life. He doesn't just read the Good Book. He tries to live by it, and it shows. He even learned to forgive and love the people who hated his dad. You have to admire that! We can't help but like him."

Jessa sighed. "I'm glad he's got support. After listening to the radio, it seemed like he wasn't capable of running an investigation."

"No one really believes the radio. I mean the radio suggested that Liam Bennett had something to do with it. That kid has got issues, but . . . well, he's not the killer type. Anyhow, I got to go re-fill the coffee pot. You want a cup?"

A smile crept across her face. Laci had warned her that these small towns were friendly, but she'd never seen a man invite a total stranger into his house for coffee.

"My wife just pulled some gingerbread from the oven and she won't let me touch it, but if you come over, she'll be more than happy to let us eat it!" The man grinned. "Do you drink coffee? Or are you too young for that? How old are you? Eighteen?"

Jessa gave a slight shrug. "I'm thirty-one, and I can't turn down a cup of coffee. Besides, I'm curious to know what you think of the suspects. Who is this Liam Bennett?"

Clay let Bertha clutch his arm as they descended the narrow staircase.

"I knew Vicklund could be trusted!" Donna said.

Clay escorted them into his humble living room, and motioned towards the sagging, floral print, couch. "I'm not sure he's going to be able to pull this off."

"Of course, he can!" Donna grinned. "Vicklund's old enough to know how important it is to keep our image. Laughing off a professional detective won't look good for our town. But Vicklund's smart. We'll solve this one under Kramer's nose."

Clay slid a leg up on his perfectly clean desk and half sat on it.

"You need a wife!" Donna said. "This home has no décor! It looks like a prison cell. Did you know that Christmas is almost here? Where's your tree?"

Bertha rubbed a hand across the hand-knitted afghan. "Your mother would be proud of how clean you keep this place, but she wouldn't be happy that you don't have Christmas decorations. Of course, if you were still living with us, you wouldn't have to worry about it. I at least wish you'd visit more often."

Clay leaned forward. "Aunties! Are you even listening to yourselves? You've been accused of murder, and all you can talk about is my décor! Okay, so maybe I'm the Grinch. You've been accused of murder! It doesn't matter what my house looks like."

"Oh, Clay. Dearie, you can't worry about us, we'll get our names cleared if you solve this case!" Donna insisted. She cocked her head to the side. "Are you worried because you think we did it?"

Clay slid off the desk and paced the room. "I don't believe you killed them but . . ." his words hung in the air. "Your fudge killed Austin Royce. You knew it was cyanide before I did! Your rolling pin killed Timmy. I just don't . . . I don't know how to explain away all the evidence!"

Clay ran his hands over his face, and Donna sighed. She hefted her way off the couch and approached him. "Clayton, look at me."

Clay met her gaze.

"Can you look me in the eye, and doubt my innocence? Or have you watched too much *Arsenic and Old Lace*?"

Clay's gaze shifted towards the floor, and he gave a quick shake of his head. "I know you didn't do it, but . . . what if I can't prove you're innocent?"

"Then you can send us to Happy Dale!" Donna said in a sing-song voice.

"This isn't funny! You could spend Christmas in jail! And I don't know if I can clear you." Clay stared at his aunts. "Why can't you take it more seriously?"

Bertha harrumphed. "Oh fer nonsense! Of course, you can solve it! I didn't raise you to be a nincompoop! I raised both you and your father to do the right thing, and to never give up."

Clay raked his fingers through his hair.

Donna wrapped her arms around him. "We're praying for you, son. You've got to trust God and let Him show Himself strong in your life! Just relax! God's got this."

Clay sighed.

Donna's arms tightened around him. "Listen to me, Clay. I know you've had some rough patches. I know you have a lot of guilt, but God's love is stronger! No matter what kind of failures you've had, God's love is stronger.

God's love has changed you, and it will continue to change you! You've got to trust God. He can help you solve this. He can work through you no matter what failures you've had, and no matter how bad a day gets, God's still got everything under control."

Clay sighed again. "I know, auntie. I know." He glanced around, and then straightened suddenly. "I guess if I'm hiding you from Sergeant Kramer, then I'd better set this place up for guests."

With a new confidence in his step, Clay walked around the room. "There's a lot more space down here than I use. They used to have cells down here, but when they built the new wing on the station, they quit using these, so, if I get some new mattresses down here, you can each have your own cell!"

Bertha rolled her eyes. "I'm too old for this kind of excitement!"

Donna grinned. "I always wanted to stay in a prison cell, but I didn't want to be arrested. Now, I get to stay in a cell to hide from the police!"

"You do know that we're still under arrest, don't you?" Bertha asked.

Clay laughed. "I love you two."

"We love you too," Donna said with a smile. "And I know you can solve this." She paused, and her eyes seemed unusually moist. "At least, you better solve it. I don't want to spend the rest of my life in jail."

Bertha sighed. "Already . . . what do you suppose the neighbors are saying about us? What will everyone think?"

Clay cringed. Of course, he could solve it, but would the results ruin him? If the aunts were the killers . . . no, he couldn't go there. His mind flew to his other options, and Liam's face flashed in his mind. Was the boy a killer? Was he smart enough to frame the aunties? It felt like yesterday that he'd been arrested after a tip from the aunties. Was he so desperate for revenge that he would kill to frame them?

Jessa said good-bye to her new friends and started back for her house.

"Miss Anderson!" The sheriff called.

Jessa jogged across the street. "Yes, sir?"

The sheriff glanced at the sergeant's car that was pulling away. "I need you to do something for me." He lowered his voice. "Kramer is free to make any arrest he wants. I'm trying to play it safe with him, you know, make us look good to the city. They kind of think we're a little backwoods like. Anyhow, I'm keeping the Martin sisters under Clay's custody and out of the way until the real killer is found. Kramer doesn't know where they are, but he knows they're under house arrest until he can prove they did it or find someone else."

Jessa nodded. "How can I help?"

"Would you put together some things for them? You know, pack them each a bag with some belongings and bring it to Clay's apartment? He lives in the basement of the station. There's a back door that goes directly to the basement. You can use that."

Jessa nodded. "I'd be happy too. But don't you think this is a little . . ."

"A little what?"

"Well, I mean hiding two old ladies in the basement of the police station to keep them from being arrested by a guy from the cities . . . it seems a little . . . odd."

Sheriff Vicklund laughed. "Odd you say? That's a laugh. I'm not concerned with how it seems, I'm concerned about looking out for the citizens of my good town and catching a murderer. This is my way of doing both those things." He rubbed his mustache. "Besides, things aren't looking good for the sisters. They're getting old and . . . well, some might argue that they're getting senile. I think it would be best for everyone if they disappear for a bit. I can't have them snooping around asking awkward questions. And if they are the killers . . . well, we need to keep them from doing it again."

Jessa nodded. "I gotcha."

"Here's a key." The sheriff fished a key out of his pocket. "If the sisters need anything from here, you'll be their carrier."

"How do you know you can trust me?" Jessa asked. "I mean you're a tight-knit community, why are you asking me, instead of one of your own? I'm the new girl on the block."

Sheriff Vicklund shrugged. "If you need a reason besides the fact that you're family . . . well, you teach violin and flute. Most old-maid music teachers aren't too likely to cause problems. Not that you're an old-maid but . . . well, I guess that's exactly what you are, but no offence of course."

"None taken." She could feel her cheeks warming. Like he said, they were family, if she couldn't take the truth from family, then who could she take it from?

"And, the sisters think you'd be a good one for Clay, so I'm willing to give you a chance. I mean some of the girls they've picked have been . . . interesting. But they've all been trustworthy."

"Did they tell you that?" Jessa asked. Who else knew that they'd match-made her?

The sheriff laughed a nervous sort of laugh. "Well, not in so many words, but the whole town knows."

Jessa forced a smile. "Well, if you happen to run into the town's people. Go ahead and let them know that I'm *not* dating Officer Martin."

"I reckon they know that," the sheriff said. "After the talking you gave him the other day when he was trying to give you a ticket . . ." the sheriff turned slightly red. "I think I'd better go before I put my foot in my mouth."

He turned and stalked away and Jessa took a deep breath. A small town had sounded good, but this was too small. Laci wouldn't be pleased that she wasn't staying off the radar.

With a sigh, Jessa headed for the house. She would just have to make the best of it. Three weeks wasn't that long. If she could stick it out till then, she could leave and no one would ever have to know where she went.

Although she wanted to get the ladies' things and leave as quickly as possible, she couldn't resist taking a look at the crime scene. The body was gone, as well as the rolling pin. Part of her wanted to clean up the kitchen, and put away the cookies, but thinking better of it, she backed away from the counter. She shouldn't even be in here, but . . . she pulled out her phone. Snapping pictures, she walked around the kitchen for different angles.

"Stop this!" she said pushing the home screen button on her phone. "You need to stay out of this!"

Sliding her phone into her pocket, she sighed. *Why can't I ignore this case?* she wondered. Of course, she couldn't ignore it. As long as people's lives were in danger, she couldn't ignore it.

Chapter Nine

Part of her felt strange going through other people's clothes, but at the same time, it seemed so natural. How often had she packed things for her mother?

As soon as the bags were packed, she hurried to the station. The back door was locked, so she knocked. As soon as she did, she frowned. What if the sergeant heard her knock? How could she explain? She glanced over her shoulder and caught movement along the landscaped hedge. It looked like a teen boy and a little girl. She took a step towards them, when the door opened, and Clay stepped out.

"What are you doing here?" His eyes narrowed.

"I've brought the sisters' things."

Clay glanced up and down the back street, and then took one of the bags from Jessa. "Come in."

The moment the door was shut behind her, she met Clay's serious gaze. "I was being watched."

Clay's eyebrows dipped down. "By whom?"

Jessa shrugged. "I don't know. It looked like a high-school boy and a little girl."

Clay's brow wrinkled. "That would be Liam and Clara Bennett."

"Why were they watching me?"

"Beats me," Clay said with a shrug.

Jessa followed Clay down the metal stairs, and through a doorway into a clean, neatly organized, yet prison like, living room. She couldn't stop thinking about the kids. What if Liam was the killer, and the reason he was watching her was because she was the next victim?

The two women were sitting on a couch. Donna held a notebook and pen and was writing frantically.

"Jessaca, dear!" Bertha said. "Did you bring my Christmas afghan?"

"No, I didn't," Jessa said. "But I can go back and get anything you ladies want."

"Oh, Bertha," Donna said. "We should have her bring some of our decorations for this dingy apartment. We could put a little tree in the corner and garland around the stair railing!"

The women started going back and forth about all the things they could possibly want, and making a list.

Clay finally cleared his throat. "Look, aunties, I know this place isn't the most cheerful for you, but do you realize that Miss Anderson has already brought you both a large bag full of stuff? How much more could you possibly need? I mean you're not moving in permanently!"

"Maybe if you'd been living with us, we wouldn't be in this fix at all!" Bertha said.

Clay's jaw muscles tightened. "Or maybe you'd be dead by now."

Donna turned to Jessa with a sigh. "One time. Onc time, someone came gunning for Clay at our house, and he's been afraid to be near us ever since."

"You could have been hurt," Clay said. "If Sheriff Vicklund hadn't showed up who knows what would have happened."

Bertha held up her hands. "Let's not have this argument again. The fact is, we're stuck here until the murderer is caught. Until then, we'll want the comforts of home, and the cheer of Christmas!"

Clay ran a hand through his hair. "Do you know what nick knacks do? They collect dust. I don't need more stuff to dust."

Footsteps rattled on the metal staircase, and Clay hurried to the living room doorway. "Sheriff Vicklund."

The sheriff entered the room and nodded towards the ladies. "I'm sorry about the uprooting, but I didn't do this just to keep our little town looking good to the higher ups. We're going to keep you two off the grid because the way I see it, someone is trying to frame you. If you're off the grid, whoever is committing these murders, won't have you to blame, so they won't be committing any more murders. We need to stop this killer, and if moving you two out of the picture keeps our killer from showing his hand, we'll hide you two until he's found. Plus, you're under house arrest. With all the evidence . . . you do look guilty. So, if you can just stay here, that would be great."

Bertha and Donna nodded.

"Of course, we'll do anything. As long as you're not hiding us to keep us from investigating," Donna said.

The sheriff paused. His silence told them that it was part of the reason. "Let's just say that we're trying to solve this without any more casualties."

"What about me?" Clay asked. "Am I really off the case?"

Sheriff Vicklund leaned against the wall with a hand on his hip. "No. You're still on it, but you're out of the office."

Clay cocked his head to the side like Callie did when Jessa offered a treat, and Jessa bit back a smile at the image.

"Sir?" Clay asked. "I'm not sure I understand you."

The sheriff took a few steps forward and leaned his hands on the desk. "Let's shoot straight here. We have a killer walking around our town. I'm not worried about our reputation as a police force, but I do worry about the people in this town. One of them is a killer, and we have to stop him at all costs. I don't care about what the books suggest. We have to do what works. I think our best bet is to have you working undercover. By this time, everyone knows that you've been suspended. You can do your job better now. You just have to be more careful about how you go about it. Kramer will work from the police side, and you can work undercover with the people. Everyone in town feels bad for you, probably even the killer. Use that to solve this case. Between you, and Kramer, this thing had better be figured out soon."

Clay rubbed his hands across his face. "I'll do my best, sir."

"That's all I ask," Sheriff Vicklund said. He turned to go, and then paused. "If I were you, I'd have Jessa help you."

Jessa watched Clay's face. His eyebrows lowered, and he followed the sheriff with his eyes. Finally, he turned to her. "Okay, Miss Anderson, who are you?"

"What do you mean?" Jessa asked.

139

"I mean how are you friends with sheriff Vicklund? You're the only person I've ever heard call him Don. Why does he trust you and why would he suggest you help me? Why can't I find anything about you from before you showed up here? Who are you?"

Jessa sighed. "Officer Martin, I don't know you, but I trust you. I trust you to do your best on this case. I trust you to do the right thing. All I'm asking is that you trust me. I can't tell you why my life is a secret, but I'm asking you to believe me."

Clay's eyes seemed to search hers, and finally he nodded. "Fair enough."

"Hey, Isaiah." Clay leaned against his friend's car. "Do you know anything about Jessa?"

Isaiah gave his usual lopsided grin. "Why do you want to know? Do you like her or something? It is about time you work up the nerve to try again."

"That's not what this is about," Clay insisted.

"Cause you do need to get married someday," Isaiah said. "I mean just look at Shelby and me, we've both had problems, but we've worked through them, and are stronger because of it. You need to work through things too. Jessa seems like she'd be a good one for you to work through problems with."

"Isaiah," Clay used his best threatening tone. "I'm serious, this isn't about me wanting to get to know her! The sheriff asked me to work with her. I need to know that I can trust her. You don't know anything about her do you?"

Isaiah's face sobered. "I did hear Sheriff Vicklund mention to Alfred that Jessa could be key to this investigation because of her experience, but besides that, I don't know anything you don't."

"She's a detective?" Clay leaned forward even more.

"How should I know? You know as much as I do and more! Trust me."

Clay clenched his fists and sighed. "Trust me. Every time you say that, I always get into trouble."

Isaiah's grin widened. "But at least it's fun trouble!"

Movement across the street drew his attention. He caught sight of Liam right before he disappeared around the corner. He took a deep breath. Despite Liam's shady history and obvious issues, Clay couldn't bring himself to believe that Liam had done it. But he also couldn't ignore how much he was hanging around. Something was up.

"I'll be back." Clay took off on foot and worked his way towards where he figured he could intercept Liam.

Sure enough, he spotted Liam coming.

"Liam!"

Liam's head jerked up, and his eyes flashed with something like flight instinct.

Clay held up his hands in a non-threatening way. "I just want to talk."

Liam's eyes darted back and forth, but he didn't move as Clay walked the last few steps and stood in front of him.

"What's wrong?"

Liam snorted. "Nothing."

Clay took a deep breath. "I'm under the impression that your home life isn't very good. Should I be calling in the social services?"

Although his face remained calm, fear flashed in Liam's eyes. "No," he kept his voice even. "It's not that bad."

"Why have you been hanging around the station?"

Liam shrugged, and looked away.

Clay hesitated, and then reached out, and put a gentle hand on Liam's shoulder.

Liam tensed, and his gaze flew to Clay's face. For a moment, Clay felt sure he would bolt, but he didn't. He slowly relaxed under the reassuring hand.

"I'm not a killer," Liam said. His voice cracked. "I just . . . Mr. Royce was a friend of mine, and I want to know who killed him. I figured watching you guys was the surest way to find out."

"Royce was your friend?"

Liam shrugged. "He didn't care that our dad's in jail or that our mom is . . ." Liam's eyes widened.

"Or that your mom is what?"

Liam shrugged his hand off and took a step back. "Officer Martin, I . . ." His eyes flashed longing.

"You can tell me anything," Clay said. "You know that, right?" In the times they'd been together after Liam's arrests, Clay had always fought to befriend the boy, and from the look on Liam's face, he remembered it.

"Thank you for everything you've done for me but . . ." Liam sighed, and his face hardened. "This is the only place there's any excitement! You can't blame a guy for enjoying that. I have to go." He turned and sprinted away.

Jessa re-filled Callie's water dish and then reached for her phone. It was time to call Laci.

After hitting her speed-dial, she waited.

"Hey, Jessa, what's up?" a chipper female voice blared in the speaker.

Jessa sank onto the couch. "You have no idea what a relief it is to hear your voice."

"Rough first week in town huh? I knew you'd have trouble settling in, but a parking ticket in your first week? I always said you were a bad driver."

With Laci's smile coming through in her voice, Jessa couldn't stop her own smile. "Hey now! How'd you know about that?"

"I have connections."

"Then you know about the murders."

The line went silent.

"Please tell me you didn't say murders," Laci finally said.

Jessa sighed. "How can you know about the parking ticket, but not know about the murder?"

"I actually guessed on the parking ticket. I've been checking your credit card statements."

Jessa started in on the story and explained everything. "I know I'm supposed to stay off the radar, but I feel like I need to help on this one. I've only been here a few days, and I already feel like this is home. These people . . . they're special. I want to help. I have to help. So far, all I've been doing is running loads of stuff

144

back and forth between the Martin's house, and Clay's basement, but I might need to get more involved."

"Is it the people that are special, or a person? You've mentioned this Officer Clay several times. Is he cute?"

"Looks have nothing to do with it!" Jessa paused. "Okay, so he's been a distraction. But don't worry, I'm dealing with it."

"You know I love you, Sis. If he becomes a problem, I'll talk to him."

"And say what? My big sister likes you but she doesn't want to risk her heart being broken so you'd better commit to marry her before she'll speak to you? Don't be silly."

Laci laughed. "It's my job to worry about you. When you made a commitment to keep your heart until you knew for sure if you'd found the right one, I made a commitment to help protect you. If you're not going to risk breaking a guy's heart, I'm not going to let someone break your heart. If the sheriff asked you to work with this guy, then go for it, I'll keep an eye on him. And if things get too bad, I'll call in reinforcements. Josh would want to know about him. He takes his job as protective brother *very* seriously."

"Don't be ridiculous! There's nothing to tell!" Jessa paused. "Anyway, back to my situation here. What about the whole staying-under-the-radar thing?"

The line was silent for a bit. "Dad would understand," Laci finally said.

"What if it puts him and Michelle in danger?"

"They both knew how dangerous it was when they left. They're prepared for anything, and I don't think Dad would want you to let your skills go to waste."

Jessa sighed. "I feel so disconnected."

"Well, if you'd become a doctor like Josh . . . or even if you'd have been content to work with the family, we could have stayed together. But no, you had to go and become a music teacher. A music teacher! And not just some side-job music teacher, you want to teach an entire school!"

"It's not just that we're apart, it's that . . . that she's with him." Jessa paused. "Do you ever feel like she stole dad?"

"I used to, but not anymore. Michelle is a good woman. Dad needed someone to look after him."

Jessa stared at the floor.

"Jessa? Are you still there?" Laci sighed. "I know you miss Mom. I do too. But I think she would like Michelle. If Mom had known that she was going to die that day, she probably would have told us not to let Dad stay single forever. Dad needs a woman to keep him from working himself to death."

Lexi paused, but Jessa didn't say anything. She couldn't.

"Okay, spit it out. What's bothering you? I can't handle your silence. We've talked about Dad before. We agreed he should get remarried. What's the trouble?"

"It's just that . . . well, for ten years after Mom died, I did all of Dad's cooking, cleaning, laundry . . . everything. I took care of him. I took care of you! I miss my job. Since he married Michelle, he doesn't need me anymore, and you're too grown up to let your big sister take care of you anymore."

A slight snicker came through the phone. "You need to get married, Sis."

"You're one to talk. When are you going to get married?"

"Oh, come on! I'm your little sister! I'm waiting for you to get married. As long as you're single, Josh and I are going to be your protectors and make sure no guys break your heart. When I'm not needed, I'll think about it."

Jessa couldn't stop the laugh. "If that isn't the most ridiculous thing you've ever said I don't know what is! You've never let me stop you from doing anything!"

"Okay, so maybe you're my excuse. I just haven't found anyone yet."

Jessa sighed. "Poor Dad! There's three of us. Three of us! And not a one of us has found the right one. Do you think we're too picky?"

"Too picky? No. I mean we've got to spend the rest of our life with whoever we marry so I guess we can . . ."

Callie's bark interrupted and Jessa tensed. Years of difficult situations had taught her to follow her instincts, and her instincts screamed that something was wrong from the way Callie was barking. "Hey, I gotta go," she cut Laci off.

"Is everything okay?" Laci asked.

"I'm not sure. I love you, sis." She hung up before Laci could argue. With heart rate speeding, she eased her way towards the kitchen.

"Quiet, Callie," she whispered. "Kennel."

The dog obediently quit barking, and hurried to its kennel.

Jessa flipped the light switch off, and scanned the yard. Whatever Callie had been barking at was outside.

A navy car sat in the Martin's driveway. Jessa paused. Instinct made her want to go find out who it was, but common sense told her that it could be the killer and she should call the police. With resignation, she called the police.

As Jessa hung up, a man exited the house.

Jessa paused. She'd seen a picture of this man before. She frowned. What was his name? Nels. Nels Christianson. Middle Ridge School's superintendent.

He paused at his vehicle, and then headed straight towards Jessa's house.

Jessa froze. The police would be here any second, but would she be dead by then? She peaked through the curtains and relaxed slightly. The neighbors across the street were also watching.

The doorbell rang, and after taking a deep breath, she opened it a crack.

"Miss Anderson?" he said. "I've got a flyer for the Christmas school benefit."

Jessa stared at him.

"We changed the date to this Saturday night, and I'm going around to let people know. You're certainly welcome to do a music demonstration for the school board. They'll want to know that you're capable of teaching all the music classes, as you would be our only music teacher. I got the papers you left me and have passed them along to the school board. I should let you know that there is one other person who is also trying to get hired on as a music teacher. I'm giving that information to the board at the meeting, and that may delay their decision. Dennis Nordlum can answer any questions about it, if you have any."

Jessa forced a smile. "Thank you. I appreciate the warning."

A police car pulled up beside the Martin's house.

"Nels frowned. "Is something going on over there?"

Jessa blinked rapidly. Had he seriously not heard? Or was he playing dumb? "A murder was committed there today, and they've been watching the place. I'm sure they're there to figure out who is visiting."

Nels paled. "I'd better go explain."

Jessa watched the man hurry over to explain to the officer. He could be telling the truth, but he had been *inside* the Martin house. If he'd been dropping off a flyer, wouldn't he have left the flyer at the door when no one answered his knock? It made sense that he had been trying to find something. Or hide something.

Chapter Ten

DECEMBER 22nd

Donna hung up and dropped her phone on the counter with a grin. "Jessa is on her way."

Bertha frowned. "Yesterday, she found a body in our kitchen, and this morning, you're calling her at a ridiculous hour of the morning. Don't you think you should give her a break?"

"For all we know, she could be the killer, and I've heard that in solving a case, you should get close to the suspects. By calling her over at this hour, she'll think we really trust her."

Clay stepped out of the bathroom with his wireless razor in hand. "You think Jessaca Anderson is the killer? Even though Sheriff Vicklund trusts her?"

Donna shook her head. "I don't think so, but she could be. We can't rule her out. I mean she could have hit Timmy on the head. She could have been at the school that morning."

Clay shook his head. "I don't think she had motive. I mean why would she have even been at the school. And if she was the murderer, then why would she tell me to find the truth?"

"And we don't know when whoever put the cyanide in the fudge did it." Bertha grabbed a coffee mug. "All we know is that the fudge was good when we brought it the night before the murder. Fact is, it was some of our best fudge! I mean all our fudge is good but, well you know what they say about our cookie dough fudge!"

Clay's face tensed, and Donna frowned.

"Clay . . . you're not thinking that we poisoned our own fudge, are you? I thought we went over this?"

Clay shook his head. "No. But then . . . it was your fudge, and you had a lot to gain by Royce's death. Like you said, no one else makes cookie dough fudge like you two do."

Donna took an orange from the fruit bowl on the table and began peeling it. "So, you think we killed him."

"I didn't say that! I . . ." he sighed. "I don't think you did it, but the evidence . . . I mean you knew it was cyanide before we did!"

"That was just a lucky guess," Donna said. "But I'll grant you that we do look guilty. Evidence points to us, which is exactly why you can be sure we didn't do it. Do you really think we're stupid enough to poison someone with our own fudge? I mean if I was going to kill someone, I certainly wouldn't waste my good fudge to do it!"

Clay's face relaxed. "No. I don't think you're stupid. You've read enough murder mysteries that if you were going to do it, I daresay you'd have done a better job."

Donna smirked. "Thank you for the compliment."

Bertha sat down in a folding chair by the desk. "Did you just say that we'd be smart murderers?"

Clay turned back to the bathroom and the buzz of his razor was the only sound.

Bertha shook her head. "That nephew of ours . . . he's a chip off the old block."

Donna tore the orange in half and slowly chewed a slice. "Do you suppose," she finally said, "that he would be much different if his folks hadn't died?"

Bertha shrugged. "I don't know. We did our best raising him. I'm sure his folks wouldn't have a problem with how he turned out. Would we be much different if our folks hadn't died? I mean we remember them, but what about Clay's parents? He doesn't hardly remember them. I guess he would be different."

Footsteps came from the staircase, and Donna hurried to the door and opened it. "Jessa! Come on in."

Jessa smiled at the room. The aunts hadn't been in the apartment for a full twenty-four hours and the place already looked like one of Fezziwig's Christmas parties.

A pine scented candle flickered on the counter, and an ancient record player softly played a Bing Crosby Christmas album.

"I brought donuts," Jessa said setting it on the table.

Bertha frowned. "The whiter the bread, the quicker you're dead."

Donna grabbed a roll of paper towel, ripped off a square, and folded it like a napkin. "I'll take a donut."

Clay stepped into the room, and Jessa fought to keep the surprise off her face. Without his uniform, he looked so young! It was hard to imagine that he was older than her.

154

"Donuts." He grinned. "Did you bring those because of the cop stereotype?"

Jessa paused. He didn't seem riled about it. In fact, his eyes seemed to twinkle a little. "No, sir. I brought donuts because I like them and I figured that most people do."

Clay reached for one. "It was kind of you. I'm afraid when it comes to donuts, I'm definitely a stereotypical cop."

Jessa nodded but didn't really believe it. A man as lean and solid as Clay, couldn't indulge in donuts very frequently. Although with his jeans and hoodie, he didn't look like a cop at all, stereotype or otherwise.

"Help yourself to the coffee," Bertha said.

Jessa glanced at the three of them. This could get really awkward. Then again, if she acted natural, it wouldn't have to be at all awkward.

Grabbing a mug of coffee, and a mint creme filled donut, she leaned her hip against the counter and took a sip.

Bing Crosby's voice blared out *I'll Be Home for Christmas*, and Jessa sighed. Would she see her family at Christmas? "So, how is progress on the case?" She asked, to take her mind off her lonely Christmas prospect.

She couldn't ignore the guarded look that crossed Clay's face. Heat crept up towards her scalp. He didn't trust her. It was obvious enough, but why? Did he know that she had been at the school?

"Well, I haven't crossed anyone off my list." Donna grabbed a notebook from the desk and flipped it open. "But I think we could cross Sally and Ken off. I mean they have motive, but they don't seem like killers."

"What does that have to do with anything?" Jessa frowned. "Do you know how many people that don't seem like criminals have committed horrible crimes? You can't write someone off because they don't seem like they're the killing type."

Donna nodded. "You're right. But how are we supposed to catch the killer if we never eliminate anyone as a suspect?"

Jessa glanced at Clay. He smirked slightly. Bertha's eyes were wide, and Donna leaned forward.

Jessa cleared her throat. If they wanted to hear how she'd do it, there was nothing to do but tell them. "Sherlock Holmes had many rules for solving a mystery. Three of them apply to every case you encounter, homicide or other. One, define the mystery. We've done that. Austin Royce and Timmy Berg were both homicide victims. The mystery is who did it. That's simple enough. The second rule, is to approach the mystery with a blank mind. In other words, we have to look at facts, not feelings. We can't write people off because we know them, or because they don't seem like a killer. We have to take all the evidence, and see it for what it is, not for what we think it should be. And number three, never underestimate anyone."

Clay swirled his coffee and raised an eyebrow.

Jessa tried to ignore his skeptical gaze and focused on Bertha and Donna. "Evidence, points to the two of you, which is what Sergeant Kramer is looking at. His problem, is that he's only looking at some of the evidence because his mind is made up. He's ignoring the rest of the evidence."

"Are you pretending this is a mystery book, or do you have experience? From the way you're talking I can't tell." Clay reached for another donut. "I'm sorry. That sounded wrong." He paused. "Okay, let's be frank with each other. I don't know if I can trust you. Like you said, never underestimate. You could be the killer." He stared into her eyes, and she felt her cheeks warming under his scrutinizing gaze. Even when he looked upset, his eyes still shone with handsome honesty.

He cleared his throat. "But . . . if you're not a killer, and you have the experience Sheriff Vicklund thinks you have, I'd like to hear your thoughts."

Jessa nodded. Of course, he didn't trust her. "Okay, first things first, do you happen to have a large marker board down here and an erasable marker?"

Clay set his coffee down and left the room.

"May I see your list?" Jessa asked.

Donna handed the notebook over and Jessa glanced across it. Sipping her coffee, she formed a plan. She allowed her investigation mood to sink in, and mentally prepared herself for what this could lead to.

Clay came back a few minutes later. "I couldn't find a marker board, will this work?" He leaned a glass door against the wall. "I never realized what strange things we have stored down here."

Jessa nodded. "That will work."

After the door was tipped on its side and set up at eye-level, Jessa grabbed a marker, and began writing the suspects along the top of the glass.

"What's the science to your order of names?" Donna asked. "You're writing them in a different order than I had them in the notebook."

Jessa nodded. "I'm putting the most obvious suspects in the center, and the least likely suspects further out."

Jessa sensed movement beside her and glanced up. Clay stared at the glass with lowered eyebrows.

"Is there a problem?" she asked.

Clay shrugged. "Nels Christianson can be crossed off. He was out of town that night, and he flew into Bakerville at three a.m. the morning of the murder. We can prove that, and he couldn't have possible gotten to the school till six o'clock, which is *after* the estimated time of death. According to Nels, he entered his office at that time, and didn't leave it until the police came to get him."

"And you believe him?" Jessa asked.

"We don't have a reason not to. Besides, he doesn't have motive."

Jessa frowned. If she told him that Nels was lying, she'd jump to the center of the investigation, but if she didn't, a possible killer could go free. Taking a deep breath, she set the marker down, and stepped back.

"And why did you put yourself so close to the center?" he asked.

"I put myself near the center because I'm the new girl on the block, none of you know anything about my past, and I know a lot about killing people. And mostly, I'm at the center for the same reason Nels is. Because I happen to know he's lying about being in his office all morning."

"You were at the school the morning of the murder?" Bertha asked. "I declare! Now you're a suspect."

Clay's frown deepened. "And why are you just telling me this now?"

Jessa leaned back against the desk. If she was going to get involved, she'd have to shoot straight. "I was at the school to drop off some credentials for the school board. The superintendent wasn't in his office when I left the papers. That was right when Donna and Bertha were coming in. I saw the body."

Clay opened his mouth, but no words came out. "You . . . you . . ." he finally stuttered.

Jessa closed her eyes. Laci would not be happy about this.

Clay stared at the young woman. Her face was honest, but she had just admitted to finding a body and not telling the police! And just when he was starting to think he could enjoy working with her. "You do know you will probably be arrested for withholding evidence that could be crucial to solving a homicide investigation?"

Jessa nodded. "I realize that could happen, but if we catch the killer, it won't happen."

"How can you be so sure? You could be the killer! And even after the case is solved, you will still have to answer."

As mad as he was with her for keeping this from him, he couldn't help but trust her. Something about her was . . . authentic. Her eyes didn't seem to be hiding anything. But hadn't she just told him not to underestimate?

Running his fingers through his hair, he tried to decide what to do. Should he turn her in? Send her to the sergeant?

"Before you decide to have me arrested, remember that you're not allowed to be in the station right now. You've been suspended. You can't arrest me, so let's help each other."

Clay nodded. "Continue." He glanced at his aunts. Was he putting them in danger by allowing her to be here? Would the sheriff be furious if he kept this a secret? Or did the sheriff already know? Was that why they had met behind closed doors?

Jessa uncapped the marker and began writing facts along the bottom of the glass. With a shake of her head, she stepped back. "No. That can't be right."

"What?" Clay asked. Her tone suggested that she had thought of something. Something important.

Jessa dug in her purse and pulled out her phone. "We need to go back to the scene of the crime."

"I'm not allowed in my office," Clay said. "So, we can't access my information board. Unless of course we wait till tonight when Sergeant Kramer is out."

161

Jessa bit her lip. "I'm not trying to dig myself into a deeper hole, but I have pictures of your office wall."

"You what?" Clay looked like he'd swallowed a glass of rotten egg nog.

Jessa nodded. "Okay, you're about to find out a lot of stuff about me that will surprise you, but for today, can we agree that you're not going to get mad at me?" She searched his face for acceptance. He frowned. "Do you have a laptop we can use?"

Clay slowly nodded. "Okay, we'll agree to trust each other today." He hurried from the room and returned with a laptop.

"Do you have Bluetooth? Or should I e-mail the pictures to your computer?"

Clay hesitated, and then rattled off an e-mail address.

"Sorry if we're boring you ladies," Jessa said to Donna. She handed her phone to Clay and let him type in his e-mail address.

"Oh, we're not bored!" Donna refilled her mug. "I'm enjoying the show."

"Speak for yourself," Bertha said. "Catching a murderer with technology is ridiculous, but then so is murder so, continue."

Clay handed the phone back, and Jessa e-mailed the pictures. All the pictures. She felt her cheeks warm as she downloaded the pictures to his computer, and then zoomed in.

"You have pictures of . . ." he paused. "Everything." She couldn't tell if he was surprised, or angry, but either way, he didn't stop her from zooming in on the pictures.

"Okay, so here we have the first wide shot of the first crime scene." Jessa pointed in on the note. "Austin Royce eating the poisoned fudge that was meant for the school board to sample. I've been trying to keep my fingers out of this pie, but since I'm involved, I've got to know, why is everyone convinced that Austin Royce was the victim?"

Clay raked his fingers through his hair in his characteristic way, and then raked it back into place. "Of course, the note makes it look like the board members were the victims, but whoever poisoned the fudge knew that Royce would be patrolling the displays on school security. Whoever did it, knew that Royce would help himself to more than one piece."

Jessa shook her head. "It seems that everyone hated Royce, but no one could guarantee he would eat the fudge. I don't think Royce was the intended victim."

163

Clay turned and paced the room. How could he have been so blind? Then again, Royce had to be the victim. Didn't he? "There wasn't enough poison in any of the pieces to kill a person. And everyone knows that our school board is very thrifty. Not a single one of them would have taken more than one piece. Besides, I've thought it through. There's no motive to kill the school board. There were plenty of motives to kill Royce."

Donna grabbed a knife and sliced a corner of one of the donuts off. "What if the killer wanted to kill the whole school board, but didn't put enough poison in each piece? They could have miscalculated the amount of cyanide."

Bertha leaned forward. "I don't think so. Whoever committed this crime paid enough attention to the details, that I don't think they would have made a mistake like that."

Donna licked her fingers. "What if they didn't mean to kill anyone? What if they deliberately only put in enough poison to make the school board sick and hospitalize them temporarily?"

Bertha slapped her hand on the desk. "That's it! No one was supposed to get killed, only sick, then Austin Royce ruined the plan by snitching the fudge. Timmy must have known who the killer was, so they had to get rid of him to keep themselves in the clear."

Clay shook his head. "Part of me is furious that I didn't figure that out sooner. At the same time, I'm not sure that Royce wasn't the intended victim. I mean if we go with the theory that the school board was being targeted, we need a motive."

"Maybe an upset parent, or an upset student like Liam," Donna suggested. "But either way, I'm sure the killer wasn't after Royce. We didn't put that card there for the school board. The killer must have done it."

Chapter Eleven

Clay stared at the computer screen. He vaguely remembered being told that the aunties hadn't filled out the display card, but in the chaos, it had slipped his mind. Now he chided himself for this oversight. It could have cost Timmy his life. It was no one's fault but his own. Sinking onto the couch in the corner, Clay fought the guilt. "No, Royce had to be the victim. There's motive for that, but who would have a motive to make the school board get sick?"

"I might have."

Clay glanced up at the soft voice. Jessa stood with her hands folded on the desk. Her long dark hair fell around her shoulders, and her tone sounded helpless, but the look in her eye was nothing like helpless. Determination filled her gaze. "The school board has a meeting tomorrow. Maybe someone was trying to postpone that meeting."

Clay ran his hands over the knees of his jeans. "Why?"

Jessa shrugged. "The meeting was supposed to be a low-key affair. They were going to vote on me being hired as a music teacher. Nels told me that someone else was looking at the job. Maybe they wanted to put the meeting off for some reason."

"Who?" Donna asked. "I don't think anyone else in town has the training to become a music teacher."

Jessa shrugged. "Search me. He said he was going to tell the board about it at the meeting. Whoever it was, probably wanted to put off that meeting. Then again, it could just be someone who said it would be fun to teach music, and he interpreted it to mean they wanted the job. You never know."

"So, we catch whoever it was, and we have our killer?" Clay asked. "That's too simple."

"It gives us someplace to start." Jessa raised an eyebrow. "Now are you going to call Nels, or should I?"

Clay reached for his phone, just as it started to ring. "Officer Martin."

Jessa and the aunties faded as he heard the sheriff's voice. "Martin, Nels Christiansen is missing. His wife said he didn't come home last night, and he never showed up at the school today."

Clay gasped. Was Nels dead? Was he hurt? Was this a result of his negligence?

The sheriff gave the basic details and then paused. "Are you hearing me, Martin?"

With a jerky nod, he swallowed hard. "Yes, sir."

"Isaiah and Shelby have got all the info on it, they'll be coming to see you soon. Martin, I'm counting on you. This has got to stop."

"Yes sir."

"I've got you on the case, I've got Kramer on the case, and everyone else in the station is trying to do something to help. We can't assume it's linked to the murders, but I wouldn't rule that out. If we can't stop this within the week, I'm going to have to call in a full-scale homicide team from the cities. If that happens, I'm not going to be re-elected, and then Josef Schwink would be elected. Our town would change overnight."

"I know that, sir. I . . ."

"Do you?" Sheriff Vicklund sounded mad. "Do you have any idea what this town used to be like? Do you have any idea what will happen if this killer stays on the loose? Stop him, Martin. You're the only one that I think is capable of finding him. And do it quick."

From the sound of it, Vicklund slammed the phone onto the receiver, and Clay slowly set his phone down.

"What's wrong?" Donna asked.

"Nels is missing." Clay got up and hurried to his desk. "We've got to do something."

"Like what?" Bertha asked. "It's not like you're not trying!"

Clay slammed the palms of his hands onto the desk. "I should have been able to prevent this. If Nels is dead, it's my fault."

"Clay." Jessa waited until Clay looked up. "Do you know who the killer is?"

What kind of question was that? Clay frowned. Who was this impertinent girl to ask such a stupid question? "No! Of course, I don't know!"

"Then how could it possibly be your fault?" Jessa asked. "If you knew who the killer was, and you didn't do anything, then it would be your fault, but as long as you're trying, don't beat up on yourself."

Something about her soothing voice calmed him. He took a deep breath. "Isaiah and Shelby are coming with all the statements. We've got to have a system to get through this information as quickly as we can. We're running out of time."

Jessa nodded. "Alright. Donna and Bertha are whizzes with books and papers. How about we have them go through the papers, with Isaiah and Shelby. You can go around and question people. Get alibis, and that kind of stuff. I can work on connecting the deaths and the disappearance to one of our suspects, as well as figuring out who might have had it in for the school board."

Clay couldn't help the slight grin. Jessa thought so much like him it was almost creepy. "That is exactly what I was going to say."

Footsteps sounded on the stairs, and a moment later, Isaiah and Shelby entered. They both stopped, open mouthed.

"Clay?" Isaiah started laughing. "This place looks nice! Merry Christmas! How did you ladies ever convince him to decorate?"

Clay cleared his throat. "Back to business."

"Business," Shelby said. "It looks like the elves were here!"

Clay frowned. "To the problem at hand." He explained his plan of action.

Shelby agreed to stay and go over papers, but Isaiah wanted to go with Clay.

Isaiah left with Clay to do some footwork, and Jessa turned back to the laptop, and the list of suspects. Pouring over pictures, she looked for anything that didn't look right. She'd always felt that the key to solving a mystery was paying attention to the details. She was also the first to admit that useless details could kill a case.

"Think, Jessa, think," she whispered to herself. With a sigh, she paused. *Okay, God. I'm in a fix. I can't jeopardize my mission, but I need to help. Please, help me see whatever I need to see.*

She'd seen things before that had distracted her and caused her to endanger the lives of those she loved. She couldn't get off on rabbit trails now.

After three cups of coffee and staring at crime scene pictures till her head ached, Jessa left the living room and kitchen area and wandered around the basement to relax. Walking up and down the old cell area, she prayed for endurance, wisdom, and answers.

Finally, she sank down in one of the old cells. Cobwebs hung from the ceiling, dust bunnies chased around the floor at her feet, and the grey walls seemed to be closing in. "Why me?" She whispered.

She leaned her head back against the cool cement walls. How could she ever hope to live a normal life when she kept getting involved with crimes? Was she a magnet for crime or what? Why couldn't she just settle down and forget about criminals?

With a clank, the prison door slammed shut.

"Hey!" Jessa jumped to her feet and banged on the steel door. "Open the door!"

A face size window at the top of the door swung open, and Bertha peaked in.

"Miss Anderson. We're holding you for the murder of Austin Royce, and Timmy Berg." Bertha's eyes crinkled with excitement.

"You're not serious!" Jessa paused. Bertha gave a slight nod, and Jessa's shoulders sagged. "You are serious. Why? I didn't do it."

"We'll leave that to Clay, whenever he gets back, he'll look at our evidence, and decide whether you're the right one or not, but we can't take any chances."

Bertha started to shut the window, but Jessa pressed her face up to the opening. "Please, just a moment. If I have to sit in an old holding cell, I'd at least like to know what evidence is against me."

Bertha paused. "You had access to both bodies before anyone else. You have reason to kill them both, and the only thing missing from Nels office, are your papers. That was the last place he was seen, and he had your papers there. Whoever took him, took your papers. It makes sense that it was you. Who else would want to take your papers?"

172

"Seriously? You think I did it because my papers are missing along with Nels? Did it never cross your mind that he might have run off on his own, and that he might have put my papers somewhere else?"

Bertha shook her head. "The folder that your papers were in was still there, but the actual papers were gone. Why would he take the papers and leave the folder?"

"Why would anyone take just the papers?" Jessa thought hard. She had to keep Bertha talking. "Do you have any idea where Nels is? I mean have you checked his phone records, his credit card statements, and have you found his car?"

Bertha sighed. "How do you make such a complicated thing sound so simple?"

Bertha slammed the window closed, and Jessa's shoulders drooped. Would Bertha forget that she'd locked Jessa up? How long would she be locked up?

Ducking behind the dumpster, Clay grabbed Isaiah's arm. With a jerk of his head, he indicated where Brad was. At least he was easy to trail. His ancient fedora made him stick out like a Santa Claus in July. After leaving the school, he'd led them to Ken and Sally's house, where he'd spent a few minutes, and then back to town, and behind Lund's Cafe, where he knocked on a back door, and waited.

Larry Erickson stepped out the back door and took a few papers from Brad. He stroked his mustache as he looked over the papers.

Clay and Isaiah exchanged a look. Why would Brad be sneaking around talking to the top suspects? Larry and Brad spoke a few words, but Clay couldn't make them out. Brad held a box out for Larry, but after looking in the box, Larry backed away. More words were spoken, then, Brad tapped his hat back a few centimeters, and headed back to his car. Larry surveyed the mostly empty parking lot. He backed into the building without taking his eyes off Brad.

Clay glanced from the closing door, to Brad's car. "You follow Brad, and I'll try to get a look at those papers Larry has."

Isaiah gave a quick nod with a grin. "Reminds me of the old days." He slipped away to the car, and Clay headed for the alley.

He caught a glimpse of Liam ducking out of the alley, and he frowned. Should he follow Liam or talk to Larry.

He exited the alley, but there was no sign of Liam, so he turned to the café.

A bell chimed when he entered, and he paused to let his eyes adjust. If there was anything he despised about his job, it was play acting. But sometimes, it seemed the only way. Holly and mistletoe hung in the center of the cafe, and soft Christmas carols wafted over the sound system. A slight frown came to his face as he saw the red berries on the mistletoe. Even without the white berries, he didn't want to be caught under it.

Clay started forward, and then paused. Leaning against the front counter, Sergeant Kramer seemed to be having a friendly conversation with Larry. Clay debated leaving and coming back, but before he could make up his mind, Kramer turned and saw him.

"If it isn't the discharged Clay Martin." His eyes lit up. "So, you have nothing now to do but hang out at the café? You been filling up on donuts and coffee like a good cop? I mean, a good ex-cop."

Clay grimaced. No sense in leaving now, he'd already been seen. *God, you're going to have to help me be civil to him.* Surveying the room, he approached the counter. The place was pretty well empty, with the exception of a few old farmers around a back table with coffee and pie.

"Sergeant Kramer." Clay nodded. "How's your work coming?"

Despite Clay's attempt at a friendly tone, Kramer's eyes narrowed into slits. "That is none of your business."

175

Clay slid onto one of the stools. "Alright. I just find it a little odd that you're in here this time of day. The place is pretty empty. Then again, maybe you're here to interrogate Larry."

Larry's posture went rigid.

Kramer scowled. "Come on, I'm just having a chat with someone who knows the town. There's no crime in that. And I'm drinking coffee, so we're all good."

From the look Larry was giving Kramer, he probably thought it was just a friendly conversation, until Clay made his statement about interrogating. Larry backed away from Kramer, and grabbed a rag. With more vigor than necessary, he began buffing the glass counter top.

As he moved away, Kramer slid off his stool, and moved to the stool beside Clay. "I should have you arrested for obstructing justice." His tone was hard as rock, and his eyes narrowed into slits. Muscles in his neck bulged as he leaned towards Clay.

Clay ignored Kramer and turned to Larry. "Hey, Larry, does Tami still make that gingerbread pie?"

Larry leaned his hands on the counter and snorted. "Why?"

"Because I'd like to buy a slice of pie and a can of pop." He smiled to himself. It felt like yesterday that he'd walked into the café with his mom. She'd said he could order anything he wanted. At six years old, he'd thought pie and pop sounded good. That had been the last afternoon he spent with his mom. Three days after the accident, the aunties had taken him there and he'd ordered the same thing. It reminded him of his mom, and it always would. Weird or not, he would drink pop with his pie till the day he died.

Larry frowned, but stepped into the back.

Clay turned to Kramer with a grin. "See? I'm buying something, you can't kick me out."

Kramer shook a fist in Clay's face. "Stay out of my investigation. I'm not afraid to press charges against you." With one last glare, Kramer headed for the door.

Clay turned back to the counter as Larry approached. "Is cream soda okay?"

Clay nodded. "You know it's my favorite. How much do I owe you?"

Larry sighed. "It's on the house. Thanks for letting me know what Kramer was up to. He started in on this nice conversation about how sorry he was that I was struggling. How he understood how hard it was to work two jobs. Then he started asking questions. I didn't even realize he was interrogating me. I didn't think you'd help me like that seeing as how you were a cop, but I reckon you're pretty sore at the sheriff and his department."

Clay shrugged. "I just don't like to see him schmooze other people like that when I know he's just trying to save his neck. This case means a lot to him." Clay paused as he popped the can open. He took a sip while watching Larry out of the corner of his eye. Larry was frowning at the place where Kramer had sat while absently stroking his mustache.

Trying to get information from someone who is mad at being questioned wasn't going to be easy unless . . . Clay forced the grin down. "Thanks for the pop, Larry. I should probably go." He slowly began sliding off the stool. "Not that I have anywhere to go now that I've been suspended from work." Clay sighed as loudly as he could without letting it sound forced.

He was halfway to the door before Larry called. "Clay, you're welcome to sit here a spell. Besides, you haven't gotten your pie yet."

Clay hesitated. If Larry thought he wanted to stay, it could ruin everything. "I'd better not. You don't want my company. Nobody does."

Larry rounded the counter and stepped in front of Clay. "Please, stay. Kramer's been badgering me and . . . well, if you're here, he won't be. As soon as my shift here is done I have to go to my next grocery store shift, I'm sure he'll be there, and I'd just assume not sit alone waiting to run into him again."

Clay gave a nonchalant shrug, let his shoulders droop, and slowly eased his way back to the counter. Propping his chin on one hand, and his elbow on the counter, he tried to look bored.

"So, you drink pop with your pie?" Larry finally broke the silence. He stroked his Charlie Chaplin-like mustache, and raised an eyebrow.

Clay gave a half shrug. "Yep." The harder Larry had to work to get him to talk, the more likely he was to say something that could be important.

Larry leaned on the counter. "Isn't that a bit odd?"

"Nope." Clay took another sip of his pop, and then did something he knew would make the aunties cringe. Swallowing his dignity, he belched as loudly as he could. If he'd learned anything about getting people to talk, it was to make them feel that you're not a threat.

Larry seemed to relax completely at Clay's sloppy manners.

"You know, there must be something wrong with that Kramer guy, he thinks I'm a top suspect in these murders!"

Clay didn't dare ask questions yet. Larry would surely close down. "Yeah, he told my aunties the same thing. He would arrest them if he could find them." Clay forced a scowl.

"It's all ridiculous." His phone vibrated in his pocket, but he ignored it.

Larry sighed, and put his head in his hands. "As if I don't have enough problems without the police asking me dumb questions." He glanced up. "Pardon the comment, but the way I see it, you're probably pretty sore with the police right now too. I think everyone in town is. I mean two people have been killed, a third missing. Who will be next?"

Clay took another swig of his pop and let out another belch. "Yeah."

"You know, if I were the police, I'd be focusing on Ken Landean."

Clay fought to keep his face straight. "I don't know, he seems nice enough. Now about my pie . . ."

"Nice?" Larry shook his head. "You don't know him like I do. He's a loan shark. 'Course, you being a cop and all, he probably stayed away from you."

Clay wiped his mouth with the back of his hand to keep the grin off. "Yeah, but I'm telling you, there's been times I could have used a guy like him. The police salary isn't exactly something to brag about."

Larry chuckled. "No, but it's probably better than a part time grocery clerk, and part time café worker. I guess if I'd stayed away from Royce and his gambling I'd have been alright."

Clay yawned. Larry was going for the bait, hook line and sinker. "Yeah, I heard he was really getting on you about paying those debts." His tone was slow and relaxed. He rubbed a thumb along the edge of the counter as if he wasn't paying attention to the conversation. As if he didn't care about the answer to his statement.

Larry snorted. "You can say that again! That's why I ended up going to Ken, but Ken and Royce worked together sometimes, and so they had a deal that they wouldn't give me money! I guess Royce really wanted to break me."

"You and everybody else." Clay swished the last of the pop around in his can.

Larry crossed his arms, and his face hardened. "Not like me. He hated me. If Brad hadn't offered to help with the money I don't know what I'd have done. I guess it doesn't matter now. Royce doesn't have anyone to collect his debts, so I'm clear. At least, I will be once Brad quits hounding me. He seems to want me to take the money even though I don't need it anymore. I'm not going to take money like that ever again. I'd probably spend it and be in the same fix I was before Royce died."

Clay wrinkled his brow. It made perfect sense, but at the same time . . . something wasn't right.

Chapter Twelve

Larry's eyebrows raised slightly. "Hey, Clay, I kinda forgot that you were a cop. You're not going to tell Kramer what I said, are you?"

Clay snorted. "Nope. I'm not any more eager to tell him anything than you are."

Larry relaxed and went back to his mustache rubbing. "Good. Cause I wouldn't want him to know about Ken loaning money. Ken would kill me if he knew I told a cop about that."

Clay shrugged. "Like you said. I'm suspended, and I'm not on friendly terms with Kramer."

Larry nodded. "Yeah, that's good. Say, you're in an interesting place, you're not a cop, but you know a lot about what they do. Could I get some advice?"

Clay gave a shrug. "I'm not sure how much help I'd be, but I can try."

"What do you do if someone is trying to give you money, and they're very persistent about it, but you think it might be stolen and you don't want to get in trouble? I mean, supposing you want to help a friend, but you're worried that if you do, you'll get caught with stolen goods?"

"If I was in uniform, I'd tell you to go to the police, but . . ." Clay sighed. "I'm not in uniform so . . . I guess it doesn't matter if I give you other advice. You could refuse, you could take it and hide it, or you could take it, and give it to someone else. Someone you'd like to get in trouble."

Larry glanced around, and then dropped his voice to a whisper. "You mean give it to someone, and then call the police?"

"It'd be your word against his," Clay said. "From what you've said, Ken might be just the person to dump it on."

Larry rubbed his chin. "I don't know. I was thinking maybe Zoe."

Clay frowned. "Zoe? As in the wannabe-news-reporter Zoe?"

"Yeah," Larry said. "She comes across as a sweet chick, but have you ever seen her lose her temper?"

Clay shook his head, and Larry continued. "I've seen her and Nels going at it a few times over the last few weeks.

Course, Nels is her mom's ex, and she was always mad at him over leaving her, but she's been really letting him have it the last few weeks. I don't like people who yell at my friends, and Nels is my friend. At least I hope he is. If he's still alive he is. I'm thinking Brad might have done him in."

Clay frowned. Larry was starting to speculate, and he had to be careful how much he paid attention.

"I mean Brad stops by today and gives me loan papers that I asked for two weeks ago. Isn't he smart enough to know I don't' need them now? He's obviously a little off in the head. It wouldn't surprise me at all if he's the killer."

Clay's phone vibrated again. He downed the rest of his pop and sighed. "Well, I guess I'd better get back to my little hole in the ground."

Larry gave a half smile. "Thanks for chatting. You made a long afternoon much shorter. Just remember not to tell Kramer anything."

Clay nodded. "I won't. And about my pie, I'll be back for it later."

Larry grinned. "Sorry. I got talking and . . . well, see ya, Clay. Merry Christmas."

"Merry Christmas to you too." Clay exited the cafe and pulled out his phone. Four missed calls. All from a blocked number.

Clay started heading for the radio station to see if he could run into Isaiah when his phone started vibrating again. He swiped his screen, and the same blocked number notification popped up on the screen. Whoever it was, was persistent. Clay tapped the green button and held it to his ear. "Officer Martin speaking how may I help you?"

"Where is she?" a disturbed female voice demanded.

"Where's who?" Clay kicked a clod of snow towards a blown-up yard sleigh and reindeer.

"You know who I mean!"

Clay cleared his throat. "Ma'am, you need to remain calm. If you're dealing with a missing person, you need to call the police."

"Clay, you are the police. Now tell me where my sister is."

Clay stopped and kicked at another chunk of snow. "I don't know who your sister is."

"Jessa. Jessaca Anderson. I've called her dozens of times in the last three hours, and she hasn't answered. I know something is wrong."

Clay shoved his free hand into his pocket to protect it from the biting wind. Jessa's sister. That was interesting. "Who are you?" Clay demanded. "I've never heard of you before."

Silence stretched out. "Are you still there?" Clay finally asked.

"I'm Laci Anderson. Dr. Josh Anderson, and Miss Jessa Anderson are my siblings. Now tell me what you've done with my sister."

"Your sister is fine," Clay said. "I left her at my apartment a few hours ago. I'm sure everything's alright." In that moment, he began to wonder. Was everything alright? What if Kramer had gone into the basement? What if Jessa was the killer? Were his aunts safe? Or what if the real killer had killed them all?

"Your apartment? Why is she at your apartment?" Laci bit off each word. "Tell me why my sister is at your apartment this early in the morning? Tell me!"

Clay eased the phone away from his ear so the yelling wasn't so loud. "She came over to compare notes with my aunts and me. She's helping on a case." *At least, I think she is,* he added to himself. *If she's not the killer.*

"Do you know anything about her capabilities?" Laci's voice had changed from anger, to scorn. "Do you?

You have no idea how lucky you are to have her in your town. If something happens to her . . . you'll be sorry."

Clay switched hands so that his right hand could warm up in his pocket. "Look, Laci, I don't know you, and you don't know me, but I know your sister, and I'm not going to let anything happen to her."

"You don't know my sister. Not like you think you do."

"You could enlighten me," Clay suggested. "It would make my job easier if I knew who I was dealing with."

There was a pause. "Martin, you're not in a room that could be bugged, are you?"

Clay glanced around. "No . . . I'm outside freezing my face off."

"Good. Now listen and listen close because I'm not repeating this, and you'd better never repeat it either. Jessa is on a mission for the Anderson Family Investigation Bureau."

"She's what?" Clay nearly dropped the phone. "She's with a detective agency?" Clay frowned. Jessa clearly didn't want people knowing that. "Why are you telling me?"

"Because I worry about her, and I can't be there right now. When I couldn't get a hold of Jessa, I researched you. I know more about you than you probably know about yourself, and I trust you. Take care of my sister."

"What do you mean she's working for a detective bureau? Middle Ridge isn't that big. I think if something was going on,

I'd know about it." Clay stomped his feet and the snow crunched beneath his heavy boots and numb toes. The cold wasn't bad as long as he was moving, but this standing still was too much.

"I sent her to Middle Ridge and told her to stay under the radar. Dad's life could depend on the results of her time there."

"What does that mean?"

Silence.

"Miss Anderson, if I'm to help your sister, I need to know what I'm dealing with."

"My sister knows the risks. She's tested Dad's experiments before, but she doesn't know just how much danger Dad is in."

"Where is your father? Why is he in danger?" Clay's breath hung in a cloud as he waited for an answer.

"I can't give you an exact location, but he's in a foreign country on a top-secret mission to save the life of an American that's going to be executed as a political prisoner. If Jessa is found by the wrong people, they'll know the secret to sabotaging Dad's mission. I have to let you go. Find my sister and have her call me. I need to speak to her. She needs to know that things are warming up."

There was a beep, and then nothing. Clay pushed the lock screen setting, and then paused. Jessa had her cell phone with her in the living room when he'd left. If she wasn't answering then . . .

Clay sprinted for the station. Nothing else mattered. He had to find out if they were okay.

Donna put her hands on her hips and glared at Shelby. "What do you mean she is innocent? Have you not heard anything I've said in the last two hours? She's guilty. She tried to poison the school board to delay the meeting. When Timmy was going to go to the police, she lured him to our house and killed him."

Shelby shook her head. "And like I've been telling you for the last two hours, none of that makes sense. How would she know you weren't home? Why would she try to frame you two? She's not the killer."

Bertha nodded. "I'm beginning to agree with Shelby. Jessa is too sweet to kill anyone."

"Didn't you hear her talking about not underestimating people?" Donna tapped her foot on the floor. "I just don't believe anyone from our town would do something like this."

Footsteps banged down the stairs, and the door flung open. Clay bolted into the room with his gun drawn.

"Wow! What's chasing you?" Donna asked.

Clay's face was tense. "Where is she?"

"I knew the police would see she was guilty eventually." Donna grinned, but Clay's face didn't show any relief. He stepped across the room to the desk and picked up Jessa's cellphone. "Why doesn't she have her phone?"

Bertha pushed in front of Donna. "She left it here, it's been vibrating almost non-stop!"

"Where did she go?" Clay's face was showing lines that Donna didn't remember seeing.

Donna crossed her arms. "Why are you getting so worked up over her? She's in one of the holding cells. Bertha locked her in so she couldn't escape. I think she's your killer."

Clay's face showed instant relief. "And you're all okay?"

"Of course, we are!" Donna said. "Whatever is the matter?"

Clay shook his head. "It's nothing. Which cell?"

Bertha led the way, and Donna followed behind Clay.

"How was your investigating?" Donna asked.

Clay shrugged. "I need time to sort out the useful information from the red herrings, but I think we've got some leads."

Bertha stopped in front of one of the cells, unlocked the door, and swung it open.

Donna peeked around Clay, Jessa was lying on the steel bedframe without a mattress. Her eyes were closed, her face was pale, and she wasn't moving.

Clay bolted in and sat beside her. "Jessa." His voice was tense. "Jessa!" He shook her shoulders.

With her dark tresses flowing over her shoulders, her eyes fluttered open. Clay let his breath out in a ragged sigh.

"Are you okay?" Donna moved in beside her.

Jessa let Clay help her sit up. "Yeah. Why wouldn't I be?"

"But you weren't moving . . . you were . . . ." Clay stopped.

Donna slapped her forehead. "I declare! After finding a dead body, and then seeing you lying there so still, we thought you were dead!"

Jessa giggled. "Dead? No. I just got tired of talking through things that weren't making sense, so I closed my eyes and must have fallen asleep." She glanced from Clay's tense face to Donna's. "Is something wrong?"

Clay handed Jessa her cellphone. "You need to call your sister."

Jessa took the phone and with odd glances between them, she called.

"Let's get out of here," Clay said. "Give her some space."

Clay herded Donna out of the room, and they headed back for the living area.

"What's going on?" Donna asked.

Clay sighed. "I don't know for sure. I bet Sheriff Vicklund could explain." Clay began raking his fingers through his hair.

Donna frowned. What wasn't he telling her?

Jessa said good-bye to Laci and headed for Clay's living area.

"Well?" Donna asked, the moment she entered the room. "Are you going to tell us what's going on?"

Jessa glanced around. Laci had said she could tell Clay, but what about the aunts and Shelby? "I'm afraid it's on a need-to-know basis. Clay, may I speak to you alone?"

Clay nodded and reached for her coat. "Outside."

"What about us?" Bertha asked. "We're involved!"

Handing the coat to Jessa, he shook his head. "Sorry, Aunties, but you need to stay out of this. Shelby, keep them here."

Outside, Jessa stepped away from the building. She couldn't risk being over heard. Clay followed her to an open spot in the back-parking lot.

"Laci told you what I'm doing?" she asked.

Clay shook his head. "Only part of it. She didn't tell me what exactly you were doing, or how it affects your father."

Jessa sighed. "Dad and Mom ran a private detective bureau. I grew up in the world of crime, lawyers, and danger. Mom backed off when us kids were growing up, but as soon as my little brother, Josh, headed for medical school, she went back to the bureau. That's when Laci and I got involved. Mom was killed a few years later on a mission. Up to that point, I'd helped Dad whenever I could, but he tried to keep us girls out of the red zone. After Mom's death, I backed off, and became a music teacher. I've slowly been working my way back into the team. Laci has stuck with Dad all the way through. She does most of his paperwork, and is a natural at dealing with people."

Jessa glanced around, making sure no one was close enough to hear. "A little over a year ago, Dad re-married. His new wife is Michelle Connors. Sheriff Vicklund's only cousin. Dad and Michelle are on a mission in . . . another country."

"That's how you and the sheriff are connected."
Clay nodded slowly. "I'd have never guessed. But how
does Michelle feel about being involved in your dad's
missions when your mom died on one?"

Jessa couldn't stop the slight eye-roll. "Dad wanted
Michelle to stay home, but after a threat on his life, Dad
figured she'd be as safe with him as at home, and she
wanted to go. She's been undergoing training the last few
months, and I think she's ready to help dad."

"But how are you involved?" Clay prodded.

Jessa sighed. "I didn't know I was involved at first.
When Dad was preparing to go, I wanted to quit again and
focus on music teaching, I just wasn't sure I wanted
anything to do with it when Dad was in so much danger.
Laci found this position for me, and told me that I could
go teach music, and help try out a new technology at the
same time. I don't understand it all, but it's a blocker so
that, without changing my name, I can go anywhere, and
the computers won't register it. The goal being that,
someday, people might not have to completely change
their lives because of a threat. They can just get FBI
protection, and no one will be able to locate them from
any kind of searches. They'd have to actually see the
person in order to find them. My being here, is a test. Josh
wasn't told where I was going, just that I was somewhere

in the United States, he's trying to find me. So far, it's been working. There is no record of me on any sort of technology except my sister's phone. After a few days of it working for me, Dad left with the same technology protection."

"How does this endanger your dad?" Clay frowned. "I'm not connecting the dots."

Jessa nodded. "Sorry, it's complicated. Basically, this only erases information from devices outside of the county I'm in. That way, I can still get tickets, and use my credit card and stuff. But if someone comes into this county, they'll be able to get through the blocker and see my movement in this county. Technology is a dangerous tool if it gets into the hands of the wrong people. Criminals could use it too. Dad's in danger because if Josh can figure out how to undermine this technology and find me, then someone could do the same, and find Dad. The case he's on involves a lot of money and if the wrong person figured out how to undermine this technology, they would find Dad, and he wouldn't be coming home. Laci thinks Dad is in danger. She believes that someone is searching for him. If this man finds out how to find me, he'll know how to find Dad."

Clay wrinkled his forehead. "It's still not making a whole lot of sense to me."

Jessa shrugged. "It doesn't make much sense to me either. That's one thing about Dad's work, most people don't know what he does, and he doesn't talk about it unless he has to. He has a very strict client privacy policy. Some things we'll never know, but if Laci said Dad is in danger because of me, then Dad is in danger because of me."

Clay nodded. "Okay, but how can I help protect you?"

"You don't have to. It's my job to stay off the radar, not yours."

"Your sister asked me to keep you safe." Clay stared into Jessa's eyes. "So, it is my job."

Jessa took a deep breath. "Well, I guess you can finish this homicide investigation as quickly as possible. The longer this killer is on the loose, the more likely chance this town has of ending up on national television."

Clay nodded. "I guess we can start by removing you from the list of suspects."

Jessa grinned. "I don't have an alibi so you can't really remove me. Working for a family run detective bureau is no guarantee that I'm innocent."

"Okay, well, let's move you down on the list." A car pulled up, and Clay turned towards it. "And we can find out if Isaiah found anything helpful. Then we're back to digging until we find enough dirt to make an arrest."

Chapter Thirteen

"Clay!" Isaiah stepped from his car and folded his arms across his chest. "I ought to knock you one. I waited for you, or any word from you, for quite some time before I backtracked. But you weren't at the café, and no one knew where you were. Mrs. Olson said she saw you running like you had a fire in your boot. Do you know how worried I was? I tried calling you, but you didn't answer, and then my Shelby calls me and I find that you've been standing here having a nice little chat when I was worried sick!"

Jessa grinned. She didn't know Isaiah that well, but it was obvious that he wasn't really mad.

Clay frowned. "I'm sorry. I should have contacted you, I was . . ."

"You were busy doing your job." Isaiah grinned. "It's okay, buddy, just don't expect me to answer your call next time you're worrying about me."

"What did you find out?" Clay asked.

Isaiah grinned. "Brad likes diet grape pop, and he spends half his time in front of a mirror making sure his fedora stays at the same odd angle."

"Where did he go from the café?" Clay asked.

"Back to his studio. He took over for Zoe at the broadcaster desk, and there he sits till supper. He took the box in with him."

Jessa stepped forward. "Then back to the suspect board?"

Clay nodded. "We need to start narrowing down our suspects."

Isaiah started leading the way, then paused. "Was I interrupting something?"

Clay shook his head. "No, Jessa was just telling me about her dad."

Isaiah stopped. "Cool? So, who exactly are you?"

Jessa shook her head. "It's on a need to know basis."

Isaiah shrugged. "Okay, well, Clay will tell me. He tells me everything."

"Not everything." Clay cut in front of Jessa and Isaiah and held the door open for them.

Back in the basement, Jessa stared at the suspect board.

"Are you guys seriously not going to tell us what's going on?" Bertha asked.

Clay shrugged. "What's going on is that we're trying to solve a mystery.

"But what did Jessa tell you?" Donna asked.

Jessa turned back to the glass door and tapped the capped marker against her chin. If this was her dad's case, she would erase some of the names.

"What are you thinking?" Clay asked.

Jessa glanced up. "Nothing."

"Nothing means something." Isaiah nodded his head for emphasis. "Every time Shelby says she's thinking nothing, it usually means I did something wrong."

Shelby gave him a playful punch in the arm. "Hey now!"

Clay cocked an eyebrow at Jessa. "So? Did we do something wrong?"

Jessa pursed her lips. "If you must know, I think we should be removing some of these names."

"But any one of them could have done it," Bertha said.

"I know." Jessa popped the cap off the marker. "Anyone in the state could have done it. And we could be wrong about the victims too. Someone could have tried killing Royce and left

199

the note after the murder just to make it look like he wasn't the intended victim. We need to focus on the most likely people who are connected to both Royce, and the school board."

"Who are the most likely people?" Isaiah asked.

"Do we have photo documentation of this as it is?" Jessa gestured towards the glass door.

Clay pulled out his phone. "We do now."

"Great." Jessa ran her hand across the top of the glass, wiping it clean. Once all the suspects were gone, she began writing. "These are the suspects as I see them."

"Ken . . ." Clay read out loud. "Larry . . . Brad . . . Liam . . . and Nels. But Nels may be murdered too."

"Or, maybe Nels disappeared to hide because he did it." Jessa said recapping the marker.

"Not to sound obnoxious, but aren't you being a little heavy on the men side?" Isaiah asked. "I mean don't you have any female suspects?"

Jessa shook her head. "At this point I don't have any female suspects. In my book, the aunts are clean, I don't think Sally did it. She may know who did, or she may be an accomplice, but she personally didn't do it."

"Why?" Clay asked.

Jessa paused. "Well, I ran into her cousin's neighbor at the gas station this morning when I was getting the donuts. She said that Sally has Parkinson's disease. That explains her shaking hands and emotional swings. It also rules her out as a suspect. Whoever injected the fudge with poison had to be steady handed enough to gently squeeze the fudge around the needle holes so they wouldn't be obvious, without mangling the fudge. The only other female, besides myself, that's been involved is Zoe. After all, she was Nels step-daughter before he divorced her mom."

"You knew that?" Clay asked. "I've lived here all my life and I didn't know that until today. It must have happened when I was at college."

"Yeah, I heard about that," Isaiah said.

Jessa shrugged. "I've done my research."

"How?" Clay asked. "I just found that out."

Flipping her hair over her shoulder, Jessa smiled. "You have a wonderful little town, and people like to talk. All those people who hang out in the gas station, or the café, are more than happy to educate a poor city girl. And they're so friendly too. I was invited to your town lutefisk bake tonight."

"What makes you think the poison was injected?" Clay asked. "We don't know that."

Jessa shrugged. "It's the only logical answer. Plus, the fudge pieces aren't as neat and square as the aunts would have left them. They've clearly been squeezed around. A syringe would make sense. I bet if you asked the lab about it, they'd tell you the same thing. I'd guess a needle was inserted, and while it was pulled out, someone injected the needle sized hole with the liquid cyanide. It would only take a couple of drops."

"Zoe doesn't make sense. I mean, how is she connected?" Shelby asked. "Even if she's connected to Nels, how is she connected to the victims?"

"Didn't she used to go out with Timmy Berg?" Isaiah asked.

Clay nodded. "Yeah, but it wasn't like they were dating. I mean he thought it was, but she wasn't serious. With his handicaps and all, I think most every girl went out with him at some point just because they felt sorry for him."

"What about Royce?" Donna asked. "Is she connected to him?"

"That doesn't matter," Jessa said. "If the school board was the intended victims, then connections with Royce don't matter."

Clay started re-filling the coffee pot. "Then why are the people on your list, on your list?"

Jessa pointed with her marker at Ken's name. "First off, the Landeans. Ken ran for school board, but wasn't elected. I heard that he'd sent in an appeal to have the votes recounted, but nothing happened. They may have been trying to get back at the school board."

Clay nodded. "Larry told me that Ken was a loan shark. Maybe that's why he didn't get elected."

"But to use poison to make people sick just because you're mad at them is . . ." Shelby paused. "A little excessive, don't you think?"

Jessa put a question mark by their names. "We can't rule them out, but you're right, it's not likely. Of course, if Royce was the intended victim, Ken and Sally would have known better than anyone his weakness for fudge, and they could have slipped the note in later to get us on the wrong trail. Then there's Nels. He could have been the next victim. He could have run off because he is the killer. Or, he could be completely disconnected from the case, and gone for some other reason. He is the superintendent, and it's possible something urgent came up."

"What about Larry?" Bertha asked. "Sure, he had reason to do Royce in, but if Royce wasn't the intended victim, then what motive would he have? I mean just because his mustache is sinister, doesn't mean he's a killer!"

Jessa gave a lopsided grin. "I don't know. There's no science to it, it's just a feeling. He's connected somehow, and it doesn't have anything to do with his mustache."

Clay shrugged. "I doubt he's the killer, but you're right, he knows something. I'll keep working on him."

"Liam," Jessa paused. "I don't know him, but if we're profiling, I've had several people mention that he has a violent streak, and he's mad at the school and school leadership for suspending him last year. That was shortly before he was arrested.

Clay nodded. "It was, but do you really think he's still carrying a grudge against the school board? I mean he was kicked out for very real problems. Most kids would love to not have to go to school."

Jessa shrugged. "I haven't talked to him, so I don't know, but it's possible that he's been thinking about that ever since he was put in Juvie. He might very well have plotted this whole thing out from behind bars. Not because he misses school, but because he doesn't like being made into a criminal."

Clay shook his head. "I hate to believe he could do such a thing. I mean yes, he's been known for his violence, and yes, he's been into some pretty serious stuff, but I don't believe he's guilty."

"And last, but not least, we have Brad." Jessa set the marker down and crossed her arms. "Like Larry, I don't have anything concrete on Brad. But I do know that this story is helping the ratings on his radio station. I also know that he's been down on the investigation. Honest people usually like it when the police solves mysteries."

"From what I gathered from Larry this morning, Royce, Ken, and Brad were all somehow connected." Clay ran his fingers through his hair. "Something to do with money lending and gambling, but he wasn't all that clear."

"Timmy did say that he saw Brad at the school the morning of Royce's death," Donna said. "Maybe someone should question Brad again. Maybe his story has changed."

"The school benefit was re-scheduled for tomorrow evening. That gives us exactly . . ." Clay paused and looked at the ceiling in deep thought. "Thirty-three hours and seventeen minutes. We've got to find the killer before that or . . . Well, Sheriff Vicklund might lock us all up."

Jessa took a deep breath. There was so much information to go through before they could make an arrest. So many people to talk to. So many mistakes that could be made. "What's your plan?"

Clay straightened and paced in front of the glass. "We need to keep accumulating information. A crime investigation is like a puzzle. We've got to find all the pieces before we can put them together. Aunties, I know you want to get involved, but . . ."

"But you want us to stay here," Bertha said.

Clay nodded. "Yes, but you're not going to be just sitting here. You'll be our contact point. If we get information, we'll call you, and you'll keep putting it on the suspect board wherever it fits. You can also do all the calling you want. Call your friends, and find out whatever you can. Just stay off the streets and don't tell them where you are. Kramer wants to make an arrest pretty badly, and you two are on the top of his list. I can't afford bail."

"Sheriff Vicklund says Shelby and I can help you till this case is done," Isaiah said.

Clay cocked an eyebrow. "He said you could leave your usual routine?"

Isaiah grinned. "Well. . . not at first but. . ."

"But Isaiah threatened to quit if we couldn't help you," Shelby said.

Clay shook his head. "You are so . . . devious!"

Isaiah raised one shoulder in a half-shrug. "We're partners. Have been since pre-school and I'm not going to stop now."

Isaiah's boyish dimples appeared and Jessa smiled. What trauma had their poor teachers been through because of them?

Clay grinned. "Kramer is focusing on finding Nels, but I still think we should work on that angle. We need to return to the scene of the crime and do another search.

206

Finding the syringe that injected the fudge could be a huge help, or the poison. We also need to try to find out what the school board was going to discuss at that meeting. Maybe that will give us another clue. We should also get close to Larry and Brad. One of them might tell us something that could help. If Brad changes his story about the morning of Royce's death, he may just be our killer."

Shelby rubbed her temples and sighed.

"Are you doing okay?" Jessa asked.

Shelby sighed. "Yeah, I think so. I've just got a little headache."

Isaiah frowned. "This investigation is too much for you."

"No, I'm just getting tired." Shelby tried to smile, but it looked more like she was gritting her teeth.

"Why doesn't Shelby take the church?" Jessa asked. "With the lutefisk bake tonight, people will be hanging out. She could pick up all kinds of information. And if it gets boring, she's got wedding prep work to do. I'm sure she could use some time to think about her wedding. I heard Larry was going to be helping with the lutefisk bake too, so she can keep an eye on him."

Shelby shook her head. "I don't want to be a wimp. It's just that . . ."

"You've got a lot on your plate, I know," Clay said. "But the church is a good idea. Go for it."

Shelby glanced at Isaiah, and he nodded. "That would be perfect. Keep your eyes and ears open, and be careful, babe."

Shelby sighed. "Alright. I'll be early for the preparation gossip, but I'll see what I can find out. Isaiah, you're on your own for supper."

Isaiah cocked an eye. "I'm always on my own. It's been forever since you actually cooked something for me."

Shelby's eyes twinkled. "Last night was a long time ago."

Isaiah grinned. "Love ya, babe."

Shelby left, and Clay turned back to Jessa and Isaiah. "Do either of you have any preference to which paths you follow?"

Isaiah grinned. "If I get a choice, I'll try to find Nels. He could be the piece that connects the dots."

Clay nodded. "Get to it."

"Oh! I declare!" Bertha hefted herself off the couch. "It's past lunch and none of you have eaten! You'll burn out if you don't get food."

Clay sighed. "Yes, well, we don't really have time to prepare something. We can pick something up on the way to our jobs."

"You'd best come back here for snack before the lutefisk bake. They're always late starting and I don't want you guys withering away." Donna headed for the kitchen.

Clay nodded. "We'll try."

Jessa followed Clay outside.

"Can I send you to the radio station?" Clay asked.

"Sure, what do you want me to do?"

"Talk to Zoe, use discretion, but see if you can get her to talk about Brad. If anyone else is around, you can talk to them too."

Jessa nodded. "It would be my pleasure. If no one will talk, what do I do?"

"I'll be at the school. I want to search the place again for something, anything that will shed some light on this. When you're done, you can come help search."

Jessa nodded, and headed for her cruiser.

Turning the key, nothing happened.

She stepped out of the car. "Clay!"

Clay turned towards her.

"Do you have jumper cables?" Her cheeks warmed. Why did this have to happen now? Clay had more important things to do than to help a strange girl.

"Give me a sec!" Clay called back.

Once Clay had his car pulled in front of the red cruiser, and the jumper cables hooked up, he stepped out. "You planning on getting a new car someday?" He asked through her open car door.

Jessa started the PT Cruiser. "Nope. My parents gave it to me in high-school. It was my mom's dream car. I'm not parting with it until it's completely done."

Clay unhooked the cables and slammed the hood. "You're good to go!"

"Thanks!" Jessa shifted into reverse and backed out of the parking lot. It felt like yesterday that her Mom had been there. Laughing, giving advice, and keeping everything in order.

Jessa parked at the radio station and closed her eyes. "Okay, God. Please keep me safe. And help us catch this killer before anyone else gets hurt."

It had been a mission similar to this that her Mom had been on. It had seemed safe, but something went wrong, and she didn't come home.

Swallowing hard, Jessa grabbed her purse and headed inside.

"Miss Anderson!" Zoe jumped up from the desk and came around it. "Do you have a statement for the radio about finding Timmy Berg?"

Jessa paused. Would she be better off playing the professional card, or the sympathy card? Deciding on the sympathy card, Jessa sank onto one of the chairs in the front office. "It's all so awful! You know. I mean one moment he was alive and then . . . it's awful." The sympathy card wasn't going to be hard to play. She couldn't get over the awfulness of the heinous crime, and tears pooled in her eyes with no effort.

Zoe nodded. "I know. I can't imagine what you're going through. Finding a body has got to be bad enough, but finding it in the middle of the old ladies' kitchen like that must have been . . . awful. Do you have any idea who would have dumped the body there?"

Jessa shook her head. "It's all so horrible. If the police knew who did it, they'd have them in jail by now. I haven't been cleared yet, and I know they don't have any reason to believe me, but I didn't do it."

Zoe sat down beside her. "This must be horrible for you coming to town like this and being dragged into a murder."

Jessa nodded. "It's not what I was expecting out of a town like Middle Ridge, but if I can manage to stay out of jail I think I'll be okay. I just feel bad for Timmy. Did you know him well?" She couldn't let her emotions distract her from getting the job done.

Zoe looked away. "He was such a sweet guy. I mean he acted like more of a six-year-old than an almost thirty-year old, but he was sweet. The whole town will miss him. It wasn't uncommon for him to shovel or sweep sidewalks around town for free meals. He was kind of a part of the scenery, and we all loved him. I can't imagine who would want to hurt him."

Jessa frowned. "I heard that he was uncomfortable around Brad, did Brad not like him hanging around?"

"Brad hated him. Timmy had no problem pestering Brad for a job. Brad didn't like that."

"Do you think Brad could have been the killer?"

Zoe shrugged. "It could be him. I mean you can't underestimate anyone."

"What are you doing here?" Brad asked.

Jessa took a deep breath as the middle-aged man stormed into the room. "I'm a little distressed over being blamed for the killings, so I've been asking questions trying to make some sense of it."

"You think I did it?" Brad put his hands on his hips.

"No, it's just that . . . well, I'm curious as to what you saw the morning of Royce's death at the school? Something you saw could solve the mystery."

"I never went in the school." Brad's neck muscles bulged. "I was only in the alley behind the school, and I didn't see anything besides the Bennett kid leaving! I talked to Nels, and nothing else, now get out!"

Jessa stood and headed for the door. "One more thing." She turned around. "What were you talking to Nels about?"

Brad spun around and shook a fist at Jessa. "Get out of here! I didn't see anything!"

Chapter Fourteen

Jessa hurried outside. She got in the car and paused. "Was that normal behavior for an innocent man?" She turned the key, but nothing happened. "Seriously?" She slumped forward and rested her forehead on the steering wheel. "Okay, God. I can't do this anymore. I need this car to work."

She sighed, and leaned her head back against the seat. "Sorry, God. I need to learn to trust you more. You can take care of this car, and I just need to trust you." She squeezed her eyes shut. Just that morning she'd read in 1 Timothy where it says *"And having food and raiment let us be therewith content."* Why was it so hard?

A tap on the window jolted her out of her deep thought and prayer.

Clay's face filled the window. She pushed the arrow down button, but the window didn't move. With a sigh, she cracked the door open. Clay backed up, and she opened the door fully.

"Need a hand?" he asked.

Jessa forced a smile. *This isn't the worst thing in the world that could happen,* she reminded herself. "Do you still have those jumper cables?"

Clay nodded. "Pop the hood."

Jessa reached for the all too familiar button.

"You ever think about getting it into the shop and having them take a look at it?" Clay yelled from behind the open hood.

"My brother took a look at it before I came. It's got a failing starter, a weak battery, and a sluggish alternator, but I can't afford to have it fixed just yet." She turned the key, and the engine revved to life. *Thank you, God!*

"You know, if you left it running, you wouldn't get into these predicaments."

Jessa nodded. "You know running a vehicle burns gas money." Jessa cocked her head to the side. "Aren't you supposed to be at the school?"

Clay stared across the parking lot. "I went there, but then I remembered your car, and I figured you'd have trouble with it. Are you done here?"

Jessa took a deep breath and let it out slowly. "If someone shakes their fist at you, and then in an excessively loud voice demands you leave, does that count as an admission of guilt?"

Clay cocked an eyebrow. "No, but it could definitely get us on the right track. I'm assuming you're talking about Brad?"

Jessa nodded. "He admitted to being in the alley beside the school the morning of the murder. He said he was talking with Nels. I asked him what they were talking about, and he got mad."

"Nels said he didn't leave his office that morning." Clay rested one hand on her open car door.

"But when I entered his office that morning, he wasn't there. Either he was lying, or both Brad and I lied. If only Brad would tell us what he was meeting Nels about. Obviously, Nels was trying to hide his meeting, and Brad won't talk about it. Why?"

Clay shook his head. "I have no idea, but we have to remember that whatever they were talking about, it was *after* the estimated time of death."

"And another thing, Brad said that he saw Liam coming out of the school that morning. Have you questioned Liam? Why was he at the school that morning when school was out? And at that hour of the morning?"

"No, I didn't figure he'd been at the school, he is still suspended from the last drug situation." Clay paused. "But he told me Royce was his friend."

"I think it's time for you to officially question him."

Donna stared at the glass door. With the grey wall behind it, the black marker stood out. Bertha was in the kitchen area banging cupboard doors and mumbling about how Clay needed a full-time house keeper to keep him from starving.

"Has Clay talked to Janet Royce yet?" Donna finally asked.

Bertha stopped her banging. "I'm sure he did. Then again, he never mentioned it."

Donna nodded. "I'm going to give her a call."

Bertha dropped her stirring spoon. "Are you sure you're allowed to do that? I mean, we're under house arrest."

Donna gave a slight shrug. "Clay said we could." She reached into her purse and pulled out her flip-phone. "What's Janet's number?"

Bertha closed her eyes as her lips moved. "Give me a bit. It will come to me." After a bit, Bertha rattled off a number.

Donna dialed it in. How did Bertha remember numbers so well? She held the phone to her ear and waited.

"Hello?" a voice asked.

"Hey, Janet! This is Donna Martin and I've got a couple of questions."

"I'm not sure I want to answer your questions. I've already talked to the police, and I have the understanding that you're under house arrest for my cousin's murder."

"Now Janet." Donna took a deep breath. "We didn't do it. Why would we kill your cousin? It's just ridiculous!"

"He was going to take your house."

Donna paused. "Okay, so maybe we had motive, but we didn't do it. In fact, I'm not even sure that Austin was the intended victim." Donna paused. Was it right to share this information? "I think the school board might have been the intended victims."

Janet gasped.

Bertha glared at Donna.

"She'd have found out anyway," Donna mouthed. "Yes," she said into her phone. "I think someone was trying to delay your school board meeting."

"Why?" Janet asked. "It's not like we have life and death discussions."

"I don't know why, but I was wondering if you have some kind of a list with the topics for the meeting? Who was supposed to talk about what, or anything like that?"

"We don't have the meeting minutes available until two days after the meeting takes place, however we should have an agenda somewhere." There was a rustling of papers. "I'm afraid I don't have the agenda."

"But you're the secretary, shouldn't you have the agenda?"

"I usually type it up and e-mail it around to the rest of the board, but I'm in the process of training in a new secretary, and she's been typing out the agendas for the last few meetings. Dennis Nordlum fills in for Nels whenever Nels is out of town, and whenever he's in charge, he keeps making changes till the very end, and we often don't get our agendas out till the day of the meeting"

"Who is the trainee?"

"Zoe Lundum. She won't be taking over for a while, but we're thinking about moving down to Minneapolis to be closer to the kids and grandkids. We're getting too old to drive four hours every time we want to see the kids. Whenever we make the final move, she'll take over for me."

"Is there any way I can get a copy of the agenda?"

"Zoe should have e-mailed them out a few days ago, but since the meeting was postponed till Monday, she probably won't get it out till Saturday. Whenever I get it, I can forward a copy of it to you."

"Thank you, that would be great. Something in that could help us figure out who the criminal is. And, Janet, we're sorry for your loss."

After hanging up, Donna turned back to the board, and drew another line from Zoe to the school board. She wrote secretary right above the line.

Donna related the conversation to Bertha.

Bertha stuck a pan of gingerbread cookies into the oven. "We've got to see that agenda. If Nels is missing because he's guilty, then something in that agenda would probably explain why he did it."

Donna nodded and glanced at the suspect board again. "I'm still trying to figure out how Brad is connected to the school board. He seems like he could have done it but I'm not finding any connection."

"Didn't Clay say that Brad had taken out some loans from Ken? Ken's connected, maybe Brad was involved in some kind of purloining operation from the school, and Ken was going to tattle on him."

Donna stared at her sister. "You could have something there. We need more facts. We can't really blame anyone until we have more facts."

"And how are you going to get facts when you're stuck down here?" Bertha asked, reaching for a frying pan.

Donna reached for a phone book. "We'll call everyone on the school board and ask questions. Someone must know something that can shed some light on this."

Clay had stopped outside to re-check the dumpster for anything, but Jessa headed inside. The cafeteria was full of volunteers stringing more garland and hanging candy canes and paper snowflakes that the classes had made. At least the delay had given the committee more time to decorate and the final event was going to be much bigger than the original plan. The murder had peaked everyone's interest in the event.

The original crime scene had been opened, and the Martin sisters' table was still there. All the fudge had been removed, and the table sat empty. Jessa couldn't help but wonder if the sisters would ever be able to sell their baked goods again.

The smell of cleaning supplies was a stark contrast to the apartment they'd stopped at on the way to the school. Liam and Clara's home wasn't much of a home.

Jessa closed her eyes and rubbed her temples, she'd only gotten a brief glance at the inside of the apartment, but it was enough to tell her all she needed to know. The place wasn't cared for.

Although Liam hadn't been home, his mother had offered a list of suggested locations he might be. She was obviously a heavy smoker, and the thick air hadn't encouraged the idea of waiting for Liam to return. Jessa frowned. Often, murderers were from homes where they were never shown love.

"Miss Anderson?" a high school guy approached.

"Yes?"

"I'm Eric, and I go to school here. I'm working with the fundraiser."

Jessa extended her hand. "It's very nice to meet you Eric. I hope the fundraiser is a success. If there's anything I can do to help, please let me know."

"There is something." Eric glanced over his shoulder. "You're friends with the Martin dames aren't you?"

Jessa nodded. "I am, but I hope you don't call them that to their face."

Eric blushed. "Sorry. Anyway, people have been talking and . . . well, no one actually believes they had anything to do with the murder. In fact, they've become somewhat of a fascination."

"What are you saying?"

"I'm saying, some of us teens had a little meeting and we think the old ladies fudge could make a lot of money for the school. Even our out of town guests have heard of it and . . . well, can you get them to make fudge for the fundraiser? I know they're on house arrest and all but if you could bring the fudge, it would sell like crazy!"

Jessa pursed her lips into a slight frown. "How is the school board going to feel about the fudge being here? I mean they were all nearly poisoned by fudge."

Eric broke into a winsome smile. "They'll be okay with it. If anyone has any complaints, I'll give them a talking to. I mean seriously, this cookie dough fudge could become world famous!"

Jessa couldn't resist a slight smile. With Eric's innocent grin and amiable charisma, he could probably convince anyone to go along with his ideas. "Alright, I'll talk to them about it."

Erica nodded. "Great. You can set the fudge booth up here where it would have been before, and charge as much as you want. People are willing to pay. If you'd donate a platter to the silent auction that would be great too."

Jessa shrugged. "I can't even guarantee they'll want to make the fudge. I mean isn't it a little insensitive to sell fudge here after what happened?"

With another charming smile, Eric winked. "Not if it helps the school. I'll have Larry drop the ingredients off at your place tonight."

"Larry?"

"Yeah, I talked to the manager of the grocery store, and they're donating the ingredients. Since no one is supposed to know what house the old ladies are at, I figured you could get them the ingredients."

Jessa nodded. "I can do that, in exchange for some information. How well do you know Liam Bennett?"

Eric shrugged. "Not really well. No one does. He's always been a quiet kid. Keeps to himself."

"Is he a violent person?"

"Not normally," Eric said. "He pretty much kept to himself until his sister started coming to school, and then he hung out with her on break time. After his father was arrested, some of the kids teased him about his dad being a jailbird, and that's when he started losing his temper."

"Did he lose his temper often?"

"Not unless Clara was near. When he was alone, you could say whatever you wanted, and he would ignore you, but if you said anything bad about his family in front of Clara, he'd pound you for it."

"Do you know anything about his home life?" Jessa watched Eric's face. He winced slightly.

"I don't know anything, but I stopped by once to leave a school flyer, and I heard his mom inside, yelling at him. I think the reason he sticks so close to his sister, is to protect her from their mother."

Jessa's grimaced. How awful was it for a sixteen-year-old boy to have to protect his little sister from his own mother? Could something like that cause a boy to commit murder?

Eric suddenly straightened. "I've got to catch someone." He turned and hurried away. "Bob!" he called.

Jessa turned back to the empty table. The holly looked lonely, next to the empty displays, but if the displays were covered in fudge, it would look just right. Jessa walked around the area.

"At least they were thorough." No trace of the crime remained.

With a sigh, she headed out. Nels office was the next place she wanted to check. If there was something in his office that could help, she was going to find it.

The office was unlocked, and she entered it with a slightly eerie feeling. This was the last place Nels had been seen. Was he dead? Hurt? Lost somewhere?

Jessa slid her thin winter gloves from her coat pockets and slipped them on. If this became a crime scene, she wasn't going to leave finger prints all over the place.

The room was as cluttered and messy as most offices are when they've had the same occupant for many years. Nels obviously hadn't been an overly neat person, but he wasn't a total slob either.

Jessa started through the stacks of papers on the desk. Nothing seemed out of the ordinary. She slid the top drawer open. A paper fell to the floor.

Jessa reached for it. *December School Board Meeting Agenda.* She glanced across the paper. Nothing out of the ordinary, but if the school board was the target, then it could be important. Jessa went to the copying machine and opened it. A piece of paper fluttered out. She stuck in the school board paper to make a copy, and then reached for the paper on the floor.

It looked like random numbers, but it needed more examining. She set it on the desk as the copy machine spit out the copy of the school meeting agenda. She returned the original to its spot in the drawer and stuck the copy in her pocket.

The door opened, and Jessa looked up from the second drawer. "Clay! Did you find anything?"

"I found everything from A to Z, but nothing relating to the crime." Clay pulled his hat off and set it on the desk. "How are you making out?"

Jessa sighed. "I don't know. Everything seems pretty normal. Except this paper." She picked up the one on the desk. "It was in the copying machine."

Clay frowned as he studied it.

"Does it make any sense to you?"

Clay sighed. "It's some kind of money record, but it isn't making much sense. If I knew what account it was talking about, it would help. It looks like money was transferred from one account to another, but no account names or numbers are listed."

Jessa left Clay to examine the paper further, and she moved around the room. From the dust on the shelves, no one had disturbed them in at least a week or two. She moved on to the waste basket in the corner. Crumpled papers, granola bar wrappers, and empty frost Gatorade bottles filled most of the can.

"Have you guys been through this?" Jessa asked.

Clay glanced up from the paper. "We haven't had reason to. Nels hasn't been missing for twenty-four hours so Kramer can't treat it like a missing person case. And after the body was found, we had no reason to search this office."

"May I go through it?"

Clay frowned. "You've done this sort of thing before?"

Jessa nodded. At least he wasn't hostile towards her anymore. In fact, he almost seemed eager to let her help. She bit back a sigh. It would be easy to get used to working with him.

"Okay, but instead of those gloves, you should wear these." He pulled a pair of plastic gloves from his pocket.

Jessa put them on, and then started taking things out of the small garbage can. She made neat piles of each thing based on the order she took it out. Even if she didn't find anything, she wanted to return it exactly as she'd found it so that when Nels returned he wouldn't feel like his office had been gone through.

She unfolded each paper, then re-crumpled it when it proved to be unimportant. Clay began going through desk drawers.

"Are you allowed to do that?" Jessa asked. "I mean don't you need a search warrant?"

Clay paused. "I was suspended. I'm just a civilian like you, and that means I can be nosy. Sure, Nels can get mad, but I can't get into the same kind of trouble. Besides, this is a school. It's public." He turned back to the desk, and Jessa went back to her garbage digging.

At the bottom of the can, she sighed. She'd been sure she would find something. Garbage cans were often a criminal's point of forgetfulness.

She began putting things back into the can, and then paused. The grocery bag that was serving as a garbage bag was too small for the can and was slipping. On instinct, she took the bag out and looked in the bottom of the can. "Clay. Get over here."

Chapter Fifteen

Clay was at her side in a moment. "What's the matter? Did you . . ." His voice trailed off as he stared into the can where a syringe and a small bottle lay.

Clay met Jessa's gaze.

"The murder weapon?" she asked.

Clay shrugged. "It seems that way. This puts Nels as our number one suspect."

"It could be a plant," Jessa said. "What now?"

Reaching for his cellphone, he motioned Jessa back. "We don't disturb anything more. And we call Isaiah. He's the best we've got in the way of a forensic team, and he'll finger print the office and this can, as well as get the syringe and bottle to Tina at the lab in Red Brooks."

"Can't you do the finger printing and stuff?"

Clay shook his head as he led Jessa from the room. "I'm not on the police team anymore. I have to leave this kind of stuff to the people who are actually on duty." He called Isaiah, and not more than five minutes went by before Isaiah arrived. He was closely followed by Sergeant Kramer, and another officer.

"I'll thank you to stay out of this!" Kramer said as he and his man entered the office.

Isaiah cast an apologetic look towards Clay and then followed Kramer and the other officer.

"They'll do a thorough job," Clay said. "There's no reason for us to stay."

"Don't we have to give a statement or something?" Jessa asked.

Clay sighed. "Yep. But we can do that at the station. It's not like the police don't know where to find us. We can probably just go back and compare notes with the others."

Jessa sighed.

"Is something wrong?"

"I just feel like I should reenact the morning of Royce's death." Jessa paused. "I feel like if I could retrace my steps, and remember every detail, it would help."

Clay glanced at the busy office. "Now's not the best time. How about we come back later tonight, or tomorrow and do it?"

Jessa nodded. "That would be great."

Footsteps sounded on the metal stairs, and Donna helped Bertha spread the food. Jessa and Clay entered the room looking discouraged and tired.

"Help yourselves!" Donna gestured towards the counter that was cluttered with food. Minnesotan cheese-wiz and olive sandwiches on cinnamon bread, along with chips, pickles, lefsa, and jello salad made for a mouthwatering sight.

Jessa started forward. "I'm starving!" As if to prove her point, her stomach rumbled loud enough for everyone to hear.

Donna put her hands on her hips. "Let me guess, you didn't stop for lunch like you were supposed to?"

Jessa shook her head. "I got distracted."

"Donuts and coffee is hardly enough to sustain a person!" Bertha said in dismay. "Clay, hurry up and pray so we can get this poor girl some food!"

Clay bowed his head and prayed. He blessed the food, and asked God for more wisdom.

Donna made sure Clay and Jessa both had plenty on their plates, and once they were seated on the couch and eating, she began telling them what she'd done.

Clay frowned, but Jessa leaned forward.

"Is this what you were looking for?" Jessa pulled a paper from her pocket and handed it to Donna.

Donna unfolded the school board agenda and whistled in delight. "Janet said Zoe hadn't sent it out yet, but maybe Janet just hadn't gotten hers yet." Donna scanned the paper with anticipation, but nothing stood out.

"What does it say?" Bertha asked.

Donna slid the paper across the desk to Bertha. "Nothing interesting at all. Just normal business, old business, and reports."

"What were you expecting?" Bertha asked.

Donna sighed. "I don't know. Something. Anything."

"I'm sorry," Jessa said. "I was hoping it would be important."

Clay shrugged. "It could still be important."

Donna nodded. "Of course, it could." She folded it and handed it back to Jessa who put it in her purse. "It may not be the piece of information that solves the mystery, but it could be a piece to the puzzle, and it could fill in some gaps. If we only had the rest of the pieces."

"Am I the only one that noticed the school suspension line?" Bertha asked. "And the initials L. B.? That's got to be Liam Bennett. If the school board was going to discuss whether or not Liam was allowed back in school, it could have caused him to poison the fudge. Even though he probably didn't want to go to school, being told he couldn't might have made him want to hurt someone. And remember, he was at the school the morning of the murder when he was suspended from being in school!"

Jessa helped clean up, and then reached for her coat. "I'd better head home. Callie will be missing me."

"Oh, your poor dog!" Donna exclaimed. "Will she be alright in the house all alone?"

Jessa nodded. "I locked her in the back half of the house, and she has a doggy door to a fenced in back yard, so she's fine, but I still should check on her."

Clay rose to his feet. "Thank you, for all your help today."

"I'm sorry I couldn't do more. I feel like we're not getting anywhere." Jessa forced a smile. "I'll see you guys at the lutefisk bake. If we keep collecting information, we will eventually figure it out."

After Jessa left, Clay grabbed his coat and headed outside. With all the details flying around his mind, he needed fresh air. His breath hung visible in the dark air, and he sighed. Winter wasn't even half over and he was already tired of the cold.

The neighboring houses seemed to have a Christmas decorating contest going, and blown up yard ornaments covered the lawns. Hundreds of tiny lightbulbs gave the snow the appearance of glitter. Closing his eyes, he sighed. Jessa's smile flashed in his mind. If only things were different . . . if only he wasn't in the middle of a murder case.

Opening his eyes, he started walking. Above all else, he had to find the truth. The truth about the murder . . . and the truth about Jessa.

Around the edge of the station, he paused. A small figure was huddled on a snow-covered bench.

"Clara!" he called.

The little girl jumped up and met his gaze. Her eyes didn't hold the fear that Liam's did, but she did seem to be unsure whether she should stay or go.

"Is Liam here?" Clay asked as he approached.

Clara shook her head. "He said he'd be back soon."

Clay frowned. "Why aren't you home?"

"I can't tell you," Clara said. "Or you'll send the bad people to take us away."

Clay frowned. "Bad people?"

"That's what Liam said. I don't know why he thinks that because I like you, and so does Liam. We think you're nice. But he said even nice people will send the bad people to take us away. Why would you do that?"

Clay squatted down on the level of the little girl. "Clara. I would never let anyone hurt you."

"But would you let them take us away?" Clara's lips trembled. "That's why Liam went to jail because he didn't want you to put my mommy in jail. Liam says that if anything happens to Mommy before he's eighteen the bad people will come. And they'll take Liam from me and put me with strangers."

Clay frowned. Did she mean the social workers? "Clara, you have my word, that I won't let anyone separate you from Liam." He stopped. Could he do that? "Unless . . . well, unless Liam has done something wrong, then he'll have to go back to jail."

Tears rolled down her cheeks. "He didn't do anything wrong!"

"Then you won't be separated," Clay assured her.

Footsteps crunched in the snow, and Clay looked up.

Liam's cool stare caught his eye. "Why can't you leave us alone? I served my time!"

Something Clara said registered in Clay's mind, and he frowned. "Liam, you lied about the drugs in your possession, didn't you? They were your mother's, and you didn't want her to be arrested or you and Clara would be sent to foster homes."

Liam's eyes narrowed.

"You could have told me, I will do whatever I have to in order to keep you guys safe."

Liam snorted. "You don't know what you're talking about. Come on, Clara." He grabbed Clara's hand and started away, looking back over his shoulder, he shook his head. "Forget anything she told you. We just like the excitement around here. That's not a crime! We're fine."

On the way home, Jessa decided to stop at the church, and see how Shelby was faring. Callie could wait.

A group of carolers stood outside the church door, their breath hung in the air like clouds as they sang *Joy to the World*. Snow gently floated down, and Jessa paused. Snowflakes caught in her hair and melted against the warmth of her cheeks. A smile parted her lips as she listened. What a joyful thing to know that the Lord is come! She waited till the song was done, and then headed inside.

Most of the people were getting up in years, and Jessa smiled. Josh had always told her that lutefisk was something you eat when you're too old to taste. Each table she passed, seemed to be talking about the murders.

"I can't handle this suspense!" someone said.

"I've started locking my doors," another person said.

"If they don't catch the killer soon, I'm going to consider moving."

Jessa slipped past the gossiping people and headed for where Shelby was sitting near the counter. The killer had to be caught soon.

When Shelby saw Jessa, her eyes lit up. "Jessa!"

Jessa hurried over. "How's it going?"

Shelby's shoulders slumped. "There's so many people and they all have opinions. I can't hear them all at once! It doesn't help that they all get quiet when I get too close. I guess they all figure I'm here to eavesdrop."

"Do you want help?" Jessa asked.

Shelby nodded. "If you would, that would be great! I don't want to leave because Ken and Sally are close by," she whispered. "But Brad just came in, and someone should stick close to him."

Jessa nodded. "I'm on it."

She headed across the fellowship hall and stood in line behind Brad.

She was unsure of how lutefisk would taste, but she knew the lefsa and mashed potatoes would be good. After getting a plate, she found a chair that was close to Brad's.

Sitting with her back at a slight angle from him so as not to draw attention, she listened.

Jessa tried not to get impatient. It was possible that no one would speak to him. She dipped a bit of lutefisk into the sauce they'd provided. It was pretty tasteless, and she frowned. What was the big deal with it? It wasn't that good, but neither was it as awful as her brother had made it sound.

"Ladies and Gentlemen!" A voice boomed.

Jessa turned towards the mic.

"Thank you all for coming! I know people will be trickling in for a while, but we'll get started on the program. If you don't know me, I'm Pastor Kevin, and I'm glad to see you all enjoying the great food. A huge thank you to everyone who had a part in making this year another success. Now, let's not forget the reason we celebrate Christmas."

"Here we go again," Brad muttered.

"Christmas is about so much more than a baby in a manger. Jesus Christ came into this world to save us. It's a great thing to celebrate, but let's not forget the price he paid on the cross in order to offer us forgiveness for our sins. The baby in the manger is the same God that created each of us, and after giving His life for us, He rose again, to offer us life."

"Hello?" Brad said, and Jessa turned to see him holding a cellphone to his ear.

Brad hunched over his phone and whispered. "What shed?" there was a pause. "Who is this? Hello?" Brad's forehead was wrinkled. He put his phone back in his pocket and began mumbling under his breath. He got out of his chair and headed for the door.

Jessa paused. Should she get up and create a double disturbance for the pastor? Deciding that she was far enough to the side not to be too distracting, she got up and followed Brad from a distance. Whoever had made the phone call had upset Brad, and if he was going to this 'shed' that the mysterious caller told him about, it could be valuable information.

Brad didn't go for his car but cut across the alley behind the church on foot and headed towards the edge of town.

Jessa stayed in the shadows as much as she could. "If Laci could see me now," she mumbled to herself. She knew following murder suspects in the dark wasn't a good idea, but at the moment, she felt strangely safe. If Brad had wanted to hurt her, he could have done it before now. Near the edge of town, a rundown shed loomed against the backdrop of white. From the undisturbed snow around the front, it was obvious that people hadn't been using it.

Brad trudged through the knee-deep snow drifts to the door, and rattled the handle, when it didn't open, he stepped back, and began throwing his weight against it. The door gave in on the third heave, and Brad disappeared into the shed.

Chills ran up her spine as Jessa walked in his tracks up to the door and peeked in. Brad had his phone out for his flashlight and he shone it around the room. When his light picked up a figure on the floor, Brad cursed. He flipped his phone around and dialed a number. "Yes, this is an emergency. I'm at the old Miller tool shed, and I've found Nels Christensen." There was a pause. "I don't know, I haven't touched him." After another pause, Brad knelt down beside the figure and held his hand out to feel Nels' pulse. "Yes, he's still alive, but unconscious."

Jessa sagged with relief. At least he wasn't dead. Jessa entered the shed. "Brad," she said.

Brad's head jerked up.

"It's just me, Jessa." She held her gloved hands up in what she hoped came across as non-threatening. "I saw you through the door. Is everything okay?"

Brad shook his head. "Nels is hurt."

From the tone in Brad's voice, Jessa figured he wasn't a threat, so she approached, and knelt beside Nels, with the light from Brad's flashlight, she checked his vitals.

"What's wrong with him?" Brad asked.

Jessa looked up. "He was hit in the head with something." She glanced back at the lump on the side of Nels head.

"Will he be alright?"

Jessa shrugged. "I don't know."

Sirens sounded in the distance, and in another moment, the shed was bustling with activity.

Isaiah appeared, and Jessa got his attention. "Nels and whoever hit him must have come in the back door. There were no tracks out front when Brad and I got here."

Isaiah nodded. "Thanks. I'm on it." He pulled a finger print kit from his pocket and headed that way.

Jessa sighed. It probably wouldn't do any good. Only a fool would be out in this kind of weather without gloves. It made her wonder how Brad could stand to wear a fedora in the sub-zero temperatures.

"How did you come to find him here?" Kramer bellowed.

Brad seemed to shrink under Kramer's stare.

"I got a phone call . . ." Brad stammered. "I don't know who from. They said Nels was here, and that he was hurt."

"That's all they said?" Kramer asked.

Brad nodded. "I came right away."

"We'll need your phone to try to trace the caller."

Brad nodded and handed it over. He seemed shaken. "I have no idea who it was."

Kramer turned to Jessa. "And what are you doing here?" he snapped.

Jessa took a deep breath. She knew she had to tell the truth, but Brad might not like it. "I left the church, and saw Brad coming here. I thought it was strange, so I followed him."

Kramer scowled. "We don't need wannabe detectives trailing suspects. Go home. We'll question you further at a later time."

Jessa exited the building and headed home on foot. Her car was still parked at the church, but home was closer, and she wasn't even sure it would start.

Nearing her house, she caught sight of a teen boy, and a little girl. "Liam!" she called.

The figure stopped on the sidewalk, his eyes darted up and down the street as she approached.

"I'm Jessaca Anderson," she said.

The teen gave a jerky nod. "I know."

Jessa stared into his eyes until he averted his gaze. Yes, there was strong feelings there, fear, pain, and perhaps hunger, but no hate, or anger. Nothing like what she'd seen in criminal's eyes in the past.

"Isn't it a little strange to be wandering the streets after dark?" she asked.

Clara smiled at her. "We can't be home right now because Mom brought home more . . ."

"Clara!" Liam cut her off. "We'd best be going."

Jessa glanced from Clara's red nose and pale cheeks to the ice and snow in Liam's hair and made a quick decision. "I live all alone, and it gets lonely. If you're just hanging around outside, I'd be much obliged if you could stop in and keep me company."

She tried to gauge their reactions. Clara beamed, but Liam's face hardened.

"We're not looking for handouts," he said.

Jessa nodded. "I know, but I'm afraid that I am. I'd like some company." Jessa started up her sidewalk. "This is my house, and I have a little dog that doesn't get to see people very much. She'd like a visit too."

"Can we please?" Clara begged. "I want to see the doggie!"

Liam's mask of hardness slipped, and his eyes softened. "Alright, Clara, we'll go see the doggie."

Callie jumped around in excitement when Jessa entered the house. After taking a few minutes to pet the dog and assure it that she still cared about her, she introduced the dog to Liam and Clara.

Clara squealed with delight.

"Go ahead and play with her," Jessa said. "I've got something I need to take care of."

Jessa left them in the back entry with the dog and headed for the kitchen. After putting the tea kettle on to boil, she called Laci.

After two rings, she picked up. "So, how's the super sleuth doing? I hear you found the possible murder weapon?"

"How did you know that?"

"I called Clay a few minutes ago for a report on you." Jessa could hear the smile in Laci's voice. "He sounds like he's warming up to you."

"You could have just asked me," Jessa said.

"That's too easy. Besides, I'm trying to get to know Clay. He seems like a great guy." Laci paused, but Jessa didn't say anything so she went on. "Actually, I had some questions for him about the case you're on. Danger levels and that kind of thing."

Jessa sighed. "Thank you for being concerned for me, but I think I'm fine. Mom did way more dangerous stuff than this and Dad never stopped her."

"Exactly my point," Laci said. "Mom died on a mission. I know you're capable of handling dangerous situations, but so was she. I'm not going to let anything happen to you. Which is why I needed to talk to you now. To tell you to obey Clay. If he thinks something is too dangerous for you, listen to him. He wants to protect you. Let him."

Jessa pulled some mugs from the cupboard. "I will. But it was really not necessary, or your place, to tell him to protect me! You make me sound like I'm incapable of being careful! I'll remind you that I'm the big sister!"

"It's not like I don't think you're capable, but . . ." Laci sighed. "You know, with Mom and everything . . . And of course, a guy is way more likely to take notice of you if he's trying to protect you."

"You're impossible!" Jessa fought to keep from laughing. "Sometimes you act like you're still thirteen! If God wants Clay to notice me as more than just a fellow citizen of Middle Ridge, He can arrange that without our help."

She sat in silence for a bit before Laci cleared her throat. "Is that a kid I hear in the background?"

"Yes, it is."

"Where are you?"

Jessa laughed. "I'm home, and I invited some friends in."

"I'm assuming, from the way you said that, that they're either suspects, or strays, and you just met them, but you're calling them friends to put me at ease. It's not working. I ought to give you the stranger-danger speech, but since you wouldn't listen anyway I'll spare us both. How are you doing with all this? I know you wanted to back off from the investigating and working with Dad to settle down with your music. Is this too much for you?"

Jessa sighed. How did Lexi go from teasing to serious so fast? "At first, I didn't like it, but it seems like God allowed this situation here, so that I'd have to realize I still enjoy investigation work. I've never tried leaving the work, it's the memories I wanted to leave. But Dad was right, it's in my blood. I have to solve anything that resembles a mystery."

"So, are you back in the Anderson family bureau team?"

Jessa paused. "As long as I'm an Anderson, I'm on the team. I always have been. I just . . . well, I needed a few months off. And I may want to move my headquarters here to Middle Ridge . . . I love it here."

"As long as you're an Anderson? Then I guess you'll just have to marry a guy with the last name Anderson! What's Clay's last name?"

247

The doorbell rang, and Jessa turned off the pot that was beginning to whistle. "I've got to go."

"Good-bye, Jessa. Love ya, sis."

"Love you, Laci!"

Jessa slid her phone into her pocket and headed for the door.

"Miss Anderson!" Larry greeted her. Snowflakes clung to his mustache. "I'm here with a delivery."

"Thanks, Larry! Eric said you'd be stopping by. You can just put it on the kitchen counter for now."

Larry paused. "Um . . . that's not quite going to work."

"Why not?"

Larry shrugged. "There's too much stuff."

Jessa paused. "You mean . . ."

"I mean we have enough ingredients to make enough fudge for everyone in town, as well as those sugar cookie things the ladies make."

Jessa opened her mouth and then paused.

"Look," Larry said. "I know we're not supposed to know where the Martin sisters are, but I think everyone in town does, so if you're okay with me just bringing it over to Clay's, I'll do that."

"How do you even know what ingredients they need? Isn't their cookie dough fudge from a secret family recipe?"

Larry nodded. "It is, but Sally Landean got a copy of the recipe from her mom, who was good friends with the Martin family. She made me a list of the ingredients."

Jessa held up a finger. "Give me a sec, and I'll come with you."

Chapter Sixteen

She hurried back to Clara and Liam. "Sorry, but I have to leave. You can stay as long as you want. There's hot water on the stove, and hot chocolate mix beside the mugs if you're interested. There are also some snacks on the counter." Jessa paused at the conflicting looks. Clara looked eager; Liam looked skeptical. "I'd be much obliged if you could stay with Callie while I'm gone. She doesn't like to be alone, and there's no way I can eat all that food, so help yourselves."

Liam's eyes flickered with thoughts that Jessa could only guess as she grabbed her purse.

She followed Larry to his rusted pickup truck. Part of her revolted at leaving a possible murder suspect in her house. Especially when Liam was known for erratic behavior. But Clara's sweet face wouldn't leave her. It was worth any damage Liam might do, just to see Clara enjoy an evening in a warm house.

Once they were in the truck, Larry paused. "Miss Anderson, am I still a suspect?"

Jessa studied his face. There was sadness in his eyes. Something deep.

"I know, I don't have an alibi, and from the message on my answering machine, you don't think I was home that day." He paused.

Jessa frowned. How had he known about that? Was it possible to keep anything secret from the town?

"But I didn't do it!" Larry gripped the shift stick and switched into drive. "I didn't do it," he repeated more softly.

"I believe you," Jessa said. "But we don't have any proof, or alibis, so we can't totally write you off."

Larry pulled up to the back side of the police station.

"It would help, if you could tell us exactly what kind of money issues are going on between Nels, Brad, and Ken."

Larry turned the vehicle off and nodded. "Alright, after we get all this stuff inside, I'll tell you everything I know."

"What have you got there?" Bertha asked as Jessa and Larry set the first bags on the floor by the kitchen.

"Donated ingredients for the school benefit." Jessa said.

"The store has never donated them before," Donna said.

Jessa grinned. "They've got a high-schooler working with the team. Eric could sweet talk anyone into donating anything."

It took several trips to get everything into the basement, but as soon as it was all there, Bertha and Donna started baking. Clay, Isaiah, and Shelby were still gone.

After some cupboard banging, Bertha sent Jessa to pick up more pans and kitchen utensils from their kitchen. Jessa took Larry's truck, and once she was back and the sisters were happily baking, she sat down with Larry.

"So, what do you know about Brad, Nels, and Ken?"

Larry flexed his fingers. "Ken is a loan shark. He hated Royce because they both targeted the same customers. They did learn to work together so when someone needed to pay one of them off, the other wouldn't lend any money. That's what happened to me. I needed money to pay Royce, but Ken wouldn't give it to me."

"Could Ken have killed Royce to get his business?"

Larry nodded. "He could have. They did hate each other."

Jessa frowned. "Middle Ridge has a population of one-thousand, three-hundred and seven people. Where did

Royce and Ken find enough people desperate enough to ask them for money?"

Larry shrugged, his hand strayed back to his mustache. "I think they do some in the bigger cities around, but locally, they wouldn't have had any business if Royce hadn't forced people's hands. He had a way of making people get involved in gambling debts and stuff like that." Larry glanced over his shoulder. "Most of it was illegal."

"Like your gambling debt?"

Larry looked at the floor. "Yeah. But now that he's dead, I'm done. I'll never get involved in that kind of thing again."

"How do Brad and Nels figure in?"

"Brad knew I was in trouble with Royce so he came to me, told me how much he hated Royce, and offered to go to Ken for me and borrow the money in his name. Ken and Brad were on speaking terms, so it seemed like a good idea. But Brad never got me the money, and after talking to me a few weeks ago, he only just got me the loan rates from Ken today. If Royce were still alive, I'd have been roasted before Brad got me the money."

"Does Nels play in here somewhere?"

"I don't know. See, Brad came to me today and asked me to take some money from him. It was quite a large sum of money, and I wasn't comfortable taking it from him when he acted the way he did. He acted like he'd stolen it. I didn't want

253

to take it and get caught with it, so I wouldn't take it. I think the money came from Nels."

"Why would you think that?"

Larry shrugged. "Brad kept mentioning something about Nels needing help. I connected the money and Nels in my mind. I could be wrong, but I don't think so."

Footsteps on the stairs alerted Jessa that someone was coming. Clay stopped inside the doorway and stared. "What is he doing here?"

Jessa explained as best she could. "He's willing to answer questions." She met Clay's eye and gave a slight nod. "Even if he has nothing to do with the murders," she lowered her voice to a whisper. "He's sharing stuff that could help you get some illegal loaning and gambling rings out of business."

Clay stepped in front of the couch and leaned back on the desk. "So, Larry, can you explain why Royce was blackmailing you?"

Larry frowned. "I'd rather not. I mean . . . well, it had to do with gambling, and it could probably get me arrested."

Clay nodded, and toyed with a snow globe the aunts had put on his desk. "Okay, well, can you repeat everything you just told Jessa?"

Larry took a deep breath and began. When Larry finished, he excused himself to go home.

Jessa walked back to the suspect board. Nels was the logical option. "If he poisoned the board for some reason," she mumbled to herself. "He could have hidden the syringe in his garbage can, then when Timmy threatened to tell the police, he'd somehow lured him to the Martin house, and killed him there to make them look guilty. Then his partner, Brad, got mad at him and killed him . . . or maybe . . . it was staged."

"Clay!" Jessa turned around. "What if Brad and Nels were working together, and Nels poisoned the school board, and then he disappeared and had Brad hit him on the head to make him look like a victim too."

Clay frowned. "You're speculating. We need facts, not theories."

Jessa bit her lip. She was right. She could feel it, but without proof, what good did it do to think she was right?

"You should come in the kitchen!" Donna said. "Baking always gives me inspiration."

With nothing better to do, Jessa started in on the dishes. Bertha's humming of *O Holy Night* filled the kitchen, and a hint of peppermint scented the air.

When she finished the dishes, she started helping the aunts. With all three of them making three different batches, things were moving along. When Clay came in to lick a bowl, Jessa glanced at the clock. It was almost nine o'clock.

"Did anything Larry say help?" Jessa asked.

Clay shrugged. "At face value, none of it seemed overly important, but maybe, if we get more information, something he said will become important."

Jessa turned back to the bowl she was stirring. Somehow, this case seemed to be taking longer than most.

"Are you alright?" Clay asked. "You look . . . sad."

Jessa glanced up. No one but Josh and Laci had ever been able to read her like that. "This case is taking longer than I'm used to."

Clay cocked an eyebrow. "Really? Because often cases take weeks. We haven't had a bad start."

Jessa nodded. "I know, but . . . I guess I miss Dad so it seems to drag on, you know?" Jessa tucked a strand of hair behind her ear. "I know I'm in my thirties, but this is the first case I've ever worked on that I haven't been able to call my dad and talk with him about it."

"I'm sorry."

"It's not your fault." Jessa turned back to her bowl. "Donna, I think this is mixed enough."

Clay rounded the counter and stopped in front of Jessa. "You need help."

Jessa glanced around the kitchen. "Help baking or mental help?"

Clay's eyes twinkled. "Christmas help. Yes, we're involved in a serious case. Yes, we must find the truth and set the town free from fear, but we also have to remember that it's Christmas." Clay stepped even closer. "Close your eyes."

Jessa opened her mouth to protest. What was he thinking? But his twinkling eyes won the silent argument, and she closed her eyes.

"Now, take a deep breath through your nose."

Jessa followed his instructions. A slight giggle made its way out. Peppermint, and chocolate was all she could smell at first, but as she took another breath, she caught a whiff of coffee, mixed with the toasty sugar cookies.

"What do you smell?" Clay asked.

"Christmas." Jessa took another breath. "May I open my eyes?"

"Not yet. I need you to open your mouth."

Jessa fought the smile, and opened her mouth.

Something was placed in her mouth, and she chewed. The flaky sugar cookie melted on her tongue with buttery sweetness. A hint of mint lingered in her mouth.

"What do you taste?"

"Christmas," Jessa whispered.

"You can open your eyes now," Clay said.

Jessa opened her eyes, and stilled under Clay's charming smile.

"It *is* Christmas," Clay's voice dropped to scarcely more than a whisper. "A time to remember the truth, and what we've been set free from. Forget about the case and just relax for a bit. It's Christmas."

Jessa held his steady gaze for a moment. She felt her cheeks warming under his steady gaze. He wouldn't do something rash would he? Like . . . kiss her? But she hadn't thought he was the kind to set a case aside for even a moment to relax for Christmas, and yet he'd just done it!

She cleared her throat and took a step back. Turning to the sink, she rinsed a chocolate covered spoon from the counter. She watched the hot water melting the chocolate away, and she tried to calm her heartrate down. What had just happened? She glanced up. He was still watching her.

Clay stared at her. What had he done? He was trying to solve a case! He didn't have time for Christmas, or love . . .

She glanced at him from the sink, and then turned her attention back to the spoon.

What just happened? Clay glanced down at the broken sugar cookie in his hand. He wasn't supposed to act like a school boy! He frowned. *What was I thinking? I can't get involved. . . I can't love again.*

Clay shook his head slightly and popped a corner of the cookie into his own mouth. He needed to stay focused. He couldn't let Jessa be a distraction. But as he brushed the crumbs from his shirt, his gaze settled on her again.

Taking a deep breath, he headed for his laptop. "I'll just leave you ladies to your work."

Though he tried to remain focused on the job before him, Jessa's smile, framed by her blushing face, wouldn't leave his mind.

Footsteps sounded on the stairs, and Clay stood with relief.

When Isaiah and Shelby finally made it in, six pans of fudge were cooling in the fridge, and Jessa was exhausted.

"I'd better head home," Jessa said. "I'll be back first thing in the morning to help with more baking and investigating or whatever I'm needed for."

"Wait up a sec," Shelby said. "You'll want to hear what Isaiah has to say."

Jessa grabbed her coat and waited.

"So, after getting things to evidence, I was assigned to regular duties," Isaiah said. "When Nels was found, I was stationed at the hospital. I was in the room when Nels regained consciousness."

"And?" Clay prompted.

"And when I tried taking his statement, he couldn't tell me anything. He didn't know Royce had been killed, and he didn't know that he'd gotten a divorce or been remarried."

"How far back does his memory loss go?" Donna asked.

"As far as I could tell," Isaiah said. "It was sometime about two years ago."

Clay raked his fingers through his hair, leaving it standing on end. "Is he for real, or is it a scam?"

Jessa studied his face. The teasing grin was gone, and had been replaced by the look of a man with a job to do.

Isaiah shrugged. "As soon as the doctor is sure that he's not suffering too much from a concussion, he's going to do a mental evaluation to see if Nels is telling the truth. If the doctor's convinced, then we'll probably get a polygraph test on him. He had Jessa's files in his pocket, but didn't seem to know why."

Bertha eased her way down onto the couch. "If a man gets beaned on the head, isn't it natural to forget things? Why assume he's lying?"

"Because we deal with criminals," Clay explained. "Criminals do this kind of thing to get their name cleared."

Clay and Isaiah started pulling out snacks from a cupboard, and Jessa turned to Shelby. "How are you feeling?"

"Great! I mean I didn't get any wedding planning done but . . . you know, it's the job." Shelby said.

Isaiah stifled a yawn. "I should drive you home tonight. We wouldn't want you falling asleep at the wheel."

Shelby smirked. "And that two-minute drive is long enough to put someone to sleep?"

Isaiah crammed a granola bar into his mouth, then helped Shelby into her coat, and opened the door for her.

"You pay attention, Clay," Bertha said. "If you ever get hitched, you'll need to help a woman into her coat."

Clay gave a slight nod and turned back to the cupboard.

Jessa frowned. What had happened to his smile?

"I'll be going now," Jessa said. "But I'll be back first thing in the morning to help with the rest of the baking."

Clay spun around. "There's a murderer on the loose. I could drive you home . . ."

Jessa's heart fluttered and she inhaled sharply. "I . . . I'll be fine." She hurried for the stairs.

Once Jessa was outside, she took a deep breath, and tried to calm down. Why did she have to feel this way about someone who would never return the feelings?

She was halfway across the empty parking lot before she remembered her car. Not wanting to go back and bother them, or risk putting herself in another awkward situation, she decided to jog home. The air nipped at her cheeks, and burned her lungs, but it felt good. Despite the cold, she was glad she was jogging. It always cleared her brain and gave her room to think clearly.

At home, the house was still lit up, and Jessa entered quietly. All was quiet. She glanced in the kitchen. Two mugs had been used, and some snacks were gone. She stepped into the living room, and stopped. Snuggled up on the couch, Clara held Callie, and leaned against Liam's shoulder. They were both sound asleep, and Jessa smiled. She draped an afghan over them, and shut the lights out, leaving a lamp on in case they awoke.

Not wanting to wake them, she headed for her own bedroom.

DECEMBER 23rd

Darkness still enveloped the room, but Jessa forced herself to get up. She grabbed her Bible and read a few chapters by lamplight.

"The Lord thy God, in the midst of thee, is mighty." She smiled at the words. No matter what the day held, God would be there. And He was mighty!

After getting ready for the day, she took Callie to the back entry and made sure she had plenty of food and water. "I'm sorry I've got to be gone so much." She scratched Callie's tummy. "I probably won't be home till late tonight. Be a good girl for me okay?"

Callie cocked her head to the side, and Jessa giggled. At times it was as if the animal actually understood.

Liam and Clara were both still asleep, so Jessa wrote them a note, and taped it to the door. Inviting them to help themselves to anything in the kitchen and thanking them for their help.

Grabbing a cold pop tart, she headed for the car. When she saw the empty driveway, she sighed. "Of course, it's gone." Jessa stood in the middle of the driveway as she finished her pop tart, then she took off on foot. Jogging in her two-inch heeled boots had been difficult at first, but after doing it for a few years, she'd gotten used to it. She jogged to the church, and stopped.

"I left it right here." She slowly turned in a circle, but the red PT Cruiser was nowhere in sight. She pulled her cell phone out and called Sheriff Vicklund.

"What is it?" he snapped.

"Don . . . my car has been stolen."

There was a pause. "Oh? That's too bad. I'll fill out a report on it, and get out an APB. Of course, with this murder, the car gets less priority."

Jessa narrowed her eyes. His tone suggested that he didn't care a bit that her car was stolen!

After saying good-bye to the sheriff, she headed for Clay's. There was no point in getting upset or flying into a rage. Either the car would be returned, or it wouldn't. Either way, she couldn't get distracted with that today. She had to stay focused. Besides, hadn't she just complained to God about the car? Maybe His way of helping, was to show her how a broken car is better than no car.

The back door to the station was locked, and Jessa paused. She didn't relish running into Sergeant Kramer in the front office. Besides, the sisters might not even be up yet. And Clay . . . did she really want to see him? Could she risk working with him? Even if he never . . . *Stop it, Jessa! This isn't about you or Clay, you're solving a mystery, so get to it!*

The eastern sky was tinged with light, and the stars were fading as Jessa made her way around the front of the station. The station seemed pretty empty.

"Can I help you?" the older man at the reception desk asked.

Jessa noted his name tag. "Thank you, Alfred, but I'm just heading downstairs. The back door was locked and I'm supposed to be going to Clay's."

Alfred grinned. "You can go ahead and go down. I haven't heard anything from down there yet, but Clay's normally an early riser, so I'm sure he's up. If he's not, just dump some snow on him."

Jessa walked down the hall, towards the back door. She stopped in Clay's office. Someone had obviously been using his suspect board. Photos had been added, and she found herself staring at the pictures in the Martin's kitchen. One of the pictures particularly drew her attention. It had obviously been taken when she had been outside because Brad and Zoe were in the kitchen. It was a wide shot, capturing the whole kitchen. Zoe was holding out her cellphone, recording a statement from one of the officers, but Brad stood in the corner with his hands in his pockets, staring at an empty place on the counter.

Something about Brad in the picture seemed to stand out like a neon sign. She backed out of the room and rushed towards the basement. She had to double check the pictures she had.

Chapter Seventeen

The coffee pot was running, but no one was in sight.

Clay's laptop still sat on the desk, and Jessa rushed to it. She pulled up the photo she'd taken before she'd called the police and compared it with the one that she'd taken after the police had been there.

"Clay!" Jessa crossed her arms to keep her hands from trembling. If she was right, it could solve the case. But if she was wrong . . . "Clay!"

Something crashed in the next room. Clay burst through the door from his bedroom. Dark rings under his eyes hinted at a sleepless night. He still wore the same shirt and jeans, and his hair looked like he'd stuck his finger in an electrical outlet. A hint of stubble covered his face and his red eyes had a wild look. "What's wrong?"

"What's wrong?" An older voice echoed, as Bertha entered the room.

Jessa glanced from the computer screen to Clay's disoriented face. "Maybe you should wake up first."

Clay rubbed his eyes and gave a weak smile. "I'm awake."

Bertha put her hands on her hips. "Really? Young man, you look like you're sleep walking. Drop and give me twenty."

Clay gave his aunt a look of disbelief.

"Don't argue." She sounded like a drill sergeant. "Down."

Clay dropped in place and did twenty pushups. Jessa tried not to laugh. It was no wonder Bertha had been able to raise him. She had a lot of pluck.

Clay jumped back to his feet looking fully awake. His face was tinged red, and moisture built on his brow. He breathed hard for a second, then looked up. "Okay, now I'm awake. What did you find?"

Jessa turned the computer screen so Bertha and Clay could see it. "This is the shot I took when I found Timmy's body." She zoomed in. "You'll notice an object on the counter here."

Clay frowned. "What is that?"

"It's a blue travel mug from Grand Canyon State Park."

"What's the significance?" Clay asked.

"The significance is that it's not in the pictures the police have, and I don't think forensics has it at the lab. That means someone moved it." Jessa pulled up another picture. "This is after the police approached the scene. The cup is gone."

Clay's eyebrows lowered. "Okay, so if the police don't have it, that means either you took it, or someone in the department is crooked, or . . . someone was in the house when you were there, and they left after you did."

Jessa shook her head. "We've missed the most obvious. How did Brad know to get there so fast? He was in the house before the police even had time to process the scene. And in one of the pictures they have on your suspect board upstairs, it catches Brad, in the background. He's standing right by this counter and staring at the empty spot."

"Brad went on a trip to the Grand Canyon in August." Clay reached for his phone. "I'm going to see if we can get a warrant for his arrest, and we need to talk to the officers who were processing the scene." Clay disappeared into his room.

"Did I miss something?" Donna stepped into the room. "I heard excitement."

Bertha started explaining to Donna, and Jessa helped herself to the coffee. As the sisters discussed what she'd found, she returned to the pictures. Something else wasn't right. "I've

269

only been involved in a few deaths by trauma force to the head, but . . . doesn't it seem like there should be more blood? Unless . . ." Jessa frowned.

"Unless what?" Donna asked.

Jessa frowned at the computer screen. "What if he was killed somewhere else?"

"And someone dumped him in our kitchen to frame us?" Bertha nodded. "That could be!"

Donna held up her hands. "Just a minute. If Timmy was killed somewhere else, and then drug into our kitchen, it would have left a blood trail."

"The floor had been mopped." Jessa closed her eyes as she tried to re-picture the scene. "But that doesn't explain how they got him inside, if blood had dripped on the ground outside, it would have frozen, and they wouldn't have had time to scrape it up. Besides, I would have noticed that while shoveling the sidewalk."

Clay came out of his room with fresh clothes, combed hair, and a shave. His phone was still to his ear. "Yes, sir. I understand. Hold on a minute." He tipped his phone away from his mouth. "Ladies, I've got some things I need to take care of. I'll give you updates when I have them."

Grabbing his coat, he started talking in his phone again as he left.

Bertha and Donna went back to work baking, and Jessa went back to staring at the pictures. Surely, she had all the pieces of the puzzle now. But putting them together was not going to be easy. It made a lot of sense that Brad and Nels were in on it together. Brad could have left his travel mug, and remembered too late. He could have come back to get it just as the police arrived. Maybe he hadn't even meant to be there with the press, it just happened. But if that were the case, why take Zoe with him? And if he was just leaving the body, why would he have taken his travel mug in at all?

After another few minuotes of accomplishing nothing, Jessa grabbed her coat. "Ladies, I'll be back, but I've got a few things I need to do too."

"Go ahead!" Bertha said. "As long as we're baking, we're happy."

Jessa headed outside and started across town on foot. When she reached the Martin's sidewalk, she approached their house with caution. She knew the police had already searched the house and surrounding area, but they'd assumed Timmy had been killed in the kitchen. It was possible something had been overlooked.

After walking up and down the sidewalk and in and out of the house looking for any drops of blood for the seventh time, she stopped in the kitchen to think. She closed her eyes and tried to see the scene over again, but nothing made sense.

Her phone vibrated, jerking her out of her deep thought. "Hello?"

"Jessa, Clay doesn't have any nice tea towels," Bertha crooned. "I always cover my cookies with a tea towel while they cool. Could you bring us some? They're in the drawer by the sink."

"Sure, but it'll be a little while before I get back."

After saying good-bye, Jessa headed for the drawer. Jessa pulled it open and stared. The drawer was empty except for a few rags at the back that looked like they'd been stuffed there for some time.

She opened every drawer around the sink. Each one had typical kitchen items, but none had tea towels.

She returned to the empty drawer and leaned towards it. A slight smudge on the side of the drawer drew her attention. The smudge was darkish in color, and Jessa took a deep breath. "Don't jump to conclusions," she reminded herself.

She pulled out her phone, and dialed Clay's number.

"What's up?" Clay answered.

"I'm at your aunts' house and I've found something. I think it's blood, and I think it proves that Timmy was killed somewhere else."

"I'll be right there." He hung up, and Jessa took a deep breath. If Timmy had been killed somewhere else, the missing towels could have been used to wipe up any blood drops. But that would only work in the house. That meant that Timmy had to have been killed inside the house. Jessa closed her eyes. Was that important?

She glanced around the room again. Was she missing something? A slight scraping reached her ears, and she froze. Had that come from the basement?

Another slight scrape, and then steady thuds. There was no mistaking the thud of footsteps. Each sluggish beat of her heart sent ice threw her chest. Someone was coming.

Her gaze flew to the basement door. Her chest ached with the sudden tensing.

She glanced towards the entryway, but knew that she couldn't get out fast enough.

Her gaze snagged on the block of kitchen knives, and she bolted into action. The wooden handle of the knife felt cold in her grip as she pressed herself against the wall behind the basement door.

The knob turned. Jessa raised the knife and held her breath. Her hand shook as she thought through all the possible situations that could occur.

The door opened, and heavy boots stepped into the kitchen.

Jessa waited for the door to move so that she could see the intruder. The door didn't move immediately, so she took a deep breath, and smashed into it.

A grunt came from the other side of the door, and a man stumbled into the kitchen.

"I'm armed and . . ." her voice trailed off. "Clay?"

Clay turned to face her. Gingerly rubbing his arm, he raised an eyebrow. "Are you going to stab me?"

Jessa glanced at the blade in her trembling hand, and slowly lowered the blade. "What were you doing down there?" Jessa held a hand to her heart.

"I was searching. I know that forensics went over the house, but I grew up here so I thought I'd see if I couldn't find something odd."

Jessa let the knife slide from her fingers and leaned back against the wall, breathing deeply.

"Are you alright?" Clay asked.

Jessa forced a nod. "Yeah. You just scared me."

"I'm sorry," he said simply. He reached down and grasped the knife. "I don't think you'll need this." He returned it to the block, and then turned to examined the drawer.

"Call Vicklund," he said.

Jessa's finger still shook as she pulled out her phone.

"Are you sure you're okay?" Clay asked.

Jessa nodded again. This time, it came more naturally.

It wasn't long before the front door banged open. "Clay?" Sheriff Vicklund called.

"In here," Clay called back.

The sheriff stepped into the kitchen, and looked straight at Jessa. "Tell us exactly what happened." Sheriff Vicklund sure didn't waste time getting down to business.

Jessa explained her theory and showed them the empty drawer with the potential blood stain. As she spoke, her heartrate finally returned to normal, and she focused on the task at hand. Making the truth known.

"What exactly is the point?" Sheriff Vicklund asked.

"The point is that Timmy may have been killed somewhere else. If he was killed somewhere else, or even in another room, we could find more evidence at the actual crime scene. Something that could point to the killer. Something that could prove Brad is guilty."

"We've got a warrant out for his arrest." The sheriff glanced around the house. "Martin, you're back in. Get a team down here and search this place again. Do whatever forensic work you need and get stuff down to the lab."

"What about Kramer?" Clay asked.

"Kramer is working on the Nels angle. But you're no longer needed undercover so get your team and get to work.

275

Jessa, I'm going to assign you a few people and I want you to go to Brad's place and search it."

"Sir?" Jessa frowned.

"I had a little chat with Laci this morning. You've got too many credentials to waste."

Jessa took a deep breath. God hadn't just opened the door, He'd practically put a neon sign in front of it. "Yes, sir." Jessa smiled slightly. Laci would just have to work around it, and she'd have to trust God to keep her parents safe. "One more thing, I hate to bring this up in the middle of a homicide investigation, but my car has been stolen."

Sheriff Vicklund grunted. "You've already mentioned that. We'll deal with it later. It's a small town, and a red eye-sore like that thing couldn't have gone unnoticed. I'm sure someone will turn it in soon. You can fill out a report at the station. Now, back to work. The town wants to know they're safe, and I want to be able to tell them tonight at the school that it's all taken care of."

The corners of Clay's mouth turned up slightly. Jessa arched an eyebrow. "You like routine combing of evidence and re-questioning witnesses, don't you?"

Clay shrugged, but his face betrayed him.

Jessa turned and headed for the door. She'd always been more of an outside-the-box sort of detective, but she respected those who could enjoy the mundane routine. That's how her Mom had been. Always doing the routine work, and typically ending up way ahead of everyone who was trying to jump around.

"Holm and Norberg are over there." Sheriff Vicklund said. He scratched a note on a paper. "This is Brad's address. They'll be your team when you get there." His radio beeped and he turned up the volume. "10-9" he asked the person on the radio to repeat.

"Brad is 10-95" the radio said.

"10-4." Sheriff Vicklund turned back to Clay. "You heard that Martin? Brad's in custody so get on the details. We need enough to convince the D.A. that we've got an open and shut case. Jessa, I'll drop you off at Brad's house."

Donna slid the last pan of cookies onto a cooling rack and let out a sigh. "We'll have to clean this place up." Flour, sugar, and other ingredients sprinkled the counter and dotted the floor.

"If you weren't so messy, it wouldn't be a problem." Bertha wiped her hands on her nearly spotless apron.

Donna ignored her sister's remark and double counted the containers. "That gives us enough cookies for everyone in town to sample one, and we've still got enough to make up several platters for the sale."

Bertha pulled another pan of fudge from the fridge and reached for a knife. "I think we've got enough fudge to give out samples, but we'd better make a few more pans for selling."

"A few more pans?" Donna looked at the mountain of remaining ingredients. "We'd better make a lot more pans of fudge."

Bertha nodded. "Okay, well, we've got several hours before the benefit. You make more cookies; I'll make more fudge."

Donna nodded. "I'm on it." She reached for a mixing bowl.

"I need to get off my feet for a bit," Bertha said.

Donna watched Bertha make her way to the couch and sink down onto it. "Is all this too much for you?"

Bertha harrumphed. "Nonsense. I'm not ninety you know. At least, not yet."

"Sometimes you act like it," Donna said.

Bertha ignored her and stared at the computer screen. Donna watched her for a moment. "Are you sure you're okay? If you need a nap or something . . ."

"Donna!" Bertha leaned forward. "Where's the owl?"

"Owl?" Donna moved around the kitchen island. "Do you need to see a doctor?"

"Oh nonsense. I'm not crazy." Bertha pointed at the computer screen. "How do you make a picture come back?"

Donna watched the computer screen, as pictures slid by. "How should I know?" She reached for the touch pad that Clay was always rubbing his finger over, and the screen changed. "I think that was what you call a screensaver," Donna said. "Which picture did you want to see?"

"The one of our entryway, going into the kitchen."

Donna clicked around several different files before she found the minimized file of pictures from their house. "This one?"

Bertha nodded. "Where's the owl?"

Donna studied the picture. For years, an owl, chiseled out of stone, had rested on that table, but in the picture, it was gone.

An e-mail notification appeared in the right corner of the screen, and Donna clicked on it. "Bertha!" Donna scanned the e-mail. "Tina from forensics e-mailed Clay about our rolling pin."

"And?"

"And even though it had blood on it, they don't believe it was the murder weapon. It doesn't show any signs of a hard hit. Maybe the owl was!"

"Don't just sit there, call Clay!"

Donna reached for her cellphone.

Jessa adjusted her gloves and left the bedroom. While there were plenty of disturbing items in the room, there hadn't been one thing that indicated any connection between Brad or any of the victims.

Stopping at a hall closet, Jessa listened. Holm and Newberg didn't know the meaning of quiet. She shook her head. The two of them were . . . well, some kind of cross between Andy and Barney, or Abbot and Costello.

Jessa opened the closet and wasn't surprised to find it packed. She sighed. In order to do a thorough job, she couldn't overlook anything. She snapped a picture of the closet before touching anything, and then she began pulling things out one by one.

All manner of strange objects filled the closet, and she tried hard not to waste time looking at things that didn't matter.

A grocery bag on the floor drew her attention and she pulled it out. A rock figurine of an owl. Hadn't she seen this before? She closed her eyes for a moment as she tried to remember where she'd seen it. "The Martins!" She stared at the owl. It was chipped, and a dark flakey substance on it indicated blood. "The murder weapon." Her mind raced. Could Brad have hidden the murder weapon in his own house? Or was it a plant?

"Anderson!" Holm yelled.

Jessa grabbed the bag and headed downstairs.

"You need to see this," Holm said. He led her towards the garage. The top garbage bag in a can had been opened, and blood-stained tea towels were on the top. "Is that proof, or is that proof?" Holm grinned.

"Bag them for the lab," Jessa said. "And do this while you're at it." She set down the owl. "I think this was the murder weapon."

Despite Holm and Newberg's unique personalities, she had no doubt that they could do their jobs with efficiency.

"Where are you going?" Newberg asked.

"I'm going to the station." Jessa headed outside, and after getting off the icy driveway onto the cleared sidewalk, she started running.

"Clay, Nels got his memory back," Shelby said as Clay entered his office. "He woke up this morning with full recollection. Apparently, it's semi-normal for head wounds like that to cause temporary memory loss."

"Did he say who did it?" Clay asked.

"No, Kramer's been questioning him all morning, but no leads. He finally pulled the lawyer card and isn't going to say anything more."

Clay frowned. If he was innocent, then telling the police who did it shouldn't have been a problem. "Where's Kramer now?"

"He's in the interrogation room talking to Brad."

Raking his fingers through his hair, Clay sighed.

"Something wrong?" Shelby asked.

Clay shrugged. "I don't know. I just feel like something isn't right." He held up a hand. "Before you give me the whole spiel about feelings not always being accurate, I've got to say that I know it's not logical, but my feelings have helped us on cases before."

Shelby leaned back. "I'm not saying anything. Except that if someone as organized and precise as you, has feelings keeping him from being happy with an investigation, they'd better do something about it."

"What?"

"I don't know. Something? Just prove your feelings right or wrong, and then you'll be happy."

"That man!" Kramer's voice echoed through the offices. He rounded the corner and almost ran Clay over. "What are you doing here?"

Clay opened his mouth, but the sheriff beat him to it.

"Kramer," Sheriff Vicklund stuck his head into the office. "Martin is part of my department. He's been undercover, but he's still on the case, and before you get mad at him, you can thank him for being the one to connect Nels and Brad. He's gotten more done in his short time undercover than you have as the lead investigator, so don't you dare say anything against him."

Kramer sent a scathing look at Clay, but kept his mouth shut.

"Kramer." Sheriff Vicklund paused. "I've put up with you to avoid problems, but I don't think we'll be needing your services anymore."

"But I . . ." Kramer stopped. "This whole town is like a backwoods bush town. The higher ups are going to hear about this."

"Let them." The sheriff stepped the rest of the way into the room. "I was elected by the people of this town, and as long as they're happy with me, I don't really care what you think."

Kramer pushed past the sheriff and left the office.

Chapter Eighteen

"Whew." Shelby tapped a pen against the desk. "That man has got some issues!"

Sheriff Vicklund nodded. "I do apologize. I know having him here hasn't been easy on anyone, but he did us a huge favor."

Clay grinned. "I don't think he'd take kindly to being told that he's a red herring."

The sheriff winked. "No, I don't suppose he would, but it worked. Brad and Nels were so busy avoiding him that they ignored you and your efforts."

"What is Brad saying?" Clay asked.

Sheriff Vicklund shook his head. "He's denying everything to do with the murders."

"Figures," Shelby said. "Most criminals do deny everything."

"We need to get him to talk," Clay said. "How about I go in there and put the heat on?"

The sheriff shook his head. "I want you to get down to the hospital. Kramer said Nels won't talk, but maybe, if you put on the charm you might be able to pull a confession out of him."

Clay nodded. "I'll try. And Brad?"

"I got a call from Newberg, Jessa should be here soon, and I think she's got just the information, and charisma to get Brad talking." The sheriff took a deep breath and let it out slowly. "I'm going to be glad when this is over."

Clay nodded. It would take weeks for all the final results from the forensic lab, and the DNA samples gathered from the crime scene to get back. Results that were necessary if they couldn't get a confession. Results that were necessary to get a conviction.

Jessa arrived at the station just as Clay was leaving. She waved at him, and then headed inside.

"Anderson, we need to talk." Sheriff Vicklund walked down the hall, and Jessa followed.

"Newberg told me about your discoveries. I need you to confront Brad."

Jessa frowned. "Me? Why me? I'm not a part of this town!"

"You are now. You've been here for over a week, and you're family. Besides, Brad doesn't know you well. If you go in there with your credentials, and your information with the bloody rags and the owl, you may be able to get a confession that the rest of us couldn't get. He hasn't known you all his life, and he's going to be reserved around you."

Jessa nodded. "I can try, but I'm not even sure he has anything to confess. It was too obvious. The evidence could have been planted."

"Well, you can find out. Follow me." The sheriff started down another hall and ended in front of a one-way glass. Brad sat at a table in the room. His balding head was in his hands, and his fedora sat beside him on the table. He held his head in his hands, and his shoulder's drooped.

"Do me a favor," Jessa said. "Go in there and ask him if he wants a drink of water."

"Why?"

"I need to see his attitude before I know how to approach him."

"You got it." The sheriff swiped a card and opened the door. "Brad, can I get you anything?"

Brad looked up. Wrinkles surrounded his eyes and his shoulders sagged. "No, thank you."

"You sure?" the sheriff asked.

Brad nodded and leaned his head down onto his folded hands.

The sheriff came out and crossed his arms. "Well?"

"He's broken. He feels alone and rejected. He needs a friend."

"What are you, a psychiatrist?"

Jessa smiled. "No, but Dad often had me do suspect interrogations, and you learn things with time. When someone is arrogant, you need to be firm, but when they're a wilting mess, you can either scare them into saying things that might not be true, or you can become their friend, and get an honest confession."

"Are you finished with your analysis?"

Jessa nodded. "Yep, and I don't want to interrogate him in there. He's scared. Do I have the liberty to set up Clay's living room for the interrogation? I feel like he would be more talkative in a more relaxed setting."

The sheriff nodded. "It's a little out of our ordinary routine but go ahead. Clay's gone, but he won't mind. You'll have to get the sisters out of there. They shouldn't go home till the crime scene is opened, but if you want to send them to your house, that's fine. And of course, we'll have someone down there with you to make sure you're safe."

Jessa nodded. "I'll be up when the room is ready, and you can have someone escort him down."

Jessa hurried downstairs and moved the suspect board.

"What are you doing?" Bertha asked.

"I'm inviting the murderer here for a little chat. You ladies can go stay at my place."

"But we're not done baking!" Donna protested. "We'll stay in our rooms until you're done."

"Are you sure?" Jessa closed the laptop.

"Of course, we're sure," Bertha said.

Jessa glanced around, it was homey and lived in, but would probably put him at ease. "Am I allowed to take a few of your cookies?"

"Of course!" Donna grabbed a plate and stacked a few cookies on it. "There, that should do it." She put the plate on the coffee table.

"Alright, ladies," Jessa put her hands on her hips.

"We know, make ourselves scarce." Donna winked. "Don't take all afternoon, we've still got some work to do before tonight."

The ladies left, and Jessa headed upstairs. After notifying the sheriff, she went back downstairs, and tipped the easy chair towards the couch. She sat down on the couch and curled her legs up under her in a relaxed position.

Moments later, Brad entered, followed by Isaiah. Jessa smiled up at them. "Hey. Have a seat Brad." She motioned towards the chair with her head. "Isaiah, you can wait outside."

Isaiah paused, and then nodded. He left the door open, and Jessa was sure that he was listening, and taking his orders very seriously to keep Brad under close watch.

Brad's eyes darted around the room. "Why am I here?" His voice was tense, and from the way he wrung his fedora, it seemed likely that it would fall apart.

Jessa shrugged. From the way he was looking around, he was nervous, that could be good; it could be bad. The setting was obviously not what he was expecting.

Jessa unwound her legs and headed for the coffee pot. "Do you take cream or sugar?"

Brad stared at her like she had two heads. "Huh?"

Jessa poured two mugs of coffee. "In your coffee, do you like cream or sugar?"

"No." he shook his head in a jerky motion. "I drink it black."

Jessa handed him one of the mugs. His hands were trembling and his coffee sloshed.

"You'd better drink some before you spill it." Jessa reached for a cookie. "And help yourself to the cookies." She fought to keep her voice to a conversational tone.

Brad sipped his coffee, and eyed Jessa as she nibbled at one of the Christmas sugar cookies. "I love the frosting on these," she said with a little smile.

Brad's brow furrowed. "Okay, so what's the deal here? Is this some good-cop routine or what?"

Jessa took a deep breath. "I'm not exactly a cop. I want to be perfectly honest with you. Brad, you've been accused of murder. There's a lot of evidence against you. If you're guilty, it will be proven, but if you're innocent, I want to help you." Jessa sipped her coffee. "I'll be frank with you, I'm not just the new wannabe music teacher. I've worked with a very effective detective agency, and I want to help."

Brad's eyebrows arched. "Are you serious?"

Jessa nibbled at the cookie. "I'm serious. But I can't help unless you'll talk to me."

Brad sighed. "Okay."

Jessa reached for her phone. "Is it alright with you if we record this conversation."

Brad hesitated. "Why?"

"Because sometimes we have to go back and follow our tracks. We don't want to have to hound you by asking you the same questions over and over."

Brad nodded. "Okay."

Jessa paused. If she started with an easy question, it would put him at ease, but at the same time, she didn't have time to waste. "Do you want to discuss the weather, or get right down to business?"

"You're so blunt," Brad leaned back. "I like it. Let's cut to the chase. You want to know if I'm a killer. I'm not."

"Would you mind explaining to me what you were talking to Nels about in the alley the day of Royce's death?"

Brad tensed. "I'd rather not say."

"Brad," Jessa gave her best sympathetic look. "You're being accused of murder. The murder weapon, and some bloody rags were found in your house, and pictures prove that your travel mug was at the scene of Timmy's death. Nothing you say at this point is going to get you in more trouble, but it could help clear things up."

Brad set his mug on the table. "I don't know what you're talking about! I didn't do it. If the murder weapon was found at my house, then it was planted, and as to my travel mug, I've got so many of them, and they're all over the radio station, anyone could have taken one. I'm innocent."

"So, what were you talking to Nels about?" Jessa asked. "We know you're hiding something with him. Something to do with loans, and gambling debts."

Brad sagged back against the chair, and toyed with the edge of his fedora. "Okay, so Nels and I were involved in Royce's gambling scheme. It was under the rug, and illegal. I'll admit to that. But all I did that morning, was give him money from Ken. Ken didn't know that I was borrowing money from him to help Larry and Nels. That's why Nels told everyone he didn't leave his office that morning. He didn't want anyone to know why we were meeting."

Jessa pulled up the picture of the Martin's kitchen on her phone and zoomed in on the mug. "Do you recognize that mug?"

Brad paled. "It's mine. But I haven't used it in weeks, honest!"

"Where was the last place you remember having it?"

Brad put his head in his hands and groaned. "I don't know . . . maybe at the radio station?"

Jessa leaned forward slightly. "It's alright. You can't tell us what you don't know." Jessa silently prayed for wisdom, as she began re-questioning him about the previous days, his connection with Nels, and the mysterious caller who'd notified him about Nels."

Clay paced his office with his phone to his ear. "Are you sure you can't speed it up?"

"It doesn't work that way," Tina said. "We're going as fast as we can, but do you have any idea just how much evidence we have to process? And it's not just all the evidence you've gotten to us, it's the multiple tests that have to be done on each item. Those rags, first we have to verify that it's blood, then we have to do a DNA test to find out who's blood it is, then, we have to sort through it all and see if there's any DNA left from the killer and get that tested. And that's all from one item. We can't just speed up the process."

"I know." Clay stopped pacing and leaned against the desk. "I appreciate how hard you're working."

After saying good-bye, Clay went back to staring at the board. It should all be sealed tight. The murder weapons would be verified, Nels and Brad would get convicted, everything would turn out. As much as he wanted to believe it, Clay couldn't stop the uneasiness. *I'm missing something,* he thought.

"Learn anything from Nels?" Shelby asked.

Clay looked up as she walked in and plopped into a chair. "No. He pulled the lawyer card. He's not talking."

"Does he have a lawyer?"

Clay shrugged. "He said he does, but he hasn't contacted him yet."

"And we don't know who hit him on the head?"

With a shake of the head, Clay glanced back at the board. "Either he doesn't know who did it, or he's protecting someone." Smashing his right fist into the palm of his left hand, he sighed. "I feel like we're missing the obvious, but what could be more obvious than Nels and Brad?"

"What about Larry? It seems like you've kind of stopped suspecting him."

Clay shook his head. "I just don't think he did it. The way he opened up about the gambling and things doesn't line up if he's the killer."

"Don't you remember what Jessa said? Never underestimate anyone." Shelby drummed the tips of her fingers together. "And what about Liam? Have you written him off? I mean if we're not supposed to underestimate anyone, we can't forget about Liam. With that kind of thinking, I could have done it."

Clay cocked his head to the side and stared at Shelby.

"What?" her face went serious. "Do you think I did it? Because I didn't! I've got a wedding to plan, I don't have time for murder!"

Clay shook his head. "No, but you could be right. Maybe we're missing the most obvious. Maybe Nels's partner is someone that none of us have thought of?"

Shelby nodded. "It warrants thinking about. Do you think it could be Liam? I mean he was seen at the school that morning. Do you know why?"

Clay shook his head. "I've stopped by his house a few times between calls, but he's never there. I have reason to believe that his mom is doing illegal drugs, but he won't say anything about it. He's worried I'll call social services and he'll be taken away from Clara."

"If she's doing drugs, she'll go to jail, and Liam and Clara will need a home. Shouldn't you call social services and have them look into it?"

Clay ran a hand through his hair. "I don't have any real evidence. I mean, part of me thinks I should, but on the other hand, I feel like Liam and Clara might be opening up to me. Clara admitted that they liked me. I need to talk to Liam again before I do anything. If he knows I'm going to take care of them, he might be willing to tell me what's going on. If I talk to him and he doesn't want to tell me anything, then we'll take it up with social services, and get a search warrant for illegal drugs."

"You're going to take care of them?" Shelby shook her head. "You've never been a foster parent!"

Clay nodded. "I know, but those kids . . . I care about them."

"Do you think it's safe to wait?" Shelby asked. "I mean, if there's illegal drugs in the home . . . will they be alright?"

Clay sighed. He'd battled his decision to wait, but it just felt right. "Liam will take care of Clara, and I'm going to talk to him as soon as I can. I think it will be better for both Liam and Clara if they bring things out into the open instead of us marching into their lives and upsetting everything. Especially since we don't have any real proof that anything is wrong."

"Martin!" Mitch stuck his head in the room. "We need you at the interrogation room. Sally Landean just confessed."

Jessa followed Brad upstairs to his cell. "Thank you for talking with me," she said. "We will try to help you."

Jessa headed for Clay's office, but Shelby stopped her. "You should see this."

Jessa followed Shelby into the outer area of the interrogation room where she could see through the one-way glass. Sally sat at the table with her head in her hands. Her shoulders shook with sobs. Clay sat across from her.

Clay's voice was quiet so Shelby turned up the volume on the sound system.

"Would you like to tell me why you're admitting to the deaths of Austin and Timmy?" Clay's voice carried clearly through the system.

"Because I did it." Sally's voice was weak, and she reached for another tissue. "I hated Austin. He deserved to die. I just didn't expect Timmy to see me leaving the school that day. He threatened to go to the police, so I had to kill him too."

"Why was Timmy's body found at the Martin's house?"

Sally's eyes flickered with something. "Well . . ." She faltered. "Timmy trusted them. He was going to go to them and tell them to call the police. I followed him there. No one was home, so he just went in. I followed. We had words, and I hit him with the rolling pin."

Jessa frowned. "She didn't do it." Jessa headed back to the basement. Even if she didn't do it, Clay would have to thoroughly question her and they'd probably have to book her.

"What's going on up there?" Donna asked.

Jessa headed for the sink. The pile of dishes wasn't going to go away on its own. "Sally just confessed to murder." Jessa squirted soap into the empty sink and began running water into it.

Bertha removed the pot she was stirring from the stove and set it on a cooling rack. "I knew she could be a suspect, but . . . I never thought she'd actually do something like this."

Donna slid a pan of fudge into the fridge. "Our younger sister, Gloria, went to school with her and . . . besides her trouble in high-school, she was always a good girl."

Jessa paused. "Trouble in high-school? What kind of trouble?"

"I don't really know," Donna said. "She was suspended from school for the eleventh grade, but no one would say why. She moved in with a friend in Red Brooks and didn't go back till her senior year."

"And you don't know why?" Jessa rinsed a pot and set it on the drying rack.

"Well, there was speculation, but no facts." Donna grabbed the plastic wrap and began wrapping up plates of fudge that were done. "Another guy was suspended at the same time, but his parents moved the same week and no one's heard of him since. At first, people thought that she was expecting, but if that was the case, she must have had an abortion because when she came back, she didn't have a baby. Then there was the rumor that she'd been involved with a drug ring, but no one really believed that because that year, there was less drug problems than any other year. Some said she was cheating on tests, but she was pretty smart and I don't think she would have had to cheat to get straight A's."

Jessa turned back to the pan in the sink and vigorously scrubbed. "If Sally did it, she's more senile then we thought. From what I heard of her interview, she doesn't even have the facts straight. She thinks the rolling pin was what killed Timmy, and she said they were having words when she hit him. If that was true, Timmy would have been hit on the front of the head, not the back. And other things about her story . . . it just doesn't line up. Why would she confess to a crime she didn't commit?"

"According to Sherlock Holmes, people lie to gain, to cover, or to protect," Donna said. "I don't think Sally would gain anything by the deaths, and I doubt she has anything to cover. She's got to be protecting someone."

Bertha straightened. "Maybe she found out that Ken did it, and she turned herself in to protect him! Unless, of course, her Parkinson's disease is worse than we thought. Maybe she had nothing to do with it, but because of her mental state, she thinks she did?"

When the dishes were done, Jessa helped the aunts with the rest of the fudge, and when they had enough fudge and cookies for the whole town, she went back to the suspect board. "It could have been Ken."

Footsteps on the metal stairs alerted Jessa that someone was coming. She stepped towards the open doorway and glanced out. "Clay! How did the interrogation finish up?"

"It finished up as an interview, not an interrogation." Clay walked around the kitchen island and snitched a cookie. "There were so many discrepancies in her story. But we can't rule her out. She insists that she did it."

"What are you going to do with her?" Bertha asked.

"We booked her, and we're having a psychological evaluation test tomorrow. It's possible that she did it despite the discrepancies. People's stories often change over time, and she is older so it's possible she's getting things mixed up. Plus, she's been known to have . . . odd behavior. Just this morning, Larry saw her going through someone's car. At first he thought it was his because it was a black Honda, so naturally he got upset at her, but once he saw it wasn't his car, he called Ken to take her home. He said she was acting pretty strange."

"What about Nels and Brad?" Donna asked.

Clay sighed. "I can't really let them go, but at the same time, if Sally really did do it, I can't hold them."

"What if we let them all loose tonight?" Jessa asked.

Chapter Nineteen

Clay raised an eyebrow. After a pause, he frowned. "I'm assuming you have a reason for suggesting that?"

"Think about it! The whole town will be there. No matter who is the guilty party, if they think it's their last night of freedom, they may try to contact their partner."

Clay stoked his chin. "Maybe . . ."

"And, all the off-duty cops are going to be there anyway, they can all be assigned to a suspect to shadow."

"I think Jessa is right," Bertha said. "If you bring all the suspects together like that, people are bound to talk, and we could learn something valuable."

Clay took a deep breath and let it out slowly. "The idea is intriguing, but I'll have to talk it over with Sheriff Vicklund."

"Mail delivery service!" a voice called from the top of the stairs.

Clay stepped to the open doorway. "Shelby? Since when have you been the mailman?"

"Since packages were delivered to the office addressed to Donna Martin. Catch."

Clay caught the package. "Thanks!" He stepped back into the living room area. "Auntie, the package is for you."

Donna and Bertha exchanged a look and beamed smiles.

"Oh goodie!" Donna grabbed the package. "Clay, you'd better go talk to the sheriff and anyone else who needs to be in on tonight's shebang."

Clay glanced at his watch and let out a low whistle. "You're right. We've only got a little over an hour before everyone starts showing up." He grabbed another cookie and left.

Donna tore into the package and pulled out a sweater. "I'm sorry it isn't wrapped, but with Christmas only two days away, we wanted to get you a gift."

"Oh, you didn't need to do that!" Jessa said. "I didn't get either of you anything."

"That's alright," Bertha said. "We'd better get ready for tonight. Why don't you wear this sweater tonight?"

Jessa took the cherry red sweater and held it up. Half of a Christmas tree covered the front.

"I wonder why they didn't put the whole tree on it?" Bertha asked.

Jessa shrugged. "Who knows why people do what they do? Anyway, I'd be happy to wear it tonight." She swallowed hard. At least she'd be happy to wear it if no one saw her in it. Then again, the sisters had been so welcoming to her. It would be wrong not to accept their gift.

"We'd better get ready and start hauling things to the school." Donna glanced at the clock. "We should be there and set up within the hour. Jessa, why don't you run on home and check in on Callie. I'm sure you'd like the opportunity to freshen up before tonight."

Jessa sighed. "I would, but someone stole my car, and until this homicide investigation is over, I don't think I'll be seeing it."

"Get our car," Bertha said. "Then you can pick us up and we can haul everything over in it. The keys are in it."

Jessa nodded. "Okay, I'll have to hurry." She shoved the sweater into her backpack-like purse and slung it over her shoulder.

She ran home, said hello to Callie, and then jumped in the shower. Liam and Clara were gone, but Jessa couldn't stop thinking about them. It was nice having kids in the house. Within a half-hour, her blow-dried hair was curled, and half pulled back, and she was ready to go. She jogged next door and hopped in the Martin's Cadillac.

Back at the station, with ten minutes to load up and get to the school, she backed up to the back door, and started making trips. Her legs burned from running up and down the stairs so many times, but once the trunk and a good deal of the backseat were filled, the aunts came out, and they headed for the school.

Other booths were already setting up, and Jessa grabbed a few high-schoolers to help haul boxes in. It didn't take long to get the samples set out and the other cookies and fudge marked for sale.

Jessa let out a sigh of relief. "We made it!"

"Of course, we did!" Donna said.

"We must be just in time," Bertha said. "Santa Claus is already here."

"Ho, ho, ho!" a voice drifted across the room, and Jessa smiled at the sight of a man in a Santa Claus suit trying to do one of the carnival games.

It wasn't long before people started flooding in. Samples seemed to fly off the plates, and sales were being made.

"Jessa, Donna and I want to walk around," Bertha said. "We may buy some things, and we want to do so before everything is sold. If we send Clay over to help, can the two of you handle this booth?"

Jessa flashed a grin at yet another customer. "Go ahead, ladies. I've got this covered."

The two elderly women slowly walked off, and Jessa took a deep breath. She was glad there was so much excitement in the air, and the school band was blaring Christmas carols. At least her flashy red sweater wasn't out of place.

"Jessa?" Zoe approached. "I promised your aunts that I would get this to them." She held out a piece of paper. "Can you give it to them when you see them?"

Jessa nodded. "I'd be happy to."

Zoe smiled slightly. "So, you're here with Clay?"

Jessa wrinkled her forehead. "No. I haven't even seen him yet. He might not be able to make it."

Zoe's grin widened, and she looked away.

Jessa frowned. If something was funny, she didn't see it. "Would you like a sample? The fudge is subline!"

Zoe stared at the fudge, and her smile vanished. "No, thank you. It's not in my diet." She turned and hurried away.

Jessa glanced down at the paper. "The school meeting agenda. We already have this." She looked up sharply, but no one was around. She let out her breath slowly. How long would it take for her to learn not to talk to herself out loud in public?

She glanced across the agenda. "It's all the same," she whispered. She flipped the page, and frowned. It seemed shorter. Like something was missing.

"I'll take a plate of cookies," a voice said.

Jessa set the paper down and reached for a plate of cookies. "Thank you for helping out the school!"

The woman took the plate of cookies and smiled as she put twice the suggested donation money in the box. "And thank you for helping out!"

The woman walked away and Jessa reached for her purse. She rummaged until she found the photocopied paper with the school's agenda. There was a slight lull in the crowd, so she compared the papers.

"The aunties said to come help you and . . ." Clay's voice stopped.

Jessa spun around. "You've got to look at this and . . ." she gasped. "You've got to be kidding me!"

Clay chuckled and shook his head. "I'm guessing my aunties gave you that sweater?"

Jessa nodded. "Of course, they gave you a matching sweater with the other half of my Christmas tree!" No wonder people had assumed they were together!

Clay stepped behind the table. "I guess we'll have to humor them for a little while. I'm supposed to make some remarks at the closing, so I brought along something else to wear later. I'll humor my aunts behind a table, but there's no way I'm getting up in front of everyone wearing a blindingly red Christmas sweater!"

Jessa caught a few people glancing their way with giggles, and she groaned. "The whole town thinks we're here together!"

Clay shrugged. "Let them think. Technically, we're here, and we're standing together, so . . . never mind. You don't date."

"This is *not* a date. Like I said before, I'm not going to go on a date with a guy unless I think he's the man I'm going to marry. And in that case, I want him to talk to my dad first, because if he makes it past Dad, I'll know he's worth considering."

Clay's eyes twinkled as he opened his mouth, but whatever he was going to say, he swallowed and turned to another customer.

"You were saying something when I arrived." He turned back from the customer. "Something I needed to look at?"

"Oh! Yes. This is the school meeting agenda that I copied from Nels's office." She held out the paper. "And this is the one that Zoe just gave me."

Clay scanned both papers. "And?"

"And on the one that Zoe gave me, something is missing. On Nels's copy, it says that Dennis Nordlum had an unknown proposal to discuss, but on Zoe's copy, it doesn't say anything about that."

Clay opened his mouth, but a group of ladies approached the table, and he closed his mouth.

"Do you really think anyone will buy that fudge?" one of the ladies asked. "I mean if the Martin sisters were the murderers, is it safe?"

"I'm going to buy some," one of the other ladies said. "If for no other reason than to spite that Sergeant Kramer. Besides, if the Martin sisters had done it, they'd be in jail by now."

"I'll buy some too. After all, it is a benefit for the school, but I'm not going to eat it. I may never eat a piece of fudge again!"

The group of ladies stopped at the table and began picking which plates of fudge they wanted.

Jessa slowly let her breath out. Being impatient with them wouldn't help. Besides, it was a benefit for the school, the more they sold, the better.

"Do you think the fudge is safe?" one of the ladies asked Jessa.

She smiled. "I know it is." To prove her point, she reached for a piece off of the sample table and took a bite.

Clay reached for one too. "It's great! I hope there are leftovers for me to take home."

One of the ladies that was holding one plate of fudge reached for two more. "I'll get three. After all, everyone in town knows about the famous Martin sister's cookie dough fudge! I'll not be left in the dark."

As soon as the ladies had moved on, Jessa turned back to Clay. "So, what do you think Dennis Nordlum wanted to talk to the school board about?"

Clay shook his head. "I have no idea. Dennis fills in as treasurer when Nels is gone."

"We need to talk to him and find out what he wanted to talk about. It could have been nothing, but it could help."

Clay nodded and glanced around. "Nels was released from the hospital, and Sheriff Vicklund is going to bring him, Brad, and Sally here. I have to be on call when they get here." Clay glanced at his watch. "I'd better go change now, so that I'm ready when they get here. I'll stop by Dennis's office on my way. If he's not there, that means he's out here somewhere. You'll recognize him because he has a very distinct laugh, and if you see him, talk to him. Find out what he was going to talk about."

Jessa watched as Clay left. Moments later, she heard a laugh. She glanced around, and a middle-aged man off to the right was cracking jokes.

"Did you hear the one about Rudolph's trainer?" The man started laughing and didn't finish his joke.

"Dennis!" Jessa called. The man looked around, and Jessa waved him over. Clay was right, that *laugh* was very distinct. Somewhere between a strangled rooster, a giggling girl, and a deep grunting snort.

"I don't believe we've had the pleasure of meeting." The man bowed and held out his hand. "Sir Dennis Nordlum at your service. Although some might tell you that I'm just a fill in treasurer, don't be fooled. I'm Santa's personal eyes and ears in this town. Have you been good?"

Jessa couldn't help but smile at the man. Crinkles around his eyes as he smiled, showed that he smiled frequently, and that he took life from a unique and humorous point of view. "I need to talk to you." Jessa straightened. She couldn't get sidetracked by his fun personality. "What were you planning on speaking to the school board about at the next meeting?"

Dennis's laughing eyes turned serious, and he glanced around. "It's not important now."

"It could be." Jessa said.

Dennis glanced over his shoulder again. "Well, I was going over the school's books, and it seemed to me that large

311

amounts of money were disappearing. I was going to ask to have a professional accountant come in and examine our accounts. Nels was against it, but I thought it was best. Then, with all the chaos, I decided to re-examine the accounts myself before bothering the school with more trouble, and I found the rest of the money there, it had just been moved to a different school account. So now, I don't need to bother anyone with it. Besides," his eyes sparkled again. "We can't waste Christmas worrying about things like that!" His eyes crinkled with laughter. "I'd better keep going or I'll miss my sleigh. Ho, ho, ho!"

Jessa watched Dennis leave, and frowned. What if the money had actually been gone? What if Nels had taken it, and then poisoned the school board to delay the meeting until he had time to return it?

Sheriff Vicklund, Isaiah, and two other officers entered the cafeteria with Nels, Brad, and Sally.

It appeared like the sheriff told them to go ahead and mingle, but Jessa shook her head. There was no way they would lead to anything if they were being followed like they were.

Ken ran up to Sally, but instead of a tender greeting, they started fighting. Jessa couldn't hear their words above the music and crowd, but she could see that neither of them were happy.

Nels looked a little peaked, and he glared around the room like everyone was his personal enemy. Larry approached him, but whatever they said was in undertones. The officer behind Nels moved in, and Larry left.

Brad was the only one acting normal. He walked around and talked to everyone like they were his best friends. As he approached the table, Jessa heard him tell a few people that he'd been framed, but that he was innocent. If he really was the crook, mingling with the townspeople sowing sympathy could make a jury be more lenient. Especially as he removed his fedora like a gentleman.

Jessa frowned. What if this had all been a bad idea? What if something went wrong.

Clay approached in a khaki suit jacket. Jessa felt her cheeks warming. Now people would think they broke up! But Clay did look dapper. In fact . . . *Stop it, Jessa!* She told herself. *He's never going to be interested, so you better not get too attached!*

"You hoo! Clay, darling!" Bertha called.

Clay and the sisters reached the table at about the same time.

"Clay, we bought you something!" Donna said.

Bertha held out a Santa Claus hat.

Clay frowned. "I have to get up in front of everyone and talk. It's not really professional to wear that kind of hat."

"It's in the spirit of Christmas!" Bertha said. "You don't want people to think that you're Scrooge, do you?"

Clay held up his hands. "It's not a good idea."

"Clay." Bertha's voice was firm. "I'll not have people thinking you're some stuffy young man. Loosen up and have fun for a change! Jessa doesn't want to walk around with Ebenezer Scrooge! Now, put on that hat!"

Clay glanced at Jessa, then reluctantly put on the hat. "Alright, if you insist."

"We can take care of the table now." Donna stepped behind Jessa. "You two go have some fun."

Bertha waved her cane, and Jessa moved out of the space behind the table.

Glancing at Clay, she shrugged. "I guess we don't have much choice."

As they moved away from the table, Clay stepped closer and lowered his voice. "Did you talk to Dennis?"

Jessa stopped walking and looked around. "He said that a bunch of money was missing from the school and he wanted to call in a professional accountant to go over the accounts, but then he double checked, and the money was there, only in a different account."

Clay frowned.

"I know you need facts, not speculations, but what if Nels stole money from the school. Then he found out that he was going to be caught, so he poisoned the fudge to delay the meeting long enough for him to get money to replace the money he'd stolen?"

Clay glanced towards where Nels sat glaring at everyone. "That makes almost too much sense. But why would he have killed Timmy? Timmy wouldn't have thought anything strange about seeing Nels at the school."

"Martin!" Sheriff Vicklund approached. "Mayor Jonson is about to open the program. He wants you to talk right after his intro. Your job is to assure the people that we're doing our job. The whole town knows that we have people in custody, but I don't want you talking about that. We don't need more gossip."

"Sir." Clay adjusted his suit. "Why am I the one doing this? You're the sheriff."

Sheriff Vicklund nodded. "You're better at calming people than I am. I tend to make everyone feel like criminals. You can make them all feel safe."

Clay nodded. "I'll do my best."

"How is it going with the suspects here?" Jessa asked.

"Not much has happened," Sheriff Vicklund said. "Ken and Sally got in a fight, and Ken left in a huff. I've got someone trailing him. Larry talked to Nels, but we don't know what they said. We're watching them, but besides constant staring at each other, they haven't approached each other since the beginning. And Brad, well, he's pawning up sympathy everywhere."

315

"I'm sorry if it was a bad idea," Jessa said. "I guess I didn't think all the way through it."

Sheriff Vicklund shrugged. "It's too early to tell. We could get some valuable information yet."

Jessa frowned. "Do I have permission to confront Nels about something?"

Sheriff Vicklund lifted his hands in a helpless gesture. "It's Martin's case."

Jessa looked to Clay.

"Go ahead. Just don't confront him in some back alley somewhere. I want you to stay safe."

Jessa smiled to herself and headed towards where Nels sat, alone, and guarded.

"Nels, can we talk?" Jessa asked.

Nels stiffened. "You're not my lawyer."

Jessa nodded. "I know." She grabbed a chair and pulled it in front of him. Almost knee to knee, she leaned forward, letting her hair fall over her shoulders in a casual way. "I want to help."

"What can you do?" Although his voice was harsh, something like hope flickered in his eyes.

"I can't make you any promises, but I think we could make things go a lot easier for you, if you could do just one thing."

"What's that?" He narrowed his eyes.

316

"Admit that you stole three-hundred-dollars from the Martin sisters."

Nels's face went blank. "Huh? I didn't take any money from them."

Jessa let out a sigh of relief. He'd responded as she'd hoped, now for the next question.

Nels's face still held confusion when Jessa leaned forward with her next question. "Okay, so you didn't steal from them. What about the school. If you could admit to stealing the money . . ."

Nels was on his feet before she could finish. "How dare you!" he glanced around and then lowered his voice. "There isn't any money missing from the school," he said through gritted teeth.

Jessa lifted the school agenda.

"Where did you get that?" he snapped.

"Zoe gave it to me."

"Zoe?" his eyes hardened.

"She gave me a copy of the agenda and I compared it with the one in your office. Dennis doesn't have to speak anymore because the money is there. The money that you stole. That's why you wanted the meeting delayed, so you had time to get the money from Ken through Brad. You needed time to get the stolen money out of your possession."

Nels's face was livid. He clenched his fists and took a step towards her, and then paused. Glancing around, he slowly relaxed. "I don't know what you're talking about. Now leave me alone!"

He stalked off to another chair as the band quieted down for the mayor to give his speech.

Jessa glanced over and saw Sally sitting all alone. She approached cautiously. "Sally? May I talk to you?"

Sally glanced up, tears pooled in her eyes. "Talking won't help anything."

"I'm a good listener." Jessa sat down beside Sally. Being careful to whisper so that anyone listening to the mayor wouldn't be distracted, she leaned towards Sally. "I don't believe you killed Timmy."

Sally's face hardened. "I did. And I poisoned Royce too."

"Where did you get the poison?"

Sally opened her mouth, and her face went blank. "Well . . . I . . . I found it. It was an old can of pesticides. I dusted the fudge with the poison."

Jessa forced herself not to roll her eyes at the blatant lie. "Do you own a black Honda?"

Sally tensed. "No. Why?"

"I heard you were caught going through one earlier today. Is there a reason for that?"

Sally turned back towards the platform. "Shh, I'm trying to listen."

Jessa debated whether or not she should push for more information, but decided against it, and moved towards the platform as Clay got up to speak.

Seeing Zoe off to the side, she headed that way. It looked like she'd have a good view from there.

Zoe glanced around and saw something that made her go tense. She started fidgeting, and Jessa followed her gaze.

Nels had stood to his feet and was making his way towards her. The scathing look he was giving her made Jessa shiver.

Zoe paled, and slipped into the crowd. With many backwards glances, she made her way towards the front of the crowd. Nels stopped his pursuit.

Moving towards the front left, Zoe approached an exit.

Jessa slipped out a near door, and ran down the hall, reaching the exit door, she hurried outside, and went around the building to wait for Zoe's exit. Surely, Zoe knew something about Nels. Something that Nels didn't want known.

Chapter Twenty

Jessa scanned the parking lot. Two black Hondas were parked near each other close to the exit door that she expected Zoe to use.

Making her way towards them, she tried to rationalize. Searching vehicles without a search warrant wasn't right, then again, glancing through a window couldn't hurt could it? Pulling out her phone, she turned on the flashlight, and shone it through the window of the first car she came to. It obviously belonged to a bachelor. The back seat looked like a garbage can, and judging by the faded camo seat covers, the car probably wasn't usually parked in a garage.

A hunting magazine drew her attention and she pressed her face against the glass. It had been mailed to

Larry. If that wasn't enough to confirm the owner of the car, a small can of mustache wax rested in the cup holder.

Jessa glanced around. Zoe hadn't left the school yet. Maybe she had gone to the ladies' room.

"Sally wasn't in Larry's car," she whispered to herself. "So, whatever disturbed her wasn't in this car."

She went on to the next black Honda. What had Sally seen that disturbed her? Holding her light to the car window, she looked inside. Although cleaner than Larry's car, it was still in need of a good cleaning.

Glancing over her shoulder, she sighed. Since she wasn't technically with the police, she could probably get by snooping. Besides, apparently no one was coming outside.

Like all the cars in the small, trusting town, it wasn't locked, so she opened the back door, and reached for a crumpled brochure on the floor. "The Grand Canyon." She frowned. Was this Brad's car?

Shining her light around, she searched for something. Anything that could have caused Sally alarm.

Nothing else in the back seat seemed important, so she went on to the trunk. It was empty. Completely empty, except a baseball bat. Jessa frowned. What kind of person kept a clean trunk, but a messy car? She leaned close to the bat. Was that blood and hair on it?

Glancing at the school, she frowned. As long as Clay kept talking, and whatever other program events kept going, she should be safe.

She slammed the trunk and headed for the glove box.

The glove box stuck, but after a bit of maneuvering, it fell open. Napkins, ketchup packets, and mints, as well as a few papers tumbled out.

Jessa shone her light back into the glove box. Was all this stuff here because someone hadn't had time to empty it, or was someone trying to hide something? She pulled out a few more papers, a car manual, a comb, and a handful of pens before she saw it. At the back of the glove compartment, was a can of pesticides.

Jessa pulled a glove from her pocket and slipped it on before grabbing the can. Flipping the can over, she read the label. Cyanide was the main ingredient, followed by other things that, if this was the poison, would have shown up on the toxicology report.

Jessa wracked her brain. Were there any good reasons for hiding pesticides in the back of a glove compartment other than a fear of being caught with it?

Jessa put everything back in the glove compartment as best she could. When she was done, she shone her light around the front seat. She hadn't found a title to the car, but it couldn't be Brad's because he had come with the police.

Jessa surveyed the rest of the front seat. In the middle console, she found the title, and the pieces fell into place. "Why didn't I see this sooner?" she asked herself. "And the evidence was right under our noses."

"That's because you're a pathetic detective," a female voice came.

Jessa cringed. How could she have been so stupid to place herself in the hands of the killer when everyone else was too busy to come help?

"Get out of the car," the voice commanded. "And put your hands up."

Jessa slowly backed out of the car and shut the door behind her. Turning to Zoe with her hands up, she forced her face to remain calm, despite the gun that was pointed at her. "I might be a slow detective, but I always get my man. Or in this case, the woman." She frowned and glanced towards the door she'd expected Zoe to exit. "I didn't see you come out." She tried to swallow, but her mouth felt like cotton.

"I took another door. Now, how did you know it was me?" Zoe asked.

"You were Nels's stepdaughter, and you were on his side through the divorce. When he told you that he could get caught for purloining money from the school, and you knew that he would spend years in prison, you came up with a scheme to save his neck." Jessa held eye contact as she talked, but her fingers moved over her phone screen, trying to call Clay. "Then when Timmy saw you at the school, and went to tell the Martin sisters, you killed him. But why didn't you leave his body in the entryway where you killed him?"

"Drop the phone." Zoe motioned to it with her gun. Jessa paused.

"Drop it!" she yelled.

Jessa cringed as she let the phone slide through her fingers. There was no way of getting help now. Her gaze slid back to the gun. Who would have to tell Lexi? Jessa fought to keep her face calm. She couldn't let Zoe see the fear. She couldn't think about the finger on the trigger.

Taking a deep breath, Jessa tried to project confidence. "That's what gave you away. When you moved the body and tried to frame Brad. If Brad had been the killer, he wouldn't have brought the murder weapon home and hidden it in his closet. He wouldn't have put a pile of bloody rags in his garage. Plus, you asked me the other day who would have dumped his body in the kitchen. Everyone else assumed that he'd been killed there, but not you. You knew better. You knew that you hadn't killed him in the kitchen."

Zoe motioned towards the sidewalk. "Start walking."

Jessa forced herself to put one foot in front of the other. Where would Zoe kill her? How long would it take someone to notice she was gone? Who would find her body? Her heart threatened to pound its way through her chest. *You have to calm down, Jessa,* she thought. "Why did you move Timmy's body?" *I might as well die knowing the facts.*

With a slight grunt, Zoe poked the gun into Jessa's back. "Because if I'd have left the body face down in the entryway, no one would have suspected the old dames. Why would they walk into their entryway and kill a man on the spot? He needed to be in the kitchen, so it looked like they'd been talking."

"How did you know the aunts weren't home?"

"I saw them at the neighbors when I was following Timmy. He just walked in."

"But you were in such a hurry to get it cleaned up, and get out of there, that you left your travel mug. Why would you have your travel mug in there anyway?"

"I don't even know if it was mine. Brad has one just like it, and we both had them at the radio station. Timmy borrowed them once in a while. After cleaning up the hall, I left, but I forgot that I'd set his mug on the counter."

"And you figured that everyone would assume the mug was yours, and not Timmy's. Then, when you realized that people might think it was Brad's, you tried to frame him. But we would have eventually examined the pictures and figured out that Brad couldn't have concealed the mug in his clothes. You, on the other hand, had a huge purse that day. You were the only one that could have taken it, and the police would have figured it out eventually." The final puzzle pieces were falling in place. "Where did you get the bottle of cyanide? Unless you pre-meditated it for a long time, you couldn't have gotten it. It's not like you can order it overnight shipping! Especially not liquid cyanide."

"The school lab had a special project they were working on a few years ago, and they got special licenses to get it." Zoe snorted. "It's lucky for me that disposing of it is so costly! The school kept it under lock and key to spare the expense of getting rid of it."

"And of course, you put it in Nels office after he disappeared. If he was going to die anyways, you figured he might as well get some of the blame."

"Be quiet," Zoe said as they rounded the far side of the school. "We're going in here."

Jessa opened the door, and stepped in, with Zoe close behind. "Then you tried to kill Nels and pin that on Brad too. You just wanted everyone in trouble but yourself! You even went so far as to try to kill the very man you started out to save!"

"Be quiet," Zoe hissed. "Besides, Nels was worried about the investigation. He wanted me to hit him on the head, so that he would be deemed a victim, and not a possible killer."

"But you hit him harder than he wanted you too. Instead of giving him a minor injury, you tried to kill him like you did Timmy. Probably because he was the only one who knew that you had done it, and you didn't want him going to the police. Is that what the baseball bat was for? Then you called Brad, hoping that if he was the one who found the body, he'd be blamed. You left the syringe and cyanide in Nels office, knowing that it wouldn't point to you. The can of pesticides . . . If I had to guess, I'd say you found them in your house, and meant to get rid of them, just in case the police came by. You didn't know that we'd be able to tell it wasn't the murder weapon. But you forgot them in your car."

"Shut up!" Zoe poked the gun into Jessa's back. "One more word out of you, and I'll shoot."

Jessa winced. Even if Zoe was lying, she couldn't call the bluff. Not after what had happened to her mom. Not with a gun in her back.

They reached a door marked *Utility*, and Zoe pulled out a key. "Open it."

Jessa took the key and opened the door. Cement steps led down into a basement.

"With your heels, no one will be surprised that you accidently fell and killed yourself. I can't be blamed for an accident. The blow to your head will look like you got it while falling. Only I will know that you died before the fall."

Jessa opened her mouth, but Zoe cut her off. "This is the part where you say, 'you'll never get away with it!' Right?"

Jessa gave a half shrug. "It's possible for you to get away with things on this earth, but when you die, God will judge you for what you've done. You can't escape that." Her only chance was to keep Zoe talking.

Zoe snorted. "So, you're a religious fanatic? I suppose you honestly think that I'm going to burn in Hell for my sins. You're so blind! Has no one ever told you how messed up your fairy tale is? You claim that God will send us wicked people to burn in Hell forever, while at the same time telling everyone how much God loves them! Don't you know how crazy you sound? Besides, my good outweighs my bad."

"If you're caught, and you go to court for your crimes, what will happen?" Jessa asked.

Zoe shook her head. "I'm not going to get caught, because if I was caught, I'd be in jail for a long time."

"What if he was a loving judge? What if you got to court, and the judge said, 'Zoe, you've committed these crimes, but I'm a man of love, and I wouldn't want to hurt you, so I'm letting you go free. Besides, you've done a lot of good in your life, so I can excuse your crimes.'"

"You're tetched. If a judge did that, he'd be kicked out of his bench. I'm guilty, and a judge would have to give me a sentence or he'd lose his job."

Jessa shook her head slowly. Sudden moves didn't seem like a good idea. "And yet, you think God, who is perfect and holy can be a righteous judge by just shrugging off your sins, and let you into Heaven? You think the ultimate judge can just let your sin go because He's a God of love?"

Zoe's gun hand trembled slightly. "I went to Sunday school as a kid, and believe me, I know the Good Book. And it says that God is love."

"He is. That's why he made a way for our sins to be dealt with in a just way. His Son, Jesus, died on the cross to pay the price for our sin. In a way, He took our sentence upon Himself, and made it so that the judge could let us go free." Jessa silently prayed for strength. She had to keep Zoe talking till someone came. And if no one came, and this was her last conversation, maybe Zoe would come to know the truth about Christ because of it. The truth that would set her free from her past.

"Zoe, if you went to court for your crimes, and the judge sentenced you to fifty years in prison, but then someone else came along, and took your sentence, and served your time, he could let you go free because the price had been paid. That's what Jesus did for us. He is a God of love, and He gives us a choice. We can choose to take our own punishment, and let the ultimate judge sentence us for eternity, or we can accept His free gift of forgiveness. The choice is yours, Zoe. Are you going to turn to God and let Him change you? Are you going to accept his payment for your sins?"

Zoe's lips were trembling. "I've heard enough. I'm not going to get caught. Everyone will think you died in an accident. Turn around." Zoe poked Jessa in the chest with the gun. Jessa gave up trying to keep her hands steady.

"You shouldn't wear high-heels. I can't get in trouble for an accident," Zoe sneered.

"You can if I witness the accident," an elderly female voice said.

Jessa gasped. "Donna! Get back!"

"It's not a problem dear," Donna's voice was calm. "I've got it all under control."

Jessa looked back. Zoe's gun swung between Donna and Jessa, but Donna's hand gun remained steadily pointing at Zoe. Donna's purse hung open from where she'd no doubt pulled the gun.

"Drop the gun," Donna said.

Footsteps pounded down the hall, and Clay approached with his gun drawn as well. "Jessa, get back."

Zoe's gun swung towards Jessa, but the door, slammed into Zoe's elbow. The gun muzzle swung up, and a shot was fired into the ceiling. Jessa rushed forward, smashing her shoulder into Zoe, knocking her down.

Zoe, still clutching her gun, tried to bring her arm around, but a worn-out sneaker firmly planted on her wrist, pinning it down.

Jessa looked up. "Liam?"

Clay was at her side in a moment. He reached down and removed the gun from Zoe. Grabbing her arms, he pulled them behind her back, and pulled out his handcuffs. "You're under arrest. You have the right to remain silent. Anything you say can and will be used against you in a court of law. You have a right to an attorney. If you cannot afford an attorney, one will be appointed to you." Clay glanced at Jessa. "Are you alright?" His eyes flashed concern.

Liam helped her to her feet, and she smiled. "I'm fine." She held a hand to her still pounding heart and took a deep breath. It would take time to calm down, but she was still alive!

Clay's crooked hat framed his concerned face, and a giggle bubbled inside and worked its way out.

"What?" Clay's brow furrowed.

"I'm sorry Clay, it's just that . . . you have no idea how funny you look in a suit coat, with a Santa hat, making an arrest! I can literally tell people that Santa Claus saved my life!"

Clay frowned. "Forget it."

Sheriff Vicklund, and Isaiah rounded the corner with guns in hand, but when they saw Clay, they relaxed.

"We heard a shot. Is anyone hurt?" Isaiah asked.

"Just my pride," Jessa said. "I should have known earlier. All the clues were there. I'm just grateful God helped me keep her talking till help could come." She rubbed the back of her neck. "The idea of being bashed on the head and then pushed down cement stairs wasn't exactly appealing!" She glanced back. "Liam!"

Liam let the utility door fall the rest of the way shut.

"You slammed the door on Zoe and saved my life!" Jessa smiled. "Thank you."

Liam shrugged, and scuffed his shoe on the linoleum. "Thanks for not treating me like a criminal because of my dad."

Zoe glared at Jessa, and then stared at the ground.

"How did you guys know I was in trouble?" Jessa asked.

Donna slid her gun back into her purse. "Janet was droning on about school projects, and I got bored, so I went for a walk. I just happened to hear someone yell, 'shut up!' so I came to check it out."

"It's a good thing you carry that canon in your purse," Clay said, his face serious. "If I hadn't made it in time, I'm sure you could have handled it."

Donna shrugged. "I do what I have to do. After helping raise a cop, I can hold my own."

Clay grabbed Zoe's elbow, and started for the door. They all followed.

"How did you know to come?" Jessa asked.

Clay winked. "Gut instinct. I had a great view from the platform, and I noticed you watching Zoe. When she left, you left, and Nels didn't look too happy about it. I figured if you weren't back by the time I was done, I'd go check on you. When Janet got up to share, I was going to go look for you, but I got talking to the mayor. When I saw Donna leave, I knew I'd better hurry up and make sure everything was okay. Are you okay?"

"Of course." Jessa's cheeks warmed under his intense gaze. "At least . . . I will be."

"Coming around that corner, and seeing Zoe with her gun pointed at you . . ." Clay's voice trialed off, and he winced. "You're sure you're okay?"

Jessa tucked a strand of hair behind her ear and nodded. Clay was concerned . . . for her? She fought a grin, and swallowed hard. Her heart fluttered and she chided herself. She had to turn away from Clay. "So, Liam, how did you get here?" She turned to him.

Liam's cheeks flushed red. "I . . . I was cleaning. Mr. Royce was letting me help him clean the school, and he was paying me a little for it. Dennis Nordlum knew I'd helped out, so he asked me to do some cleaning before school opened again. That's what I was doing here that morning too. I was going to return a mop when I saw Zoe."

"Where's Clara?" Jessa asked.

Liam frowned. "She's at your house again. I hope you don't mind. She wanted to see Callie again, and I didn't want to leave her outside."

Jessa smiled. "Of course, I don't mind!"

After Clay left with the sheriff and Isaiah, Jessa and Donna headed back inside to help Bertha with the closing down of the now empty table.

"We made a lot of money for the school!" Bertha said, as she counted the last of it. She hobbled away on her cane to tell Dennis, who was at the foot of the stage collecting information for the big announcement.

Donna held a hand to her chest.

"Are you alright?" Jessa asked.

"I was fine until just now, but I think it caught up with me." She eased down into a chair and let her breath out slowly. "What a night. I declare, what a night."

Jessa smiled. What a woman.

Jessa sat down next to Donna and sighed. Her own heart rate was still working its way down. She wasn't afraid to die, but the mental image of someone having to tell Laci, or Dad and Josh, was . . . unthinkable.

Off to the side, Shelby held her radio to her ear, and then whispered back into it, after a bit, she headed for the other officers, and they rounded up Nels, Brad and Sally, and left.

"Are you going to be alright if I go?" Jessa asked.

"Of course, I'll be alright! Do I look like I'm going to keel over?" Donna asked.

Jessa grinned. "Thanks. And thanks for saving my life."

"Think nothing of it!"

Jessa hurried to follow Shelby. As she left the cafeteria, the mayor led the audience in *Silent Night*.

Jessa sighed. There was nothing silent about this night, but at least the danger was over.

"Do you have room for one more?" Jessa called.

Shelby turned back. "We sure do."

Jessa hopped in shotgun. Although she was relieved to not have to be involved in what she figured would be months of court appointments and paperwork, she was eager to learn the details she'd missed.

At the station, everything buzzed with activity.

"Jessa!" Sheriff Vicklund met her in the lobby. "We're dividing forces to keep this from taking all night. Do you want to take Sally?"

Jessa nodded. "Sure can."

Sally was brought to an interrogation room, and Jessa followed her in. "Okay, Mrs. Landean, let's get right to the point. Why would you admit to killing people, when you didn't?"

Despite all of Jessa's prodding, Sally remained tight-lipped. Jessa drummed her fingers on her knee for a bit before deciding to just bluff her way through the interview. "Okay, so you don't want to talk. Supposing I told you that the reason you confessed to this murder, was because of something that happened in high-school?"

Sally's face tensed. "How did you know?"

Jessa shrugged. This next statement could get a blank look or hit a button. "For the same reason that I believe you didn't mean to be searching Zoe's car this morning at the café. You meant to be searching Larry's."

"Shh!" Sally leaned forward. "Don't say that out loud!"

Jessa tried to hide the relief on her face. Her guess had been right! "You thought the car was Larry's, so when you found the poison, you assumed that Larry had done it, and you wanted to protect him."

Sally looked everywhere, except at Jessa. "Everyone kept talking, and I heard that he was a suspect, and I couldn't believe he would do such a thing! I searched his house, but didn't find anything, so I figured I'd search his car. How was I supposed to know that there was more than one black Honda in town?"

Jessa did the math in her head. If she added Larry's age, with the age that Sally was in eleventh grade . . . "Larry's your son, isn't he? You adopted him out."

Chapter Twenty-One

Sally's eyes filled with tears. "I couldn't take my own baby's life, but I couldn't raise a child! I was devastated and lost. I knew if I had only listened to my mother . . . if I'd have made right choices I wouldn't have been in that situation. Abortion was the only logical thing, but I couldn't add murder to my sin." She pressed the heels of her hands to her eyes. "I visited a crisis pregnancy center, and they did an ultra sound. When I saw him, I knew I could never kill him. I couldn't take his life because of my sin. I chose to blow it, and I had to face the consequences. I adopted him out to the Erickson family with the understanding that they wouldn't ever tell anyone where he came from."

"Does Ken know?"

Sally shook her head. "I didn't know how to tell him. Larry doesn't know either. All these years I've watched Larry grow up, I've watched him struggle through life, and I've wondered what it would have been like if I'd have kept him. When people accused him, I couldn't bear the idea of my son being a murderer. When I found the poison, I thought it was him, so to save him from going to jail, I turned myself in."

Sally's eyes widened. "But you must not tell anyone! Ken and I have three children living in the cities, and they would hate me if they knew that they had a half-brother. Ken would hate me. Even tonight, Ken was mad at me for not telling him stuff. He's been accusing me of keeping stuff from him for months now. That's part of the reason I wasn't afraid to turn myself in. Jail can't be that much worse than living with a man who doesn't trust you."

Jessa's heart ached for the hurting woman. "Mrs. Landean." Jessa laid a hand on her shoulder. "I think Ken would forgive you, and I think your children will forgive you. I think it would be better for everyone, if you told them. Hiding it is only going to hurt you more. It's the truth that sets us free. Even if the truth isn't pleasant. Besides, I'm going to have to tell the sheriff about this."

Sally's shoulder's sagged. "I just . . . I don't know how. I've hid it for so long and . . . I just don't know how. How will

Larry feel about me?" She broke down sobbing, and Jessa reached for the box of tissues.

After letting Sally cry for a few minutes, Jessa tilted her chin up. "Mrs. Landean. You can't go on like this. Would you like me to call Ken, and have him come down here?"

Sally paused, and then nodded. "Okay."

Jessa left the room and headed for the front desk. "I need to get Ken Landean here," she said.

Mitch pointed across the room. "There he is."

Jessa saw a man with an invisible burden on his shoulders. Wrinkles stood out all over Ken's face, and the corners of his mouth drooped. He looked years older than the last time she'd seen him.

"Mr. Landean." She approached him. He looked up, but his face didn't change. "Would you like to see your wife?"

He shrugged. "I don't know what good it will do."

"Then why are you here, if you don't mind my asking?"

Ken sighed, as if he didn't know why he was there either. "She's my wife," he said simply. "She might not be able to trust me with anything, but I still love her. And with her Parkinson's disease . . . she needs me."

340

Tears sprang to Jessa's eyes at the tenderness in Ken's voice. "Ken, I think she's ready to talk to you," Jessa said softly. "But before I take you to her, I want you to promise me one thing. Promise that you'll listen to her, and not get mad. You think it's been hard having her hide stuff from you, but you have no idea how hard it's been for her keeping all this stuff bottled up inside of her, and not feeling free to share it."

"She can tell me anything!" Ken said. "I promise, I'll listen."

Jessa nodded. "Right this way."

Ken hefted himself out of the chair like he was thirty years older than his age and shuffled after Jessa. They reached the interrogation room, and Jessa let Ken inside, and then stepped outside. Part of her didn't feel right watching through the one-way glass, but at the same time, she couldn't risk it turning into a violent argument.

Sally rose to meet Ken, and after a few awkward moments, she broke down in tears, and told him everything. Jessa turned off the volume so she couldn't hear them. They deserved at least that much privacy. Jessa watched, as Sally gestured and cried, and talked and wept.

Ken moved around, and Jessa saw tears on his face as well. He said something to her, and then, it was as if an invisible wall crumbled between them, and they embraced.

Jessa slipped out of the viewing room. There was no need to watch further.

"How'd it go?" Sheriff Vicklund asked.

Jessa blinked back tears. "It was beautiful."

"Beautiful? I've never heard an interrogation called beautiful before."

Jessa cleared her throat. "The actual interrogation went well." She repeated what Sally had said. "I'll type it up so she can sign her statement."

Sheriff Vicklund grinned. "At least one of my problems is done. Nels and Zoe both admitted to their parts in the crime, but they don't want to talk till they get their lawyers."

"And Brad?"

"He's going to get to go home, but he will have to appear in court. He's been involved in some illegal operations."

"And Ken?"

"We can't arrest someone just because they're rumored to be involved in illegal operations. We'll keep an eye on him, but I'm guessing this whole thing has him pretty shook up. Anyway, I'm not planning on running for re-election, so someone else can deal with it."

"You're not running again?" Jessa shook her head. "But the town loves you!"

Sheriff Vicklund sighed. "I've got kids living in California, and I'm getting old, I want to be near them. I want to see my grandkids grow up."

"That's why you made Clay do so much on this case." It all made sense now. Making Clay talk to the people. Making Clay do the undercover footwork with the people. Clay would get the glory for the solved case.

Sheriff Vicklund shrugged. "I haven't told anyone yet, but I've been secretly grooming Clay for the job. I want him to run. He's a little slow to act sometimes, but once he gets going, he's unstoppable. He really notices details. I wasn't sure if the town would go for him with all of his religious spiels, but anyone who knows him personally, knows that it just makes him a better person. I reckon he should be able to get elected. Especially with my support."

Jessa forced a smile. "We'll miss you."

"Are you seriously taking that music teaching job? I figured you'd have more to do with your talents and credentials."

"I love teaching music. And I love this town. I'd like to settle down here. That is, if I get the job. The school board still hasn't had their final meeting about me, and I heard someone else was interested in the job. Even if I get the job, it'll just be for the next semester, and after that, I'll have to make some decisions. I'm back to the family bureau, and if I can do that long-distance from here I will. If not, this might just have to become my vacation spot or something. I don't know how it's all going to work, but I'm excited to see where God takes me."

Sheriff Vicklund waved his hand like it was all nonsense. "They'll hire you and you'll never leave this town. That other person who expressed interest in the job was one of the parents of a student in band. She never actually asked for the job, she said she would fill in until the school board picked someone else. But she doesn't really want the job."

"And there's something else here . . ." she paused. "Liam and Clara. What's going on with them?"

Sheriff Vicklund sighed. "Clay caught Liam outside a few minutes ago and had a talk with him. Liam opened up about a lot of things. I've got someone over at his place now. It seems like their mother is the one that's been doing the drugs. The drugs we found in Liam's possession last year were hers. Anyway, they will need a place to stay until everything is figured out."

Jessa nodded. "That's what I thought. If it's alright, I'd like them to stay with me."

The sheriff raised an eyebrow. "That's interesting. Clay wants them to stay with him."

Clay came down the hall holding his cell phone. "Jessa, it's Laci, she wants to talk to you."

Jessa took the cell phone from Clay and stepped into a quiet corner of the lobby. "Hey, sis!"

"If Mom were here she'd take you over her knee and give you a great big spanking."

"It's nice to hear from you too!" Jessa couldn't stop the smile. "It was no big deal. It was nothing Mom wouldn't have done."

"After what happened to Mom, I'm surprised you even got involved." Laci's voice grew serious. "How are you? Really?"

Jessa sat down and closed her eyes. She breathed deeply for a few minutes and replayed the events from the night through her head. The fear. The panic. The memories of Mom. The feeling when Clay showed up. . .

"Jessa?"

"I'm okay," Jessa said. "It was hard, but I think it was good for me. It kept me distracted and helped me refocus."

"So, are you coming back to Missouri?"

"No, I'm going to take the teaching job through the spring. After that . . . well, we'll see where God leads me. But I still want to be a part of the team. There's plenty I can do long distance. Enough about me. Have you heard from Dad? And what about Josh? Is he still trying to find me?"

There was a pause. "Jessa. I don't know how to tell you this but . . ." there was another long pause, and Jessa's chest tightened.

This could only mean one thing. "What happened?"

"Well . . . you see, there was this mission, and then there was this plane ride, and now . . . well, it's all over."

Laci paused again, and Jessa wished she could reach through the phone and grab her. "Talk to me, Laci. What's over?" She fought for breath, but her chest just tightened more, squeezing the breath out of her.

"The mission, and our peace and quiet. Dad and Michelle are in the kitchen, and they're assaulting me with their awful cooking! Seriously, Jessa, you've got to come home and spare me from their cooking!"

"You mean they're home?" Her lungs came free.

Laci burst out laughing. "You're so easy to play! Yes, they're home."

"Laci Joy Anderson! If I could I'd . . ."

"You'd what?" she cut her off with laughter in his voice.

"Oh, you, you, meanie!"

"Come on, pipsqueak. Aren't we a little old to be name calling?"

"How are they home so soon? They weren't supposed to get back for another three weeks! Can I talk to Dad?"

"He's been waiting for you to ask since you started being gullible. Here he is." There was a rustling, and then her dad's voice came on.

"Hello, sweetheart. How's my girl?"

At the sound of her father's strong and cheerful voice, she teared up. "I was so worried."

"I was in God's hands," he said. "No matter what, I'm in God's hands."

"I missed you."

"We missed you too. Michelle is calling your Sheriff Vicklund now, and we're thinking about taking a trip out there. Michelle would like to see her cousin, and Josh and I wouldn't mind seeing you and your friends. Especially this one that Laci mentioned. What was his name again?"

"Dad!" Jessa giggled. It was like they'd never been apart. "Is Josh there too?"

"Yep, he came home for Christmas. But seriously, honey." His voice softened. "I missed you. I don't like these missions that are that long and dangerous. Especially when I know you're in danger. My mission went incredibly well, and from what I've heard, you've been in danger more than I was."

"I'm fine," Jessa assured him. "Besides, it was nothing Mom wouldn't have done."

"I know. That's why I worry. You're so much like your mother." He took on a dreamy tone. "If she were here, she'd scold me for worrying about you. 'Worrying is just saying you don't trust God,' is what she used to always say. If my work in the agency has taught me anything, it's that I have to trust God, even when things are hard. He can see the big picture, even when we can't."

Jessa started in on the details of the last week and told him everything. "You'll understand better when you get here and meet everyone."

"And I look forward to telling you what I can about our mission in person."

"How did Michelle do?" Jessa couldn't keep the edge out of her voice.

"She did great."

Jessa didn't respond.

A sigh carried through the phone. "Honey, Michelle isn't your mom. She'll never be like your mom, but that doesn't mean she's wrong."

"Oh, I know that! I love Michelle, but I worry that . . . that you'll trust her to watch your back like you did Mom, and that she won't be able to do it."

"I understand that Michelle doesn't have the training that your mother had, and I'm very careful what kinds of things I let her do. You don't have to worry. We make a great team."

Jessa relaxed as she heard the smile in her dad's voice. "I'm glad you found love again."

"So am I." He cleared his throat. "When your mom died, I didn't think I'd ever live again, but God is good. God's brought me through some tough times, and made me better because of it. It took me nearly forty years to learn that God is always good. Even in the hard times. I'm so proud to see that you've learned that lesson at such a young age. Well, I'd better let you go. Make sure you get your phone back up and running, and . . . clean out your guest bedrooms. We might just be there for Christmas."

"Christmas is two days away!"

He chuckled. "I know! But I miss my girl! And this Clay fellow might need some encouragement from me!"

"I love you, Dad."

"I love you too, short stuff."

"Oh, and Dad, I may have a couple of kids with me from now on." She began explaining, and the more she talked about it, the more she felt good about it. She didn't know the first thing about being a mother, but Clara and Liam needed a safe home with love. She knew she could provide that.

When she finally hung up, Jessa couldn't stop the smile that seemed set on keeping her lips apart.

"Good talk with your sister?" Clay asked when she returned the phone.

"Great talk with my dad!" she said. "He's home, safe and sound."

"It sounds like we may be seeing a lot of each other from now on." Clay paused. "In court."

"Huh?"

"It seems we both want custody of the Bennett kids."

Jessa shrugged. "Well, I have a home, not a dingy basement. They should stay with me." Her face warmed. Why did she always feel this way around him? *God, please help me keep my emotions under control!*

Clay shook his head. "I'm a cop, I can keep them safe. They should stay with me. Besides, you'll probably be gallivanting across the country solving mysteries, and they'll need a steady home."

Jessa couldn't resist the smile. "Somehow, I think it will all work out. I'm going to fight to get the kids, but not in court, and if you get them, I won't hold any hard feelings."

Clay raked his trembling fingers through his hair.

"You look tired. You should get some rest."

Clay sighed. "Yes, well, I've got a few hours of paperwork before I can go to bed, and more paperwork tomorrow and the next day, and the next."

"Clay, it's Christmas. Do your paperwork, but don't lose your spirit! No one *needs* your papers this week. Take it easy! How are you going to take care of two kids if you can't even take care of yourself? In fact, you told me just the other day, that we need to relax a little at Christmas."

Clay nodded. He shifted and looked around the room. Everywhere, except at her.

"Is something wrong?" she asked.

He took a deep breath and raked his other hand through his hair. "I don't know how to ask this, I'm kind of nervous."

"Why are you nervous?" she asked.

"I don't know. I'm just nervous."

Jessa leaned her against the wall and crossed her arms. "I don't bite. Go ahead and ask whatever it is you're afraid I'll say no too." Her heart beat a bit faster. What could he possibly have to ask her?

Clay met her gaze, and she caught her breath at the serious, yet passionate twinkle in his blue eyes.

"Miss Anderson, would you give me your father's phone number?" He straightened and stared at her with reserve.

"Sure. Why wouldn't I?" She paused. "Why do you want it? That could make a difference you know."

Clay took a deep breath and clasped his hands in an almost pleading stance. "I would like to talk to your dad and see if he's okay with me taking you out for coffee and maybe, get Christmas trees for our places. I hope you don't like Douglas fir trees. The aunties refuse to let me get one. They say everyone has one and we should be different. I also need to pick up a piece of pie and I thought . . . that is, if it's alright with you," he spoke in a rush. "If you don't want me to talk to him, I won't. If you'd rather I didn't, I could not do it. We could forget that I asked, and you could pretend that it had never happened and . . ." he paused. "I know we just met but . . .Why are you smiling like that?"

Jessa felt her cheeks warming. Poor Clay was so nervous about this. She didn't need to make it worse for him by laughing. "Officer Clay Martin, I would be delighted to have you ask my dad about taking me out for a date."

"Really?" His eyes lit up. "I want to be completely open about this, and I don't want you to think that my aunties are making me. They don't even know. They're convinced that I'll never open up again, but . . . every time I pray, God brings you to mind. I know we just met, and you don't date so, I want you to know that I'm totally serious. This is probably bad timing too, and if you need more time to think about it, that's alright. I was just thinking that maybe you didn't have Christmas plans and if we're both going for Liam and Clara we'll be seeing a lot of each other. We could both take Liam and Clara and . . ." he winced. "I shouldn't be talking to you like this. Not yet. Can I just get his number?"

Jessa pulled a notepad and pen from her purse and scratched out the number. "Here you go. And don't be so terrified. My dad doesn't bite either." She raised an eyebrow. "At least, not if he's in a good mood, and if he thinks you're a good guy. The last three guys who asked about me left with only five arms and two legs between them."

Clay's eyebrows wrinkled and his mouth opened slightly.

Jessa laughed. "Sorry. I was joking."

"Oh." Clay tried to smile, but it looked more like a wince.

"Hey, you two!" Alfred called for their attention. "You're standing under mistletoe."

Jessa tensed, and took a step back.

Clay glanced up. "It's okay, there's not white berries. You're okay for now but . . ." He flashed a grin. "I should go."

On his way from the room, Clay nearly tripped on a chair, caught himself, and cast a boyish grin back at Jessa, revealing a dimple.

Jessa let her breath out slowly, grateful that she'd taught him the true tradition of mistletoe, but she couldn't stop the fluttering of her heart.

"I'd say this is going to be a marry Christmas," Alfred piped up. "Get it? *Marry* Christmas. You know? With an 'a' instead of an 'e'?" He cackled at his own joke, and Jessa couldn't help but laugh with him. Not at the joke, but at watching him laugh. And, with what Clay had been through, and his seriousness about talking to her dad, Alfred could be right. Just thinking about it brought another smile to her face, and her cheeks warmed.

Alfred turned back to his computer and reached for a piece of cookie dough fudge from a plate nearby. Jessa smiled, and walked to the window. The snow floated down lazily, like it was in a snow globe, and she couldn't resist the urge to go outside.

She stood on the front steps, enjoying the silent snow, when she saw it. Her beloved cruiser pulling into a parking spot. "Hey!" she yelled at the guy getting out of it. "That's my car!"

He jumped back with his hands in the air, as if he thought she was going to shoot him. "I didn't take it!" he yelled. "I'm just returning it."

Jessa approached. "Who are you?"

"I'm Hunter. I just work at the car garage."

"The garage?"

"Yeah, your car was brought there the other day. We fixed it all up good as new. You should get a few thousand more miles."

"Who dropped it off? Who paid for it?" Jessa asked.

The guy shrugged. "He left a note in the car."

Jessa hurried to the cruiser and looked it over. Even the gas tank had been filled. She looked around for the note and found it on the dash.

Miss Anderson – I apologize for stealing your car, but in the Christmas spirit, I couldn't resist. May it continue to serve you faithfully like a good reindeer. One with a REALLY bright red body. Like Rudolph, only more red. With appreciation, Santa

Jessa laughed. "Clay." No wonder he'd ignored her when she said it had been stolen! Her cheeks warmed as she thought of Clay, and a smile parted her lips. She couldn't wait for her Dad to meet him.

Jessa closed her eyes and ran her hands over the steering wheel. The last few days played through her mind and for the first time since her mother's death, the idea of being involved in an investigation didn't hurt. She opened her eyes and stared at the falling snow. "No matter what happens, I'm in God's hands." She leaned her head back and smiled. That was enough. That was enough to make it a merry Christmas.

THE END

John 8:32 "And ye shall know the truth, and the truth shall make you free."

The Martin Sisters' Cookie Dough Fudge

1/3 cup melted butter

1/3 cup brown sugar

¾ cup white flour

Two pinches of salt, divided

1/3 cup mini semisweet chocolate chips

1 cup milk chocolate chips or semi-sweet

1 lb. powdered sugar (About 3 and 3/4ths cup)

8 oz. softened cream cheese

2 teaspoons vanilla

Step One – Line a 9x9 pan with foil. Be sure to leave an overhang on the sides. Lightly butter the foil or use cooking spray.

Step Two – Mix the butter and brown sugar. Stir in flour, and one pinch of salt. Stir in the 1/3 cup of mini semisweet chocolate chips. Form the dough into a ball.

Place the dough ball on plastic wrap, flatten into a disc, then wrap completely and freeze for 10 minutes, or until firm. When the dough is firm, unwrap it, cut it into ½ inch squares, and refrigerate.

Step Three – Mix together the powdered sugar, cream cheese, vanilla, and the remaining pinch of salt. Beat until smooth.

Step Four – Melt the cup of chocolate chips over low heat, stirring constantly, or microwave for thirty second intervals, stirring between until melted.

Step Five – Add the melted chocolate to the cream cheese mixture and beat until blended. Stir in the chilled cookie dough squares. Spread into the prepared pan.

Step Six – Refrigerate until firm, and then remove the fudge from the pan by lifting the foil. Cut into squares, and store in the fridge or freezer.

Enjoy!

About the Author

Priscilla J. Krahn lives on a farm in northern Minnesota, with her parents and two unmarried siblings. She is the youngest of seven siblings and always loved to read all of her older sibling's books. Her love for reading sparked a passion in her to write. If you were to ask her, Priscilla would say that her two passions are, "Writing and evangelism." Her goal is to write books that not only entertain but also share the gospel. If you have any questions or comments, she would love to hear from you. You can contact her though her website at **www.priscillajkrahn.com**. Also, check out her blog at www.priscillakrahn.blogspot.com for current updates, short stories, deleted scenes and more! She can also be found on Facebook, Goodreads, and Google+.

Also By The Same Author

The Adventures of Amy

Recommended for ages 12-18

Kidnappings, family secrets, and hospitals are the least of Amy's problems as she struggles to find the truth. The sheriff promises to help and her family wants to protect her, but will that be enough? Join Amy as she learns to trust God in the midst of danger.

Mystery at the Maze
Recommended for ages 7-12

Along with her two friends, Leah Brink charges head first into a race against time. Can they find out who's vandalizing the corn maze before Mr. Creval has to shut it down? In the midst of danger, fear, and failure, Leah wants nothing more than to do the right thing. An overly confident friend and an annoying little sister bring challenges into Leah's life that she's not ready to face, but does she really have a choice? What if the only way for Leah to find true joy and success is by trusting God? Join Leah and her friends as they work together to show God's love to others in the midst of a thrilling mystery.

Mission of a Lifetime
Teen/Young Adult Fiction

A missing airplane . . .
Hostile tribes . . .
Mysterious kidnappings . . .
Responsibility falls upon twenty-one-year-old William Rodriguez when his missionary parents disappear in the hostile jungles of Columbia. Willie knows that he has to go find them, but what will it cost him? When his dreams and his very life are on the line, Willie doesn't know whom to trust. Will he be able to overcome his past mistakes and the present failure that seems set on destroying his mission?

When Willie finds himself in the midst of a drug smuggling ring, difficult decisions are thrust upon him. Can he escape his captors before his family is killed? Can he find forgiveness in his heart for the very people who ruined his life, or will it only bring back more painful memories? Will he be able to survive the mission of a lifetime?

Ty Carson
Recommended for ages 12-18

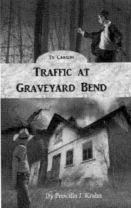

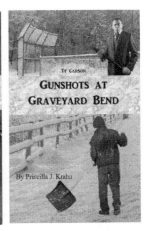

There's nothing like spending the summer with a grandpa that you don't remember ever meeting . . . especially when he's murdered the day you arrive.

Searching for clues to the alleged murder brings fourteen-year-old Ty Carson across questions that should be answered. As he tries to unravel the clues, he wants to know why he's not allowed to talk about the police hero who had died ten years before. The man that he had called 'dad'. Accused and alone, Ty realizes that the answers have to be nearby, but can he understand them? Can a baseball game, a figure dressed in black, and an old gun collection be the things that he needs to find friendship and bring him closer to God?